THE CALL OF THE CANYON

ZANE GREY

Edited by
EVA ELDRIDGE
Foreword by
JEFFREY J. MARIOTTE

WFP
WORDFIRE PRESS

Ebook ISBN: 978-1-68057-657-3
Trade Paperback ISBN: 978-1-68057-658-0
Jacketed Hardcover ISBN: 978-1-68057-659-7

Illustrations and figures are in the public domain.
Cover design by Eva Eldridge and Allyson Longueira
Cover art by Yurkovska | Depositphotos

Published by WordFire Press, LLC
P.O. Box 1840
Monument, CO 80132
Kevin J. Anderson & Rebecca Moesta, Publishers

WordFire Press Edition 2024

Printed in the USA

Join our WordFire Press Readers Group for new projects and giveaways. Sign up at wordfirepress.com.

THE CALL OF THE CANYON

FOREWORD

Jeffrey J. Mariotte

Pearl Zane Grey—who dropped the Pearl at an early age and stuck, perhaps wisely, with Zane—was a man of contradictory impulses and appetites. Born in Zanesville, Ohio, a town named for an ancestor who had been a hero of the Revolutionary War, he grew up loving fishing, baseball, writing, and women—not necessarily in that order. But when he won a baseball scholarship to the University of Pennsylvania, he studied dentistry, intending to follow in the footsteps of his dentist father. He even practiced, briefly, after college.

A trip to the Grand Canyon in 1907 rearranged his priorities and set the course for the rest of his life. He had married Lina Roth, whom he called Dolly, in 1905, before he ever saw the American west. Once he had visited, however, he kept returning, finally moving with Dolly to California in 1918. In the west, he found fertile ground for his vivid imagination to take root.

In his books he populated the west with hard-bitten loners —powerful, capable men of fierce passions and noble ideals. Through his characters, he preached a deeply conservative morality. In 1924's *The Call of the Canyon*, through the voice of protagonist Carley Burch, he railed against liquor, revealing clothing on women, birth control, jazz music, immigrants, automobiles ("the greatest evil that ever menaced American girls"), and more—but in his personal life, he began his marriage to Dolly with a warning that "I shall never lose the spirit of my interest in women," and he had numerous mistresses throughout their long union. He traveled extensively over the next decades, sometimes in the company of one mistress or another, usually while Dolly stayed home and kept the money flowing.

Throughout their marriage, Dolly handled his business affairs: negotiations with agents, contracts with publishers, movie deals. In recognition of her contribution, Grey split his substantial earnings with Dolly, right down the middle. She had plenty to do; despite being largely panned by critics of the day who wanted to see Modernist works, not those of the Romantic tradition, Grey sold millions of books worldwide; his stories have been adapted for film more than 100 times and have been the basis for three separate television series.

Considered today one of the earliest Western writers (he was heavily influenced by Owen Wister's *The Virginian*), even in his most traditional Western action tales, Grey kept most of the violence off the page and instead celebrated the beauty and restorative powers of the western landscape on his characters. *The Call of the Canyon* is a prime example of that approach.

The novel begins in New York City, where wealthy socialite Carley reads a letter from her beloved, Glenn Kilbourne. Glenn had returned from service in France during World War I "shell-shocked and gassed and otherwise incapacitated for service in the Army." He's written to tell Carley that, having relocated to Arizona, he's found peace and strength and healing, and he doesn't intend to return to New York.

Seemingly on a lark, Carley catches a train and makes her way to Glenn's homestead in Oak Creek Canyon (near Sedona). Here, Grey gets to the real point of his book—describing in lush, sometimes purple prose the beauty of the region, and its effect on Glenn's recovery. Grey's own powers of observation come into play, and anyone who has visited the area will recognize it from his descriptions, which can go on for pages.

"The murmur of falling water sounded closer. Presently Carley saw that the road turned at the notch in the canyon, and crossed a clear, swift stream. Here were huge mossy bowlders [sic], and red walls covered by lichens, and the air appeared dim and moist, and full of mellow, hollow roar. Beyond this crossing the road descended the west side of the canyon, drawing away and higher from the creek. Huge trees, the like of which Carley had never seen, began to stand majestically up out of the gorge, dwarfing the maples and white-spotted sycamores. The driver called these great trees yellow pines."

It's been more than a year since this writer last visited Oak Creek Canyon, but the road, I believe, still follows the route Grey described more than a century ago, and the sights are little changed. More buildings amidst the trees, more devil automobiles on the road, but otherwise the same.

The bulk of the story, after Carley's reunion with Glenn and her introduction to his new way of living—with nature instead of removed from it, as it is back home in New York City—revolves around Carley's discarding old ideas about her limits and her role in the world. While she's in Arizona with Glenn, they travel throughout the region, and Grey describes open desert and mountain peaks with as much detail and accuracy as he does the environs of the canyon (along with a vivid lesson on sheep-dipping).

Missing her old life, Carley eventually tells Glenn she can't stay, can't marry him, and returns to New York. But compared to the wide-open spaces of the west, she finds the city stifling, her friends shallow, her suitors of inferior stock. Even her attempt to be helpful to a friend of Glenn's from the war, a veteran who lost a leg in combat, turns sour.

Grey's depiction of New York society life rings true, but it's obvious that he finds it less interesting than the wild lands of the west. Finally, Carley has had enough and boards another train.

This time, she visits another of Arizona's canyons—the Grand Canyon. Again, Grey's rich prose brings it to life. "A transformation of color and shade appeared to be going on swiftly, as if gods were changing the scenes of a Titanic stage. As she gazed the dark fringed line of the north rim turned to burnished gold, and she watched that with fascinated eyes. It turned rose, it lost its fire, it faded to quiet cold gray. The sun had set."

One hundred years ago, Zane Grey wrote a novel that foresaw this writer's experience of those same places. The wild lands of the west *are* healing, redemptive, even transformative. They inspire awe and wonder and a sense of peace. Read *The Call of the Canyon*, hear and smell the crackling fire warming the cool night, feel the muscles of a horse racing beneath you, taste the piñon-infused breeze, and you might find yourself studying maps and making travel plans.

You won't regret it.

CHAPTER ONE

What subtle strange message had come to her out of the West?
Carley Burch laid the letter in her lap and gazed dreamily
through the window.

It was a day typical of early April in New York, rather cold
and gray, with steely sunlight. Spring breathed in the air, but the
women passing along Fifty-seventh Street wore furs and wraps.
She heard the distant clatter of an L train and then the hum of a
motor car. A hurdy-gurdy jarred into the interval of quiet.

"Glenn has been gone over a year," she mused, "three months
over a year—and of all his strange letters this seems the strangest
yet."

She lived again, for the thousandth time, the last moments
she had spent with him. It had been on New-Year's Eve, 1918.
They had called upon friends who were staying at the McAlpin,
in a suite on the twenty-first floor overlooking Broadway. And
when the last quarter hour of that eventful and tragic year began
slowly to pass with the low swell of whistles and bells, Carley's
friends had discreetly left her alone with her lover, at the open
window, to watch and hear the old year out, the new year in.

Glenn Kilbourne had returned from France early that fall,
shell-shocked and gassed, and otherwise incapacitated for

service in the army—a wreck of his former sterling self and in
many unaccountable ways a stranger to her. Cold, silent, haunted
by something, he had made her miserable with his aloofness. But
as the bells began to ring out the year that had been his ruin
Glenn had drawn her close, tenderly, passionately, and yet
strangely, too.

"Carley, look and listen!" he had whispered.

Under them stretched the great long white flare of Broadway,
with its snow-covered length glittering under a myriad of electric
lights. Sixth Avenue swerved away to the right, a less brilliant
lane of blanched snow. The L trains crept along like huge fire-
eyed serpents. The hum of the ceaseless moving line of motor
cars drifted upward faintly, almost drowned in the rising clamor
of the street. Broadway's gay and thoughtless crowds surged to
and fro, from that height merely a thick stream of black figures,
like contending columns of ants on the march. And everywhere
the monstrous electric signs flared up vivid in white and red and
green; and dimmed and paled, only to flash up again.

Ring out the Old! Ring in the New! Carley had poignantly
felt the sadness of the one, the promise of the other. As one by
one the siren factory whistles opened up with deep, hoarse
bellow, the clamor of the street and the ringing of the bells were
lost in a volume of continuous sound that swelled on high into a
magnificent roar. It was the voice of a city—of a nation. It was
the voice of a people crying out the strife and the agony of the
year—pealing forth a prayer for the future.

Glenn had put his lips to her ear: "It's like the voice in my
soul!" Never would she forget the shock of that. And how she
had stood spellbound, enveloped in the mighty volume of sound
no longer discordant, but full of great, pregnant melody, until the
white ball burst upon the tower of the Times Building, showing
the bright figures 1919.

The new year had not been many minutes old when Glenn
Kilbourne had told her he was going West to try to recover his
health.

Carley roused out of her memories to take up the letter that had so perplexed her. It bore the postmark, Flagstaff, Arizona. She reread it with slow pondering thoughtfulness.

WEST FORK, *March 25*

> *DEAR CARLEY:*
>
> It does seem my neglect in writing you is unpardonable. I used to be a pretty fair correspondent, but in that as in other things I have changed.
>
> One reason I have not answered sooner is because your letter was so sweet and loving that it made me feel an ungrateful and unappreciative wretch. Another is that this life I now lead does not induce writing. I am outdoors all day, and when I get back to this cabin at night I am too tired for anything but bed.
>
> Your imperious questions I must answer—and that must, of course, is a third reason why I have delayed my reply. First, you ask, "Don't you love me any more as you used to?". . . Frankly, I do not. I am sure my old love for you, before I went to France, was selfish, thoughtless, sentimental, and boyish. I am a man now. And my love for you is different. Let me assure you that it has been about all left to me of what is noble and beautiful. Whatever the changes in me for the worse, my love for you, at least, has grown better, finer, purer.
>
> And now for your second question, "Are you coming home as soon as you are well again?". . . Carley, I am well. I have delayed telling you this because I knew you would expect me to rush back East with the telling. But—the fact is, Carley, I am not coming—just yet. I wish it were possible for me to make you understand. For a long time I seem to have been frozen within. You know when I came back from France I couldn't talk. It's almost as bad as that now. Yet all that I was then seems to have changed again. It is only fair to you to tell you that, as I feel now, I hate the city, I hate people, and particularly I hate that dancing, drinking, lounging set you chase with. I don't want to come East until I am over that, you know. . . Suppose I never get over it? Well, Carley, you can free yourself from me by one word that I could never utter. I could never break our engagement. During the hell I went through in the war my attachment to you saved me from moral ruin, if it did not from perfect

honor and fidelity. This is another thing I despair of making you understand. And in the chaos I've wandered through since the war my love for you was my only anchor. You never guessed, did you, that I lived on your letters until I got well. And now the fact that I might get along without them is no discredit to their charm or to you.

It is all so hard to put in words, Carley. To lie down with death and get up with death was nothing. To face one's degradation was nothing. But to come home an incomprehensibly changed man—and to see my old life as strange as if it were the new life of another planet—to try to slip into the old groove—well, no words of mine can tell you how utterly impossible it was.

My old job was not open to me, even if I had been able to work. The government that I fought for left me to starve, or to die of my maladies like a dog, for all it cared. I could not live on your money, Carley. My people are poor, as you know. So there was nothing for me to do but to borrow a little money from my friends and to come West. I'm glad I had the courage to come.

What this West is I'll never try to tell you, because, loving the luxury and excitement and glitter of the city as you do, you'd think I was crazy.

Getting on here, in my condition, was as hard as trench life. But now, Carley—something has come to me out of the West. That, too, I am unable to put into words. Maybe I can give you an inkling of it. I'm strong enough to chop wood all day. No man or woman passes my cabin in a month. But I am never lonely. I love these vast red canyon walls towering above me. And the silence is so sweet. Think of the hellish din that filled my ears. Even now—sometimes, the brook here changes its babbling murmur to the roar of war. I never understood anything of the meaning of nature until I lived under these looming stone walls and whispering pines.

So, Carley, try to understand me, or at least be kind. You know they came very near writing, "Gone west!" after my name, and considering that, this "Out West" signifies for me a very fortunate difference. A tremendous difference! For the present I'll let well enough alone.

Adios. Write soon. Love from

GLENN.

Carley's second reaction to the letter was a sudden upflashing desire to see her lover—to go out West and find him. Impulses with her were rather rare and inhibited, but this one made her tremble. If Glenn was well again he must have vastly changed from the moody, stone-faced, and haunted-eyed man who had so worried and distressed her. He had embarrassed her, too, for sometimes, in her home, meeting young men there who had not gone into the service, he had seemed to retreat into himself, singularly aloof, as if his world was not theirs.

Again, with eager eyes and quivering lips, she read the letter. It contained words that lifted her heart. Her starved love greedily absorbed them. In them she had excuse for any resolve that might bring Glenn closer to her. And she pondered over this longing to go to him.

Carley had the means to come and go and live as she liked. She did not remember her father, who had died when she was a child. Her mother had left her in the care of a sister, and before the war they had divided their time between New York and Europe, the Adirondacks and Florida, Carley had gone in for Red Cross and relief work with more of sincerity than most of her set. But she was really not used to making any decision as definite and important as that of going out West alone. She had never been farther west than Jersey City; and her conception of the West was a hazy one of vast plains and rough mountains, squalid towns, cattle herds, and uncouth ill-clad men.

So she carried the letter to her aunt, a rather slight woman with a kindly face and shrewd eyes, and who appeared somewhat given to old-fashioned garments.

"Aunt Mary, here's a letter from Glenn," said Carley. "It's more of a stumper than usual. Please read it."

"Dear me! You look upset," replied the aunt, mildly, and, adjusting her spectacles, she took the letter.

Carley waited impatiently for the perusal, conscious of inward forces coming more and more to the aid of her impulse to go West. Her aunt paused once to murmur how glad she was that Glenn had gotten well. Then she read on to the close.

"Carley, that's a fine letter," she said, fervently. "Do you see through it?"

"No, I don't," replied Carley. "That's why I asked you to read it."

"Do you still love Glenn as you used to before—"

"Why, Aunt Mary!" exclaimed Carley, in surprise.

"Excuse me, Carley, if I'm blunt. But the fact is young women of modern times are very different from my kind when I was a girl. You haven't acted as though you pined for Glenn. You gad around almost the same as ever."

"What's a girl to do?" protested Carley.

"You are twenty-six years old, Carley," retorted Aunt Mary.

"Suppose I am. I'm as young—as I ever was."

"Well, let's not argue about modern girls and modern times. We never get anywhere," returned her aunt, kindly. "But I can tell you something of what Glenn Kilbourne means in that letter —if you want to hear it."

"I do—indeed."

"The war did something horrible to Glenn aside from wrecking his health. Shell-shock, they said! I don't understand that. Out of his mind, they said! But that never was true. Glenn was as sane as I am, and, my dear, that's pretty sane, I'll have you remember. But he must have suffered some terrible blight to his spirit—some blunting of his soul. For months after he returned he walked as one in a trance. Then came a change. He grew restless. Perhaps that change was for the better. At least it showed he'd roused. Glenn saw you and your friends and the life you lead, and all the present, with eyes from which the scales had dropped. He saw what was *wrong*. He never said so to me, but I knew it. It wasn't only to get well that he went West. It was to get away. . . . And, Carley Burch, if your happiness depends on him you had better be up and doing—or you'll *lose* him!"

"Aunt Mary!" gasped Carley.

"I mean it. That letter shows how near he came to the Valley of the Shadow—and how he has become a man. . . . If I were you I'd go out West. Surely there must be a place where it would be all right for you to stay."

"Oh, yes," replied Carley, eagerly. "Glenn wrote me there was a lodge where people went in nice weather—right down in the canyon not far from his place. Then, of course, the town—Flagstaff—isn't far. . . . Aunt Mary, I think I'll go."

"I would. You're certainly wasting your time here."

"But I could only go for a visit," rejoined Carley, thoughtfully. "A month, perhaps six weeks, if I could stand it."

"Seems to me if you can stand New York you could stand that place," said Aunt Mary, dryly.

"The idea of staying away from New York any length of time —why, I couldn't do it! . . . But I can stay out there long enough to bring Glenn back with me."

"That may take you longer than you think," replied her aunt, with a gleam in her shrewd eyes. "If you want my advice you will surprise Glenn. Don't write him—don't give him a chance to— well to suggest courteously that you'd better not come just yet. I don't like his words 'just yet.'"

"Auntie, you're—rather—more than blunt," said Carley, divided between resentment and amaze. "Glenn would be simply wild to have me come."

"Maybe he would. Has he ever asked you?"

"No-o—come to think of it, he hasn't," replied Carley, reluctantly. "Aunt Mary, you hurt my feelings."

"Well, child, I'm glad to learn your feelings are hurt," returned the aunt. "I'm sure, Carley, that underneath all this— this blasé ultra something you've acquired, there's a real heart. Only you must hurry and listen to it—or—"

"Or what?" queried Carley.

Aunt Mary shook her gray head sagely. "Never mind what. Carley, I'd like your idea of the most significant thing in Glenn's letter."

"Why, his love for me, of course!" replied Carley.

"Naturally you think that. But I don't. What struck me most were his words, 'out of the West.' Carley, you'd do well to ponder over them."

"I will," rejoined Carley, positively. "I'll do more. I'll go out to his wonderful West and see what he meant by them."

Carley Burch possessed in full degree the prevailing modern craze for speed. She loved a motor-car ride at sixty miles an hour along a smooth, straight road, or, better, on the level seashore of Ormond, where on moonlight nights the white blanched sand seemed to flash toward her. Therefore quite to her taste was the Twentieth Century Limited which was hurtling her on the way to Chicago. The unceasingly smooth and even rush of the train satisfied something in her. An old lady sitting in an adjoining seat with a companion amused Carley by the remark: "I wish we didn't go so fast. People nowadays haven't time to draw a comfortable breath. Suppose we should run off the track!"

Carley had no fear of express trains, or motor cars, or transatlantic liners; in fact, she prided herself in not being afraid of anything. But she wondered if this was not the false courage of association with a crowd. Before this enterprise at hand she could not remember anything she had undertaken alone. Her thrills seemed to be in abeyance to the end of her journey. That night her sleep was permeated with the steady low whirring of the wheels. Once, roused by a jerk, she lay awake in the darkness while the thought came to her that she and all her fellow passengers were really at the mercy of the engineer. Who was he, and did he stand at his throttle keen and vigilant, thinking of the lives intrusted to him? Such thoughts vaguely annoyed Carley, and she dismissed them.

A long half-day wait in Chicago was a tedious preliminary to the second part of her journey. But at last she found herself aboard the California Limited, and went to bed with a relief quite a stranger to her. The glare of the sun under the curtain awakened her. Propped up on her pillows, she looked out at apparently endless green fields or pastures, dotted now and then with little farmhouses and tree-skirted villages. This country, she thought, must be the prairie land she remembered lay west of the Mississippi.

Later, in the dining car, the steward smilingly answered her question: "This is Kansas, and those green fields out there are the wheat that feeds the nation."

Carley was not impressed. The color of the short wheat appeared soft and rich, and the boundless fields stretched away monotonously. She had not known there was so much flat land in the world, and she imagined it might be a fine country for automobile roads. When she got back to her seat she drew the blinds down and read her magazines. Then tiring of that, she went back to the observation car. Carley was accustomed to attracting attention, and did not resent it, unless she was annoyed. The train evidently had a full complement of passengers, who, as far as

Carley could see, were people not of her station in life. The glare from the many windows, and the rather crass interest of several men, drove her back to her own section. There she discovered that some one had drawn up her window shades. Carley promptly pulled them down and settled herself comfortably. Then she heard a woman speak, not particularly low: "I thought people traveled west to see the country." And a man replied, rather dryly. "Wal, not always." His companion went on: "If that girl was mine I'd let down her skirt." The man laughed and replied: "Martha, you're shore behind the times. Look at the pictures in the magazines."

Such remarks amused Carley, and later she took advantage of an opportunity to notice her neighbors. They appeared a rather quaint old couple, reminding her of the natives of country towns in the Adirondacks. She was not amused, however, when another of her woman neighbors, speaking low, referred to her as a "lunger." Carley appreciated the fact that she was pale, but she assured herself that there ended any possible resemblance she might have to a consumptive.

And she was somewhat pleased to hear this woman's male companion forcibly voice her own convictions. In fact, he was nothing if not admiring.

Kansas was interminably long to Carley, and she went to sleep before riding out of it. Next morning she found herself looking out at the rough gray and black land of New Mexico. She searched the horizon for mountains, but there did not appear to be any. She received a vague, slow-dawning impression that was hard to define. She did not like the country, though that was not the impression which eluded her. Bare gray flats, low scrub-fringed hills, bleak cliffs, jumble after jumble of rocks, and occasionally a long vista down a valley, somehow compelling—these passed before her gaze until she tired of them. Where was the West Glenn had written about? One thing seemed sure, and it was that every mile of this crude country brought her nearer to him. This recurring thought gave Carley all the pleasure she had felt so far in this endless ride. It struck her that England or France could be dropped down into New Mexico and scarcely noticed.

By and by the sun grew hot, the train wound slowly and creakingly upgrade, the car became full of dust, all of which was disagreeable to Carley. She dozed on her pillow for hours, until she was stirred by a passenger crying out, delightedly: "Look! Indians!"

Carley looked, not without interest. As a child she had read about Indians, and memory returned images both colorful and romantic. From the car window she espied dusty flat barrens, low squat mud houses, and queer-looking little people, children naked or extremely ragged and dirty, women in loose garments with flares of red, and men in white man's garb, slovenly and motley. All these strange individuals stared apathetically as the train slowly passed.

"Indians," muttered Carley, incredulously. "Well, if they are the noble red people, my illusions are dispelled." She did not look out of the window again, not even when the brakeman called out the remarkable name of Albuquerque.

Next day Carley's languid attention quickened to the name of Arizona, and to the frowning red walls of rock, and to the vast rolling stretches of cedar-dotted land. Nevertheless, it affronted her. This was no country for people to live in, and so far as she could see it was indeed uninhabited. Her sensations were not, however, limited to sight. She became aware of unfamiliar disturbing little shocks or vibrations in her ear drums, and after that a disagreeable bleeding of the nose. The porter told her this was owing to the altitude. Thus, one thing and another kept Carley most of the time away from the window, so that she really saw very little of the country. From what she had seen she drew the conviction that she had not missed much. At sunset she deliberately gazed out to discover what an Arizona sunset was like just a pale yellow flare! She had seen better than that above the Palisades. Not until reaching Winslow did she realize how near she was to her journey's end and that she would arrive at Flagstaff after dark. She grew conscious of nervousness. Suppose Flagstaff were like these other queer little towns!

Not only once, but several times before the train slowed down for her destination did Carley wish she had sent Glenn word to meet her. And when, presently, she found herself standing out in the dark, cold, windy night before a dim-lit railroad station she more than regretted her decision to surprise Glenn. But that was too late and she must make the best of her poor judgment.

Men were passing to and fro on the platform, some of whom appeared to be very dark of skin and eye, and were probably Mexicans. At length an expressman approached Carley, soliciting patronage. He took her bags and, depositing them in a wagon, he pointed up the wide street: "One block up an' turn. Hotel Wetherford." Then he drove off. Carley followed, carrying her small satchel. A cold wind, driving the dust, stung her face as she crossed the street to a high sidewalk that extended along the block. There were lights in the stores and on the corners, yet she seemed impressed by a dark, cold, windy bigness. Many people, mostly men, were passing up and down, and there were motor cars everywhere. No one paid any attention to her. Gaining the corner of the block, she turned, and was relieved to see the hotel sign. As she entered the lobby a clicking of pool balls and the discordant rasp of a phonograph assailed her ears. The expressman set down her bags and left Carley standing there. The clerk or proprietor was talking from behind his desk to several men, and there were loungers in the lobby. The air was thick with tobacco smoke. No one paid any attention to Carley until at length she stepped up to the desk and interrupted the conversation there.

"Is this a hotel?" she queried, brusquely.

The shirt-sleeved individual leisurely turned and replied, "Yes, ma'am."

And Carley said: "No one would recognize it by the courtesy shown. I have been standing here waiting to register."

With the same leisurely ease and a cool, laconic stare the clerk turned the book toward her. "Reckon people round here ask for what they want."

Carley made no further comment. She assuredly recognized that what she had been accustomed to could not be expected out here. What she most wished to do at the moment was to get close to the big open grate where a cheery red-and-gold fire cracked. It was necessary, however, to follow the clerk. He assigned her to a small drab room which contained a bed, a bureau, and a stationary washstand with one spigot. There was also a chair. While Carley removed her coat and hat the clerk went downstairs for the rest of her luggage. Upon his return Carley learned that a stage left the hotel for Oak Creek Canyon at nine o'clock next morning. And this cheered her so much that she faced the strange sense of loneliness and discomfort with something of fortitude. There was no heat in the room, and no hot water. When Carley squeezed the spigot handle there burst forth a torrent of water that spouted up out of the washbasin to deluge her. It was colder than any ice water she had ever felt. It was piercingly cold. Hard upon the surprise and shock Carley suffered a flash of temper. But then the humor of it struck her and she had to laugh.

"Serves you right—you spoiled doll of luxury!" she mocked. "This is out West. Shiver and wait on yourself!"

Never before had she undressed so swiftly nor felt grateful for thick woollen blankets on a hard bed. Gradually she grew warm. The blackness, too, seemed rather comforting.

"I'm only twenty miles from Glenn," she whispered. "How strange! I wonder will he be glad." She felt a sweet, glowing assurance of that. Sleep did not come readily. Excitement had laid hold of her nerves, and for a long time she lay awake. After a while the chug of motor cars, the click of pool balls, the murmur of low voices all ceased. Then she heard a sound of wind outside, an intermittent, low moaning, new to her ears, and somehow pleasant. Another sound greeted her—the musical clanging of a clock that struck the quarters of the hour. Some time late sleep claimed her.

Upon awakening she found she had overslept, necessitating haste upon her part. As to that, the temperature of the room did not admit of leisurely dressing. She had no adequate name for the feeling of the water. And her fingers grew so numb that she made what she considered a disgraceful matter of her attire.

Downstairs in the lobby another cheerful red fire burned in the grate. How perfectly satisfying was an open fireplace! She thrust her numb hands almost into the blaze, and simply shook with the tingling pain that slowly warmed out of them. The lobby was deserted. A sign directed her to a dining room in the basement, where of the ham and eggs and strong coffee she managed to partake a little. Then she went upstairs into the lobby and out into the street.

A cold, piercing air seemed to blow right through her.

Walking to the near corner, she paused to look around. Down the main street flowed a leisurely stream of pedestrians, horses, cars, extending between two blocks of low buildings. Across from where she stood lay a vacant lot, beyond which began a line of neat, oddly constructed houses, evidently residences of the town. And then lifting her gaze, instinctively drawn by something obstructing the sky line, she was suddenly struck with surprise and delight.

"Oh! how perfectly splendid!" she burst out.

Two magnificent mountains loomed right over her, sloping up with majestic sweep of green and black timber, to a ragged tree-fringed snow area that swept up cleaner and whiter, at last to lift pure glistening peaks, noble and sharp, and sunrise-flushed against the blue.

Carley had climbed Mont Blanc and she had seen the Matterhorn, but they had never struck such amaze and admiration from her as these twin peaks of her native land.

"What mountains are those?" she asked a passer-by.

"San Francisco Peaks, ma'am," replied the man.

"Why, they can't be over a mile away!" she said.

"Eighteen miles, ma'am," he returned, with a grin. "Shore this Arizonie air is deceivin'."

"How strange," murmured Carley. "It's not that way in the Adirondacks."

She was still gazing upward when a man approached her and said the stage for Oak Creek Canyon would soon be ready to start, and he wanted to know if her baggage was ready. Carley hurried back to her room to pack.

She had expected the stage would be a motor bus, or at least a large touring car, but it turned out to be a two-seated vehicle drawn by a team of ragged horses. The driver was a little wizen-faced man of doubtful years, and he did not appear obviously susceptible to the importance of his passenger. There was considerable freight to be hauled, besides Carley's luggage, but evidently she was the only passenger.

"Reckon it's goin' to be a bad day," said the driver. "These April days high up on the desert are windy an' cold. Mebbe it'll snow, too. Them clouds hangin' around the peaks ain't very promisin'. Now, miss, haven't you a heavier coat or somethin'?"

"No, I have not," replied Carley. "I'll have to stand it. Did you say this was desert?"

"I shore did. Wal, there's a hoss blanket under the seat, an' you can have that," he replied, and, climbing to the seat in front of Carley, he took up the reins and started the horses off at a trot.

At the first turning Carley became specifically acquainted with the driver's meaning of a bad day. A gust of wind, raw and penetrating, laden with dust and stinging sand, swept full in her face. It came so suddenly that she was scarcely quick enough to close her eyes. It took considerable clumsy effort on her part with a handkerchief, aided by relieving tears, to clear her sight again. Thus uncomfortably Carley found herself launched on the last lap of her journey.

All before her and alongside lay the squalid environs of the town. Looked back at, with the peaks rising behind, it was not unpicturesque. But the hard road with its sheets of flying dust, the bleak railroad yards, the round pens she took for cattle corrals, and the sordid debris littering the approach to a huge sawmill,—these were offensive in Carley's sight. From a tall dome-like stack rose a yellowish smoke that spread overhead, adding to the lowering aspect of the sky. Beyond the sawmill extended the open country sloping somewhat roughly, and evidently once a forest, but now a hideous bare slash, with ghastly burned stems of trees still standing, and myriads of stumps attesting to denudation.

The bleak road wound away to the southwest, and from this direction came the gusty wind. It did not blow regularly so that Carley could be on her guard. It lulled now and then, permitting her to look about, and then suddenly again whipping dust into her face. The smell of the dust was as unpleasant as the sting. It made her nostrils smart. It was penetrating, and a little more of it would have been suffocating. And as a leaden gray bank of broken clouds rolled up the wind grew stronger and the air colder. Chilled before, Carley now became thoroughly cold.

There appeared to be no end to the devastated forest land, and the farther she rode the more barren and sordid grew the landscape. Carley forgot about the impressive mountains behind her. And as the ride wore into hours, such was her discomfort and disillusion that she forgot about Glenn Kilbourne. She did not reach the point of regretting her adventure, but she grew mightily unhappy. Now and then she espied dilapidated log cabins and surroundings even more squalid than the ruined forest. What wretched abodes! Could it be possible that people had lived in them? She imagined men had but hardly women and children. Somewhere she had forgotten an idea that women and children were extremely scarce in the West.

Straggling bits of forest—yellow pines, the driver called the trees—began to encroach upon the burned-over and arid barren land. To Carley these groves, by reason of contrast and proof of what once was, only rendered the landscape more forlorn and dreary. Why had these miles and miles of forest been cut? By money grubbers, she supposed, the same as were devastating the Adirondacks. Presently, when the driver had to halt to repair or adjust something wrong with the harness, Carley was grateful for a respite from cold inaction. She got out and walked. Sleet began to fall, and when she resumed her seat in the vehicle she asked the driver for the blanket to cover her. The smell of this horse blanket was less endurable than the cold. Carley huddled down into a state of apathetic misery. Already she had enough of the West.

But the sleet storm passed, the clouds broke, the sun shone through, greatly mitigating her discomfort. By and by the road led into a section of real forest, unspoiled in any degree. Carley saw large gray squirrels with tufted ears and white bushy tails. Presently the driver pointed out a flock of huge birds, which

Carley, on second glance, recognized as turkeys, only these were sleek and glossy, with flecks of bronze and black and white, quite different from turkeys back East. "There must be a farm near," said Carley, gazing about.

"No, ma'am. Them's wild turkeys," replied the driver, "an' shore the best eatin' you ever had in your life."

A little while afterwards, as they were emerging from the woodland into more denuded country, he pointed out to Carley a herd of gray white-rumped animals that she took to be sheep.

"An' them's antelope," he said. "Once this desert was overrun by antelope. Then they nearly disappeared. An' now they're increasin' again."

More barren country, more bad weather, and especially an exceedingly rough road reduced Carley to her former state of dejection. The jolting over roots and rocks and ruts was worse than uncomfortable. She had to hold on to the seat to keep from being thrown out. The horses did not appreciably change their gait for rough sections of the road. Then a more severe jolt brought Carley's knee in violent contact with an iron bolt on the forward seat, and it hurt her so acutely that she had to bite her lips to keep from screaming. A smoother stretch of road did not come any too soon for her.

It led into forest again. And Carley soon became aware that they had at last left the cut and burned-over district of timberland behind. A cold wind moaned through the treetops and set the drops of water pattering down upon her. It lashed her wet face. Carley closed her eyes and sagged in her seat, mostly oblivious to the passing scenery. "The girls will never believe this of me," she soliloquized. And indeed she was amazed at herself. Then thought of Glenn strengthened her. It did not really matter what she suffered on the way to him. Only she was disgusted at her lack of stamina, and her appalling sensitiveness to discomfort.

"Wal, hyar's Oak Creek Canyon," called the driver.

Carley, rousing out of her weary preoccupation, opened her

eyes to see that the driver had halted at a turn of the road, where apparently it descended a fearful declivity.

The very forest-fringed earth seemed to have opened into a deep abyss, ribbed by red rock walls and choked by steep mats of green timber. The chasm was a V-shaped split and so deep that looking downward sent at once a chill and a shudder over Carley. At that point it appeared narrow and ended in a box. In the other direction, it widened and deepened, and stretched farther on between tremendous walls of red, and split its winding floor of green with glimpses of a gleaming creek, bowlder-strewn and ridged by white rapids. A low mellow roar of rushing waters floated up to Carley's ears. What a wild, lonely, terrible place! Could Glenn possibly live down there in that ragged rent in the earth? It frightened her—the sheer sudden plunge of it from the heights. Far down the gorge a purple light shone on the forested floor. And on the moment the sun burst through the clouds and sent a golden blaze down into the depths, transforming them incalculably. The great cliffs turned gold, the creek changed to glancing silver, the green of trees vividly freshened, and in the clefts rays of sunlight burned into the blue shadows. Carley had never gazed upon a scene like this. Hostile and prejudiced, she yet felt wrung from her an acknowledgment of beauty and grandeur. But wild, violent, savage! Not livable! This insulated rift in the crust of the earth was a gigantic burrow for beasts, perhaps for outlawed men—not for a civilized person—not for Glenn Kilbourne.

"Don't be scart, ma'am," spoke up the driver. "It's safe if you're careful. An' I've druv this manys the time."

Carley's heartbeats thumped at her side, rather denying her taunted assurance of fearlessness. Then the rickety vehicle started down at an angle that forced her to cling to her seat.

CHAPTER TWO

Carley, clutching her support, with abated breath and prickling skin, gazed in fascinated suspense over the rim of the gorge. Sometimes the wheels on that side of the vehicle passed within a few inches of the edge. The brakes squeaked, the wheels slid; and she could hear the scrape of the iron-shod hoofs of the horses as they held back stiff legged, obedient to the wary call of the driver.

The first hundred yards of that steep road cut out of the cliff appeared to be the worst. It began to widen, with descents less precipitous. Tips of trees rose level with her gaze, obstructing sight of the blue depths. Then brush appeared on each side of the road. Gradually Carley's strain relaxed, and also the muscular contraction by which she had braced herself in the seat. The horses began to trot again. The wheels rattled. The road wound around abrupt corners, and soon the green and red wall of the opposite side of the canyon loomed close. Low roar of running water rose to Carley's ears. When at length she looked out instead of down she could see nothing but a mass of green foliage crossed by tree trunks and branches of brown and gray. Then the vehicle bowled under dark cool shade, into a tunnel with mossy wet cliff on one side, and close-standing trees on the other.

"Reckon we're all right now, onless we meet somebody comin' up," declared the driver.

Carley relaxed. She drew a deep breath of relief. She had her first faint intimation that perhaps her extensive experience of motor cars, express trains, transatlantic liners, and even a little of airplanes, did not range over the whole of adventurous life. She was likely to meet something, entirely new and striking out here in the West.

The murmur of falling water sounded closer. Presently Carley saw that the road turned at the notch in the canyon, and crossed a clear swift stream. Here were huge mossy boulders, and red walls covered by lichens, and the air appeared dim and moist, and full of mellow, hollow roar. Beyond this crossing the road descended the west side of the canyon, drawing away and higher from the creek. Huge trees, the like of which Carley had never seen, began to stand majestically up out of the gorge, dwarfing the maples and white-spotted sycamores. The driver called these great trees yellow pines.

At last the road led down from the steep slope to the floor of the canyon. What from far above had appeared only a green timber-choked cleft proved from close relation to be a wide winding valley, tip and down, densely forested for the most part, yet having open glades and bisected from wall to wall by the creek. Every quarter of a mile or so the road crossed the stream; and at these fords Carley again held on desperately and gazed out dubiously, for the creek was deep, swift, and full of bowlders. Neither driver nor horses appeared to mind obstacles. Carley was splashed and jolted not inconsiderably. They passed through groves of oak trees, from which the creek manifestly derived its name; and under gleaming walls, cold, wet, gloomy, and silent; and between lines of solemn wide-spreading pines. Carley saw deep, still green pools eddying under huge massed jumble of cliffs, and stretches of white water, and then, high above the treetops, a wild line of canyon rim, cold against the sky. She felt shut in from the world, lost in an unscalable rut of the earth. Again the sunlight had failed, and the gray gloom of the canyon oppressed her. It struck Carley as singular that she could not help being affected by mere weather, mere heights and depths, mere rock walls and pine trees, and rushing water. For really, what had these to do with her? These were only physical things that she was passing. Nevertheless, although she resisted sensation, she was more and more shot through and through with the wildness and savageness of this canyon.

A sharp turn of the road to the right disclosed a slope down the creek, across which showed orchards and fields, and a cottage nestling at the base of the wall. The ford at this crossing gave Carley more concern than any that had been passed, for there was greater volume and depth of water. One of the horses slipped on the rocks, plunged up and on with great splash. They crossed, however, without more mishap to Carley than further acquaintance with this iciest of waters. From this point the driver turned back along the creek, passed between orchards and fields, and drove along the base of the red wall to come suddenly upon a large rustic house that had been hidden from Carley's sight. It sat almost against the stone cliff, from which poured a white foamy sheet of water. The house was built of slabs with the bark on, and it had a lower and upper porch running all around, at least as far as the cliff. Green growths from the rock wall overhung the upper porch. A column of blue smoke curled lazily upward from a stone chimney. On one of the porch posts hung a sign with rude lettering: "Lolomi Lodge."

"Hey, Josh, did you fetch the flour?" called a woman's voice from inside.

"Hullo I Reckon I didn't forgit nothin'," replied the man, as he got down. "An' say, Mrs. Hutter, hyar's a young lady from Noo Yorrk."

That latter speech of the driver's brought Mrs. Hutter out on the porch. "Flo, come here," she called to some one evidently near at hand. And then she smilingly greeted Carley.

"Get down an' come in, miss," she said. "I'm sure glad to see you."

Carley, being stiff and cold, did not very gracefully disengage herself from the high muddy wheel and step. When she mounted to the porch she saw that Mrs. Hutter was a woman of middle age, rather stout, with strong face full of fine wavy lines, and kind dark eyes.

"I'm Miss Burch," said Carley.

"You're the girl whose picture Glenn Kilbourne has over his fireplace," declared the woman, heartily. "I'm sure glad to meet you, an' my daughter Flo will be, too."

That about her picture pleased and warmed Carley. "Yes, I'm Glenn Kilbourne's fiancée. I've come West to surprise him. Is he here. . . . Is—is he well?"

"Fine. I saw him yesterday. He's changed a great deal from what he was at first. Most all the last few months. I reckon you won't know him. . . . But you're wet an' cold an' you look fagged. Come right in to the fire."

"Thank you; I'm all right," returned Carley.

At the doorway they encountered a girl of lithe and robust figure, quick in her movements. Carley was swift to see the youth and grace of her; and then a face that struck Carley as neither pretty nor beautiful, but still wonderfully attractive.

"Flo, here's Miss Burch," burst out Mrs. Hutter, with cheerful importance. "Glenn Kilbourne's girl come all the way from New York to surprise him!"

"Oh, Carley, I'm shore happy to meet you!" said the girl, in a voice of slow drawling richness. "I know you. Glenn has told me all about you."

If this greeting, sweet and warm as it seemed, was a shock to Carley, she gave no sign. But as she murmured something in reply she looked with all a woman's keenness into the face before her. Flo Hutter had a fair skin generously freckled; a mouth and chin too firmly cut to suggest a softer feminine beauty; and eyes of clear light hazel, penetrating, frank, fearless. Her hair was very abundant, almost silver-gold in color, and it was either rebellious or showed lack of care. Carley liked the girl's looks and liked the sincerity of her greeting; but instinctively she reacted antagonistically because of the frank suggestion of intimacy with Glenn. But for that she would have been spontaneous and friendly rather than restrained.

They ushered Carley into a big living room and up to a fire of blazing logs, where they helped divest her of the wet wraps. And all the time they talked in the solicitous way natural to women who were kind and unused to many visitors. Then Mrs. Hutter bustled off to make a cup of hot coffee while Flo talked.

"We'll shore give you the nicest room—with a sleeping porch right under the cliff where the water falls. It'll sing you to sleep. Of course you needn't use the bed outdoors until it's warmer. Spring is late here, you know, and we'll have nasty weather yet. You really happened on Oak Creek at its least attractive season. But then it's always—well, just Oak Creek. You'll come to know."

"I dare say I'll remember my first sight of it and the ride down that cliff road," said Carley, with a wan smile.

"Oh, that's nothing to what you'll see and do," returned Flo, knowingly. "We've had Eastern tenderfeet here before. And never was there a one of them who didn't come to love Arizona."

"Tenderfoot! It hadn't occurred to me. But of course—" murmured Carley.

Then Mrs. Hutter returned, carrying a tray, which she set upon a chair, and drew to Carley's side. "Eat an' drink," she said, as if these actions were the cardinally important ones of life. "Flo, you carry her bags up to that west room we always give to some particular person we want to love Lolomi." Next she threw sticks of wood upon the fire, making it crackle and blaze, then seated herself near Carley and beamed upon her.

"You'll not mind if we call you Carley?" she asked, eagerly.

"Oh, indeed no! I—I'd like it," returned Carley, made to feel friendly and at home in spite of herself.

"You see it's not as if you were just a stranger," went on Mrs. Hutter. "Tom—that's Flo's father—took a likin' to Glenn Kilbourne when he first came to Oak Creek over a year ago. I wonder if you all know how sick that soldier boy was. . . . Well, he lay on his back for two solid weeks—in the room we're givin' you. An' I for one didn't think he'd ever get up. But he did. An' he got better. An' after a while he went to work for Tom. Then six months an' more ago he invested in the sheep business with Tom. He lived with us until he built his cabin up West Fork. He an' Flo have run together a good deal, an' naturally he told her about you. So you see you're not a stranger. An' we want you to feel you're with friends."

"I thank you, Mrs. Hutter," replied Carley, feelingly. "I never could thank you enough for being good to Glenn. I did not know he was so—so sick. At first he wrote but seldom."

"Reckon he never wrote you or told you what he did in the war," declared Mrs. Hutter.

"Indeed he never did!"

"Well, I'll tell you some day. For Tom found out all about him. Got some of it from a soldier who came to Flagstaff for lung trouble. He'd been in the same company with Glenn. We didn't know this boy's name while he was in Flagstaff. But later Tom found out. John Henderson. He was only twenty-two, a fine lad. An' he died in Phœnix. We tried to get him out here. But the boy wouldn't live on charity. He was always expectin' money —a war bonus, whatever that was. It didn't come. He was a clerk at the El Tovar for a while. Then he came to Flagstaff. But it was too cold an' he stayed there too long."

"Too bad," rejoined Carley, thoughtfully. This information as to the suffering of American soldiers had augmented during the last few months, and seemed to possess strange, poignant power to depress Carley. Always she had turned away from the unpleasant. And the misery of unfortunates was as disturbing almost as direct contact with disease and squalor. But it had begun to dawn upon Carley that there might occur circumstances of life, in every way affronting her comfort and happiness, which it would be impossible to turn her back upon.

At this juncture Flo returned to the room, and again Carley was struck with the girl's singular freedom of movement and the sense of sure poise and joy that seemed to emanate from her presence.

"I've made a fire in your little stove," she said. "There's water heating. Now won't you come up and change those traveling clothes. You'll want to fix up for Glenn, won't you?"

Carley had to smile at that. This girl indeed was frank and unsophisticated, and somehow refreshing. Carley rose.

"You are both very good to receive me as a friend," she said. "I hope I shall not disappoint you. . . . Yes, I do want to improve my appearance before Glenn sees me. . . . Is there any way I can send word to him—by someone who has not seen me?"

"There shore is. I'll send Charley, one of our hired boys."

"Thank you. Then tell him to say there is a lady here from New York to see him, and it is very important."

Flo Hutter clapped her hands and laughed with glee. Her gladness gave Carley a little twinge of conscience. Jealously was an unjust and stifling thing.

Carley was conducted up a broad stairway and along a boarded hallway to a room that opened out on the porch. A steady low murmur of falling water assailed her ears. Through the open door she saw across the porch to a white tumbling lacy veil of water falling, leaping, changing, so close that it seemed to touch the heavy pole railing of the porch.

This room resembled a tent. The sides were of canvas. It had no ceiling. But the rough-hewn shingles of the roof of the house sloped down closely. The furniture was home made. An Indian rug covered the floor. The bed with its woolly clean blankets and the white pillows looked inviting.

"Is this where Glenn lay—when he was sick?" queried Carley.

"Yes," replied Flo, gravely, and a shadow darkened her eyes. "I ought to tell you all about it. I will some day. But you must not be made unhappy now. . . . Glenn nearly died here. Mother or I never left his side—for a while there—when life was so bad."

She showed Carley how to open the little stove and put the short billets of wood inside and work the damper; and cautioning her to keep an eye on it so that it would not get too hot, she left Carley to herself.

Carley found herself in an unfamiliar mood. There came a leap of her heart every time she thought of the meeting with Glenn, so soon now to be, but it was not that which was unfamiliar. She seemed to have a difficult approach to undefined and unusual thoughts. All this was so different from her regular life. Besides she was tired. But these explanations did not suffice. There was a pang in her breast which must owe its origin to the fact that Glenn Kilbourne had been ill in this little room and some other girl than Carley Burch had nursed him. "Am I jealous?" she whispered. "No!" But she knew in her heart that she lied. A woman could no more help being jealous, under such circumstances, than she could help the beat and throb of her blood. Nevertheless, Carley was glad Flo Hutter had been there, and always she would be grateful to her for that kindness.

Carley disrobed and, donning her dressing gown, she unpacked her bags and hung her things upon pegs under the curtained shelves. Then she lay down to rest, with no intention of slumber. But there was a strange magic in the fragrance of the room, like the piny tang outdoors, and in the feel of the bed, and especially in the low, dreamy hum and murmur of the waterfall. She fell asleep. When she awakened it was five o'clock. The fire in the stove was out, but the water was still warm. She bathed and dressed, not without care, yet as swiftly as was her habit at home; and she wore white because Glenn had always liked her best in white. But it was assuredly not a gown to wear in a country house where draughts of cold air filled the unheated rooms and halls. So she threw round her a warm sweater-shawl, with colorful bars becoming to her dark eyes and hair.

All the time that she dressed and thought, her very being seemed to be permeated by that soft murmuring sound of falling water. No moment of waking life there at Lolomi Lodge, or perhaps of slumber hours, could be wholly free of that sound. It vaguely tormented Carley, yet was not uncomfortable. She went out upon the porch. The small alcove space held a bed and a rustic chair. Above her the peeled poles of the roof descended to within a few feet of her head. She had to lean over the rail of the porch to look up. The green and red rock wall sheered ponderously near. The waterfall showed first at the notch of a fissure, where the cliff split; and down over smooth places the water gleamed, to narrow in a crack with little drops, and suddenly to leap into a thin white sheet.

Out from the porch the view was restricted to glimpses between the pines, and beyond to the opposite wall of the canyon. How shut-in, how walled in this home!

"In summer it might be good to spend a couple of weeks here," soliloquized Carley. "But to *live* here? Heavens! A person might as well be buried."

Heavy footsteps upon the porch below accompanied by a man's voice quickened Carley's pulse. Did they belong to Glenn? After a strained second she decided not. Nevertheless, the acceleration of her blood and an unwonted glow of excitement, long a stranger to her, persisted as she left the porch and entered the boarded hall. How gray and barn-like this upper part of the house! From the head of the stairway, however, the big living room presented a cheerful contrast. There were warm colors, some comfortable rockers, a lamp that shed a bright light, and an open fire which alone would have dispelled the raw gloom of the day.

A large man in corduroys and top boots advanced to meet Carley. He had a clean-shaven face that might have been hard and stern but for his smile, and one look into his eyes revealed their resemblance to Flo's.

"I'm Tom Hutter, an' I'm shore glad to welcome you to Lolomi, Miss Carley," he said. His voice was deep and slow. There were ease and force in his presence, and the grip he gave Carley's hand was that of a man who made no distinction in hand-shaking. Carley, quick in her perceptions, instantly liked him and sensed in him a strong personality. She greeted him in turn and expressed her thanks for his goodness to Glenn. Naturally Carley expected him to say something about her fiancé, but he did not.

"Well, Miss Carley, if you don't mind, I'll say you're prettier than your picture," said Hutter. "An' that is shore sayin' a lot. All the sheep herders in the country have taken a peep at your picture. Without permission, you understand."

"I'm greatly flattered," laughed Carley.

"We're glad you've come," replied Hutter, simply. "I just got back from the East myself. Chicago an' Kansas City. I came to Arizona from Illinois over thirty years ago. An' this was my first trip since. Reckon I've not got back my breath yet. Times have changed, Miss Carley. Times an' people!"

Mrs. Hutter bustled in from the kitchen, where manifestly she had been importantly engaged. "For the land's sakes!" she exclaimed, fervently, as she threw up her hands at sight of Carley. Her expression was indeed a compliment, but there was a suggestion of shock in it. Then Flo came in. She wore a simple gray gown that reached the top of her high shoes.

"Carley, don't mind mother," said Flo. "She means your dress is lovely. Which is my say, too. . . . But, listen. I just saw Glenn comin' up the road."

Carley ran to the open door with more haste than dignity. She saw a tall man striding along. Something about him appeared familiar. It was his walk—an erect swift carriage, with a swing of the march still visible. She recognized Glenn. And all within her seemed to become unstable. She watched him cross the road, face the house. How changed! No—this was not Glenn Kilbourne. This was a bronzed man, wide of shoulder, roughly garbed, heavy limbed, quite different from the Glenn she remembered. He mounted the porch steps. And Carley, still unseen herself, saw his face. Yes—Glenn! Hot blood seemed to be tingling liberated in her veins. Wheeling away, she backed against the wall behind the door and held up a warning finger to Flo, who stood nearest. Strange and disturbing then, to see something in Flo Hutter's eyes that could be read by a woman in only one way!

A tall form darkened the doorway. It strode in and halted.

"Flo!—who—where?" he began, breathlessly.

His voice, so well remembered, yet deeper, huskier, fell upon Carley's ears as something unconsciously longed for. His frame had so filled out that she did not recognize it. His face, too, had unbelievably changed—not in the regularity of feature that had been its chief charm, but in contour of cheek and vanishing of pallid hue and tragic line. Carley's heart swelled with joy. Beyond all else she had hoped to see the sad fixed hopelessness, the havoc, gone from his face. Therefore the restraint and nonchalance upon which Carley prided herself sustained eclipse.

"Glenn! Look—who's—here!" she called, in voice she could not have steadied to save her life. This meeting was more than she had anticipated.

Glenn whirled with an inarticulate cry. He saw Carley. Then —no matter how unreasonable or exacting had been Carley's longings, they were satisfied.

"You!" he cried, and leaped at her with radiant face.

———

Carley not only did not care about the spectators of this meeting, but forgot them utterly. More than the joy of seeing Glenn, more than the all-satisfying assurance to her woman's heart that she was still beloved, welled up a deep, strange, profound something that shook her to her depths. It was beyond selfishness. It was gratitude to God and to the West that had restored him.

"Carley! I couldn't believe it was you," he declared, releasing her from his close embrace, yet still holding her.

"Yes, Glenn—it's I—all you've left of me," she replied, tremulously, and she sought with unsteady hands to put up her dishevelled hair.

"You—you big sheep herder! You Goliath!"

"I never was so knocked off my pins," he said. "A lady to see me—from New York!. . . Of course it had to be you. But I couldn't believe. Carley, you were good to come."

Somehow the soft, warm look of his dark eyes hurt her. New and strange indeed it was to her, as were other things about him. Why had she not come West sooner? She disengaged herself from his hold and moved away, striving for the composure habitual with her. Flo Hutter was standing before the fire, looking down. Mrs. Hutter beamed upon Carley.

"Now let's have supper," she said.

"Reckon Miss Carley can't eat now, after that hug Glenn gave her," drawled Tom Hutter. "I was some worried. You see Glenn has gained seventy pounds in six months. An' he doesn't know his strength."

"Seventy pounds!" exclaimed Carley, gayly. "I thought it was more."

"Carley, you must excuse my violence," said Glenn. "I've been hugging sheep. That is, when I shear a sheep I have to hold him."

They all laughed, and so the moment of readjustment passed. Presently Carley found herself sitting at table, directly across from Flo. A pearly whiteness was slowly warming out of the girl's face. Her frank clear eyes met Carley's and they had nothing to hide. Carley's first requisite for character in a woman was that she be a thoroughbred. She lacked it often enough herself to admire it greatly in another woman. And that moment saw a birth of respect and sincere liking in her for this Western girl. If Flo Hutter ever was a rival she would be an honest one.

Not long after supper Tom Hutter winked at Carley and said he "reckoned on general principles it was his hunch to go to bed." Mrs. Hutter suddenly discovered tasks to perform elsewhere. And Flo said in her cool sweet drawl, somehow audacious and tantalizing, "Shore you two will want to spoon."

"Now, Flo, Eastern girls are no longer old-fashioned enough for that," declared Glenn.

"Too bad! Reckon I can't see how love could ever be old-fashioned. Good night, Glenn. Good night, Carley."

Flo stood an instant at the foot of the dark stairway where the light from the lamp fell upon her face. It seemed sweet and earnest to Carley. It expressed unconscious longing, but no envy. Then she ran up the stairs to disappear.

"Glenn, is that girl in love with you?" asked Carley, bluntly.

To her amaze, Glenn laughed. When had she heard him laugh? It thrilled her, yet nettled her a little.

"If that isn't like you!" he ejaculated. "Your very first words after we are left alone! It brings back the East, Carley."

"Probably recall to memory will be good for you," returned Carley. "But tell me. Is she in love with you?"

"Why, no, certainly not!" replied Glenn. "Anyway, how could I answer such a question? It just made me laugh, that's all."

"Humph! I can remember when you were not above making love to a pretty girl. You certainly had me worn to a frazzle— before we became engaged," said Carley.

"Old times! How long ago they seem!. . . Carley, it's sure wonderful to see you."

"How do you like my gown?" asked Carley, pirouetting for his benefit.

"Well, what little there is of it is beautiful," he replied, with a slow smile. "I always liked you best in white. Did you remember?"

"Yes. I got the gown for you. And I'll never wear it except for you."

"Same old coquette—same old eternal feminine," he said, half sadly. "You know when you look stunning. . . . But, Carley, the cut of that—or rather the abbreviation of it—inclines me to think that style for women's clothes has not changed for the better. In fact, it's worse than two years ago in Paris and later in New York. Where will you women draw the line?"

"Women are slaves to the prevailing mode," rejoined Carley. "I don't imagine women who dress would ever draw a line, if fashion went on dictating."

"But would they care so much—if they had to work—plenty of work—and children?" inquired Glenn, wistfully.

"Glenn! Work and children for modern women? Why, you are dreaming!" said Carley, with a laugh.

She saw him gaze thoughtfully into the glowing embers of the fire, and as she watched him her quick intuition grasped a subtle change in his mood. It brought a sternness to his face. She could hardly realize she was looking at the Glenn Kilbourne of old.

"Come close to the fire," he said, and pulled up a chair for her. Then he threw more wood upon the red coals. "You must be careful not to catch cold out here. The altitude makes a cold dangerous. And that gown is no protection."

"Glenn, one chair used to be enough for us," she said, archly, standing beside him.

But he did not respond to her hint, and, a little affronted, she accepted the proffered chair. Then he began to ask questions rapidly. He was eager for news from home—from his people— from old friends. However he did not inquire of Carley about her friends. She talked unremittingly for an hour, before she satisfied his hunger. But when her turn came to ask questions she found him reticent.

He had fallen upon rather hard days at first out here in the West; then his health had begun to improve; and as soon as he was able to work his condition rapidly changed for the better; and now he was getting along pretty well. Carley felt hurt at his apparent disinclination to confide in her. The strong cast of his face, as if it had been chiseled in bronze; the stern set of his lips and the jaw that protruded lean and square cut; the quiet masked light of his eyes; the coarse roughness of his brown hands, mute evidence of strenuous labors—these all gave a different impression from his brief remarks about himself. Lastly there was a little gray in the light-brown hair over his temples. Glenn was only twenty-seven, yet he looked ten years older. Studying him so, with the memory of earlier years in her mind, she was forced to admit that she liked him infinitely more as he was now. He seemed proven. Something had made him a man. Had it been his love for her, or the army service, or the war in France, or the struggle for life and health afterwards? Or had it been this rugged, uncouth West? Carley felt insidious jealousy of this last possibility. She feared this West. She was going to hate it. She had womanly intuition enough to see in Flo Hutter a girl somehow to be reckoned with. Still, Carley would not acknowledge to herself that his simple, unsophisticated Western girl could possibly be a rival. Carley did not need to consider the fact that she had been spoiled by the attention of men. It was not her vanity that precluded Flo Hutter as a rival.

Gradually the conversation drew to a lapse, and it suited Carley to let it be so. She watched Glenn as he gazed thoughtfully into the amber depths of the fire. What was going on in his mind? Carley's old perplexity suddenly had rebirth. And with it came an unfamiliar fear which she could not smother. Every moment that she sat there beside Glenn she was realizing more and more a yearning, passionate love for him. The unmistakable manifestation of his joy at sight of her, the strong, almost rude expression of his love, had called to some responsive, but hitherto unplumbed deeps of her. If it had not been for these undeniable facts Carley would have been panic-stricken. They reassured her, yet only made her state of mind more dissatisfied.

"Carley, do you still go in for dancing?" Glenn asked, presently, with his thoughtful eyes turning to her.

"Of course. I like dancing, and it's about all the exercise I get," she replied.

"Have the dances changed—again?"

"It's the music, perhaps, that changes the dancing. Jazz is becoming popular. And about all the crowd dances now is an infinite variation of fox-trot."

"No waltzing?"

"I don't believe I waltzed once this winter."

"Jazz? That's a sort of tinpanning, jiggly stuff, isn't it?"

"Glenn, it's the fever of the public pulse," replied Carley. "The graceful waltz, like the stately minuet, flourished back in the days when people rested rather than raced."

"More's the pity," said Glenn. Then after a moment, in which his gaze returned to the fire, he inquired rather too casually, "Does Morrison still chase after you?"

"Glenn, I'm neither old—nor married," she replied, laughing.

"No, that's true. But if you were married it wouldn't make any difference to Morrison."

Carley could not detect bitterness or jealousy in his voice. She would not have been averse to hearing either. She gathered from his remark, however, that he was going to be harder than ever to understand. What had she said or done to make him retreat within himself, aloof, impersonal, unfamiliar? He did not impress her as loverlike. What irony of fate was this that held her there yearning for his kisses and caresses as never before, while he watched the fire, and talked as to a mere acquaintance, and seemed sad and far away? Or did she merely imagine that? Only one thing could she be sure of at that moment, and it was that pride would never be her ally.

"Glenn, look here," she said, sliding her chair close to his and holding out her left hand, slim and white, with its glittering diamond on the third finger.

He took her hand in his and pressed it, and smiled at her.

"Yes, Carley, it's a beautiful, soft little hand. But I think I'd like it better if it were strong and brown, and coarse on the inside—from useful work."

"Like Flo Hutter's?" queried Carley.

"Yes."

Carley looked proudly into his eyes. "People are born in different stations. I respect your little Western friend, Glenn, but could I wash and sweep, milk cows and chop wood, and all that sort of thing?"

"I suppose you couldn't," he admitted, with a blunt little laugh.

"Would you want me to?" she asked.

"Well, that's hard to say," he replied, knitting his brows. "I hardly know. I think it depends on you. . . . But if you did do such work wouldn't you be happier?"

"Happier! Why Glenn, I'd be miserable!. . . But listen. It wasn't my beautiful and useless hand I wanted you to see. It was my engagement ring."

"Oh!—Well?" he went on, slowly.

"I've never had it off since you left New York," she said, softly. "You gave it to me four years ago. Do you remember? It was on my twenty-second birthday. You said it would take two months' salary to pay the bill."

"It sure did," he retorted, with a hint of humor.

"Glenn, during the war it was not so—so very hard to wear this ring as an engagement ring should be worn," said Carley, growing more earnest. "But after the war—especially after your departure West it was terribly hard to be true to the significance of this betrothal ring. There was a let-down in all women. Oh, no one need tell me! There was. And men were affected by that and the chaotic condition of the times. New York was wild during the year of your absence. Prohibition was a joke.—Well, I gadded, danced, dressed, drank, smoked, motored, just the same as the other women in our crowd. Something drove me to. I never rested. Excitement seemed to be happiness—Glenn, I am not making any plea to excuse all that. But I want you to know—how under trying circumstances —I was absolutely true to you. Understand me. I mean true as regards love. Through it all I loved you just the same. And now I'm with you, it seems, oh, so much more!. . . Your last letter hurt me. I don't know just how. But I came West to see you— to tell you this—and to ask you. . . . Do you want this ring back?"

"Certainly not," he replied, forcibly, with a dark flush spreading over his face.

"Then—you love me?" she whispered.

"Yes—I love you," he returned, deliberately. "And in spite of all you say—very probably more than you love me. . . . But you, like all women, make love and its expression the sole object of life. Carley, I have been concerned with keeping my body from the grave and my soul from hell."

"But—dear—you're well now?" she returned, with trembling lips.

"Yes, I've almost pulled out."

"Then what is wrong?"

"Wrong?—With me or you," he queried, with keen, enigmatical glance upon her.

"What is wrong between us? There is something."

"Carley, a man who has been on the verge—as I have been— seldom or never comes back to happiness. But perhaps—"

"You frighten me," cried Carley, and, rising, she sat upon the arm of his chair and encircled his neck with her arms. "How can I help if I do not understand? Am I so miserably little?. . . Glenn, *must* I tell you? No woman can live without love. I need to be loved. That's all that's wrong with *me*."

"Carley, you are still an imperious, mushy girl," replied Glenn, taking her into his arms. "I need to be loved, too. But that's not what is wrong with me. You'll have to find it out yourself."

"You're a dear old Sphinx," she retorted.

"Listen, Carley," he said, earnestly. "About this love-making stuff. Please don't misunderstand me. I love you. I'm starved for your kisses. But—is it right to ask them?"

"Right! Aren't we engaged? And don't I want to give them?"

"If I were only *sure* we'd be married!" he said, in low, tense voice, as if speaking more to himself.

"Married!" cried Carley, convulsively clasping him. "Of course we'll be married. Glenn, you wouldn't jilt me?"

"Carley, what I mean is that you might never really marry me," he answered, seriously.

"Oh, if that's all you need be sure of, Glenn Kilbourne, you may begin to make love to me now."

————

It was late when Carley went up to her room. And she was in such a softened mood, so happy and excited and yet disturbed in mind, that the coldness and the darkness did not matter in the least. She undressed in pitchy blackness, stumbling over chair and bed, feeling for what she needed. And in her mood this unusual proceeding was fun. When ready for bed she opened the door to take a peep out. Through the dense blackness the water-fall showed dimly opaque. Carley felt a soft mist wet her face. The low roar of the falling water seemed to envelop her. Under the cliff wall brooded impenetrable gloom. But out above the treetops shone great stars, wonderfully white and radiant and cold, with a piercing contrast to the deep clear blue of sky. The waterfall hummed into an absolutely dead silence. It emphasized the silence. Not only cold was it that made Carley shudder. How lonely, how lost, how hidden this canyon!

Then she hurried to bed, grateful for the warm woolly blankets. Relaxation and thought brought consciousness of the heat of her blood, the beat and throb and swell of her heart, of the tumult within her. In the lonely darkness of her room she might have faced the truth of her strangely renewed and augmented love for Glenn Kilbourne. But she was more concerned with her happiness. She had won him back. Her presence, her love had overcome his restraint. She thrilled in the sweet consciousness of her woman's conquest. How splendid he was! To hold back physical tenderness, the simple expressions of love, because he had feared they might unduly influence her! He had grown in many ways. She must be careful to reach up to his ideals. That about Flo Hutter's toil-hardened hands! Was that significance somehow connected with the rift in the lute? For Carley admitted to herself that there was something amiss, something incomprehensible, something intangible that obtruded its menace into her dream of future happiness. Still, what had she to fear, so long as she could be with Glenn?

And yet there were forced upon her, insistent and perplexing, the questions—was her love selfish? was she considering him? was she blind to something he could see? Tomorrow and next day and the days to come held promise of joyous companionship with Glenn, yet likewise they seemed full of a portent of trouble for her, or fight and ordeal, of lessons that would make life significant for her.

CHAPTER THREE

Carley was awakened by rattling sounds in her room. The raising of sleepy eyelids disclosed Flo on her knees before the little stove, in the act of lighting a fire.

"Mawnin', Carley," she drawled. "It's shore cold. Reckon it'll snow today, worse luck, just because you're here. Take my hunch and stay in bed till the fire burns up."

"I shall do no such thing," declared Carley, heroically.

"We're afraid you'll take cold," said Flo. "This is desert country with high altitude. Spring is here when the sun shines. But it's only shinin' in streaks these days. That means winter, really. Please be good."

"Well, it doesn't require much self-denial to stay here awhile longer," replied Carley, lazily.

Flo left with a parting admonition not to let the stove get red-hot. And Carley lay snuggled in the warm blankets, dreading the ordeal of getting out into that cold bare room. Her nose was cold. When her nose grew cold, it being a faithful barometer as to temperature, Carley knew there was frost in the air. She preferred summer. Steam-heated rooms with hothouse flowers lending their perfume had certainly not trained Carley for primitive conditions. She had a spirit, however, that was waxing a little rebellious to all this intimation as to her susceptibility to colds and her probable weakness under privation. Carley got up. Her bare feet landed upon the board floor instead of the Navajo rug, and she thought she had encountered cold stone. Stove and hot water notwithstanding, by the time she was half dressed she was also half frozen. "Some actor fellow once said w-when you w-went West you were c-camping out," chattered Carley. "Believe me, he said something."

The fact was Carley had never camped out. Her set played golf, rode horseback, motored and house-boated, but they had never gone in for uncomfortable trips. The camps and hotels in the Adirondacks were as warm and luxurious as Carley's own home. Carley now missed many things. And assuredly her flesh was weak. It cost her effort of will and real pain to finish lacing her boots. As she had made an engagement with Glenn to visit his cabin, she had donned an outdoor suit. She wondered if the cold had anything to do with the perceptible diminishing of the sound of the waterfall. Perhaps some of the water had frozen, like her fingers.

Carley went downstairs to the living room, and made no effort to resist a rush to the open fire. Flo and her mother were amused at Carley's impetuosity. "You'll like that stingin' of the air after you get used to it," said Mrs. Hutter. Carley had her doubts. When she was thoroughly thawed out she discovered an appetite quite unusual for her, and she enjoyed her breakfast. Then it was time to sally forth to meet Glenn.

"It's pretty sharp this mawnin'," said Flo. "You'll need gloves and sweater."

Having fortified herself with these, Carley asked how to find West Fork Canyon.

"It's down the road a little way," replied Flo. "A great narrow canyon opening on the right side. You can't miss it."

Flo accompanied her as far as the porch steps. A queer-looking individual was slouching along with ax over his shoulder.

"There's Charley," said Flo. "He'll show you." Then she whispered: "He's sort of dotty sometimes. A horse kicked him once. But mostly he's sensible."

At Flo's call the fellow halted with a grin. He was long, lean, loose jointed, dressed in blue overalls stuck into the tops of muddy boots, and his face was clear olive without beard or line. His brow bulged a little, and from under it peered out a pair of wistful brown eyes that reminded Carley of those of a dog she had once owned.

"Wal, it ain't a-goin' to be a nice day," remarked Charley, as he tried to accommodate his strides to Carley's steps.

"How can you tell?" asked Carley. "It looks clear and bright."

"Naw, this is a dark mawnin'. Thet's a cloudy sun. We'll hev snow on an' off."

"Do you mind bad weather?"

"Me? All the same to me. Reckon, though, I like it cold so I can loaf round a big fire at night."

"I like a big fire, too."

"Ever camped out?" he asked.

"Not what you'd call the real thing," replied Carley.

"Wal, thet's too bad. Reckon it'll be tough fer you," he went on, kindly. "There was a gurl tenderfoot heah two years ago an' she had a hell of a time. They all joked her, 'cept me, an' played tricks on her. An' on her side she was always puttin' her foot in it. I was shore sorry fer her."

"You were very kind to be an exception," murmured Carley.

"You look out fer Tom Hutter, an' I reckon Flo ain't so darn above layin' traps fer you. 'Specially as she's sweet on your beau. I seen them together a lot."

"Yes?" interrogated Carley, encouragingly.

"Kilbourne is the best fellar thet ever happened along Oak Creek. I helped him build his cabin. We've hunted some together. Did you ever hunt?"

"No."

"Wal, you've shore missed a lot of fun," he said. "Turkey

huntin'. Thet's what fetches the gurls. I reckon because turkeys
are so good to eat. The old gobblers hev begun to gobble now.
I'll take you gobbler huntin' if you'd like to go."

"I'm sure I would."

"There's good trout fishin' along heah a little later," he said,
pointing to the stream. "Crick's too high now. I like West Fork
best. I've ketched some lammin' big ones up there."

Carley was amused and interested. She could not say that
Charley had shown any indication of his mental peculiarity to
her. It took considerable restraint not to lead him to talk more
about Flo and Glenn. Presently they reached the turn in the
road, opposite the cottage Carley had noticed yesterday, and
here her loquacious escort halted.

"You take the trail heah," he said, pointing it out, "an' foller it
into West Fork. So long, an' don't forget we're goin' huntin'
turkeys."

Carley smiled her thanks, and, taking to the trail, she stepped
out briskly, now giving attention to her surroundings. The
canyon had widened, and the creek with its deep thicket of
green and white had sheered to the left. On her right the canyon
wall appeared to be lifting higher—and higher. She could not see
it well, owing to intervening treetops. The trail led her through a
grove of maples and sycamores, out into an open park-like bench
that turned to the right toward the cliff. Suddenly Carley saw a
break in the red wall. It was the intersecting canyon, West Fork.
What a narrow red-walled gateway! Huge pine trees spread wide
gnarled branches over her head. The wind made soft rush in
their tops, sending the brown needles lightly on the air. Carley
turned the bulging corner, to be halted by a magnificent spectacle. It seemed a mountain wall loomed over her. It was the
western side of this canyon, so lofty that Carley had to tip back
her head to see the top. She swept her astonished gaze down the
face of this tremendous red mountain wall and then slowly swept
it upward again. This phenomenon of a cliff seemed beyond the

comprehension of her sight. It looked a mile high. The few trees along its bold rampart resembled short spear-pointed bushes outlined against the steel gray of sky. Ledges, caves, seams, cracks, fissures, beetling red brows, yellow crumbling crags, benches of green growths and niches choked with brush, and bold points where single lonely pine trees grew perilously, and blank walls a thousand feet across their shadowed faces—these features gradually took shape in Carley's confused sight, until the colossal mountain front stood up before her in all its strange, wild, magnificent ruggedness and beauty.

"Arizona! Perhaps this is what he meant," murmured Carley. "I never dreamed of anything like this. . . . But, oh! it overshadows me—bears me down! I could never have a moment's peace under it."

It fascinated her. There were inaccessible ledges that haunted her with their remote fastnesses. How wonderful would it be to get there, rest there, if that were possible! But only eagles could reach them. There were places, then, that the desecrating hands of man could not touch. The dark caves were mystically potent in their vacant staring out at the world beneath them. The crumbling crags, the toppling ledges, the leaning rocks all threatened to come thundering down at the breath of wind. How deep and soft the red color in contrast with the green! How splendid the sheer bold uplift of gigantic steps! Carley found herself marveling at the forces that had so rudely, violently, and grandly left this monument to nature.

"Well, old Fifth Avenue gadder!" called a gay voice. "If the back wall of my yard so halts you—what will you ever do when you see the Painted Desert, or climb Sunset Peak, or look down into the Grand Canyon?"

"Oh, Glenn, where are you?" cried Carley, gazing everywhere near at hand. But he was farther away. The clearness of his voice had deceived her. Presently she espied him a little distance away, across a creek she had not before noticed.

"Come on," he called. "I want to see you cross the stepping stones."

Carley ran ahead, down a little slope of clean red rock, to the shore of the green water. It was clear, swift, deep in some places and shallow in others, with white wreathes or ripples around the rocks evidently placed there as a means to cross. Carley drew back aghast.

"Glenn, I could never make it," she called.

"Come on, my Alpine climber," he taunted. "Will you let Arizona daunt you?"

"Do you want me to fall in and catch cold?" she cried, desperately.

"Carley, big women might even cross the bad places of modern life on stepping stones of their dead selves!" he went on, with something of mockery. "Surely a few physical steps are not beyond you."

"Say, are you mangling *Tennyson* or just kidding me?" she demanded slangily.

"My love, Flo could cross here with her eyes shut."

That thrust spurred Carley to action. His words were jest, yet they held a hint of earnest. With her heart at her throat Carley stepped on the first rock, and, poising, she calculated on a running leap from stone to stone. Once launched, she felt she was falling downhill. She swayed, she splashed, she slipped; and clearing the longest leap from the last stone to shore she lost her balance and fell into Glenn's arms. His kisses drove away both her panic and her resentment.

"By Jove! I didn't think you'd even attempt it!" he declared, manifestly pleased. "I made sure I'd have to pack you over—in fact, rather liked the idea."

"I wouldn't advise you to employ any such means again—to dare me," she retorted.

"That's a nifty outdoor suit you've on," he said, admiringly. "I was wondering what you'd wear. I like short outing skirts for women, rather than trousers. The service sort of made the fair sex dippy about pants."

"It made them dippy about more than that," she replied. "You and I will never live to see the day that women recover their balance."

"I agree with you," replied Glenn.

Carley locked her arm in his. "Honey, I want to have a good time today. Cut out all the *other* women stuff. . . . Take me to see your little gray home in the West. Or is it gray?"

He laughed. "Why, yes, it's gray, just about. The logs have bleached some."

Glenn led her away up a trail that climbed between bowlders, and meandered on over piny mats of needles under great, silent, spreading pines; and closer to the impondering mountain wall, where at the base of the red rock the creek murmured strangely with hollow gurgle, where the sun had no chance to affect the cold damp gloom; and on through sweet-smelling woods, out into the sunlight again, and across a wider breadth of stream; and up a slow slope covered with stately pines, to a little cabin that faced the west.

"Here we are, sweetheart," said Glenn. "Now we shall see what you are made of."

Carley was non-committal as to that. Her intense interest precluded any humor at this moment. Not until she actually saw the log cabin Glenn had erected with his own hands had she been conscious of any great interest. But sight of it awoke something unaccustomed in Carley. As she stepped into the cabin her heart was not acting normally for a young woman who had no illusions about love in a cottage.

Glenn's cabin contained one room about fifteen feet wide by twenty long. Between the peeled logs were lines of red mud, hard dried. There was a small window opposite the door. In one corner was a couch of poles, with green tips of pine boughs peeping from under the blankets.

The floor consisted of flat rocks laid irregularly, with many spaces of earth showing between. The open fireplace appeared too large for the room, but the very bigness of it, as well as the blazing sticks and glowing embers, appealed strongly to Carley. A rough-hewn log formed the mantel, and on it Carley's picture held the place of honor. Above this a rifle lay across deer antlers. Carley paused here in her survey long enough to kiss Glenn and point to her photograph.

"You couldn't have pleased me more."

To the left of the fireplace was a rude cupboard of shelves, packed with boxes, cans, bags, and utensils. Below the cupboard, hung upon pegs, were blackened pots and pans, a long-handled skillet, and a bucket. Glenn's table was a masterpiece. There was no danger of knocking it over. It consisted of four poles driven into the ground, upon which had been nailed two wide slabs. This table showed considerable evidence of having been scrubbed scrupulously clean. There were two low stools, made out of boughs, and the seats had been covered with woolly sheep hide. In the right-hand corner stood a neat pile of firewood, cut with an ax, and beyond this hung saddle and saddle blanket, bridle and spurs. An old sombrero was hooked upon the pommel of the saddle. Upon the wall, higher up, hung a lantern, resting in a coil of rope that Carley took to be a lasso. Under a shelf upon which lay a suitcase hung some rough wearing apparel.

Carley noted that her picture and the suit case were absolutely the only physical evidences of Glenn's connection with his Eastern life. That had an unaccountable effect upon Carley. What had she expected? Then, after another survey of the room, she began to pester Glenn with questions. He had to show her the spring outside and the little bench with basin and soap. Sight of his soiled towel made her throw up her hands. She sat on the stools. She lay on the couch. She rummaged into the contents of the cupboard. She threw wood on the fire. Then, finally, having exhausted her search and inquiry, she flopped down on one of the stools to gaze at Glenn in awe and admiration and incredulity.

"Glenn—you've actually lived here!" she ejaculated.

"Since last fall before the snow came," he said, smiling.

"Snow! Did it snow?" she inquired.

"Well, I guess. I was snowed in for a week."

"Why did you choose this lonely place—way off from the Lodge?" she asked, slowly.

"I wanted to be by myself," he replied, briefly.

"You mean this is a sort of camp-out place?"

"Carley, I call it my home," he replied, and there was a low, strong sweetness in his voice she had never heard before.

That silenced her for a while. She went to the door and gazed up at the towering wall, more wonderful than ever, and more fearful, too, in her sight. Presently tears dimmed her eyes. She did not understand her feeling; she was ashamed of it; she hid it from Glenn. Indeed, there was something terribly wrong between her and Glenn, and it was not in him. This cabin he called home gave her a shock which would take time to analyze. At length she turned to him with gay utterance upon her lips. She tried to put out of her mind a dawning sense that this close-to-the-earth habitation, this primitive dwelling, held strange inscrutable power over a self she had never divined she possessed. The very stones in the hearth seemed to call out from some remote past, and the strong sweet smell of burnt wood thrilled to the marrow of her bones. How little she knew of herself! But she had intelligence enough to understand that there was a woman in her, the female of the species; and through that the sensations from logs and stones and earth and fire had strange power to call up the emotions handed down to her from the ages. The thrill, the queer heartbeat, the vague, haunting memory of something, as of a dim childhood adventure, the strange prickling sense of dread—these abided with her and augmented while she tried to show Glenn her pride in him and also how funny his cabin seemed to her.

Once or twice he hesitatingly, and somewhat appealingly, she imagined, tried to broach the subject of his work there in the

West. But Carley wanted a little while with him free of disagreeable argument. It was a foregone conclusion that she would not like his work. Her intention at first had been to begin at once to use all persuasion in her power toward having him go back East with her, or at the latest some time this year. But the rude log cabin had checked her impulse. She felt that haste would be unwise.

"Glenn Kilbourne, I told you why I came West to see you," she said, spiritedly. "Well, since you still swear allegiance to your girl from the East, you might entertain her a little bit before getting down to business talk."

"All right, Carley," he replied, laughing. "What do you want to do? The day is at your disposal. I wish it were June. Then if you didn't fall in love with West Fork you'd be no good."

"Glenn, I love people, not places," she returned.

"So I remember. And that's one thing I don't like. But let's not quarrel. What'll we do?"

"Suppose you tramp with me all around, until I'm good and hungry. Then we'll come back here—and you can cook dinner for me."

"Fine! Oh, I know you're just bursting with curiosity to see how I'll do it. Well, you may be surprised, miss."

"Let's go," she urged.

"Shall I take my gun or fishing rod?"

"You shall take nothing but *me*," retorted Carley. "What chance has a girl with a man, if he can hunt or fish?"

So they went out hand in hand. Half of the belt of sky above was obscured by swiftly moving gray clouds. The other half was blue and was being slowly encroached upon by the dark storm-like pall. How cold the air! Carley had already learned that when the sun was hidden the atmosphere was cold. Glenn led her down a trail to the brook, where he calmly picked her up in his arms, quite easily, it appeared, and leisurely packed her across, kissing her half a dozen times before he deposited her on her feet.

"Glenn, you do this sort of thing so well that it makes me imagine you have practice now and then," she said.

"No. But you are pretty and sweet, and like the girl you were four years ago. That takes me back to those days."

"I thank you. That's dear of you. I think I am something of a cat. . . . I'll be glad if this walk leads us often to the creek."

Spring might have been fresh and keen in the air, but it had not yet brought much green to the brown earth or to the trees. The cotton-woods showed a light feathery verdure. The long grass was a bleached white, and low down close to the sod fresh tiny green blades showed. The great fern leaves were sear and ragged, and they rustled in the breeze. Small gray sheath-barked trees with clumpy foliage and snags of dead branches, Glenn called cedars; and, grotesque as these were, Carley rather liked them. They were approachable, not majestic and lofty like he pines, and they smelled sweetly wild, and best of all they afforded some protection from the bitter wind. Carley rested better than she walked. The huge sections of red rock that had tumbled from above also interested Carley, especially when the sun happened to come out for a few moments and brought out their color. She enjoyed walking on the fallen pines, with Glenn below, keeping pace with her and holding her hand. Carley looked in vain for flowers and birds. The only living things she saw were rainbow trout that Glenn pointed out to her in the beautiful clear pools. The way the great gray bowlders trooped down to the brook as if they were cattle going to drink; the dark caverns under the shelving cliffs, where the water murmured with such hollow mockery; the low spear-pointed gray plants, resembling century plants, and which Glenn called mescal cactus, each with its single straight dead stalk standing on high with fluted head; the narrow gorges, perpendicularly walled in red, where the constricted brook plunged in amber and white cascades over fall after fall, tumbling, rushing, singing its water melody—these all held singular appeal for Carley as aspects of the wild land, fascinating for the moment, symbolic of the lonely

red man and his forbears, and by their raw contrast making more
necessary and desirable and elevating the comforts and conven-
tions of civilization. The cave man theory interested Carley only
as mythology.

Lonelier, wilder, grander grew Glenn's canyon. Carley was
finally forced to shift her attention from the intimate objects of
the canyon floor to the aloof and unattainable heights. Singular
to feel the difference! That which she could see close at hand,
touch if she willed, seemed to, become part of her knowledge,
could be observed and so possessed and passed by. But the gold-
red ramparts against the sky, the crannied cliffs, the crags of the
eagles, the lofty, distant blank walls, where the winds of the gods
had written their wars—these haunted because they could never
be possessed. Carley had often gazed at the Alps as at celebrated
pictures. She admired, she appreciated—then she forgot. But the
canyon heights did not affect her that way. They vaguely dissatisfied, and as she could not be sure of what they dissatisfied, she
had to conclude that it was in herself. To see, to watch, to dream,
to seek, to strive, to endure, to find! Was that what they meant?
They might make her thoughtful of the vast earth, and its
endless age, and its staggering mystery. But what more!

The storm that had threatened blackened the sky, and gray
scudding clouds buried the canyon rims, and long veils of rain
and sleet began to descend. The wind roared through the pines,
drowning the roar of the brook. Quite suddenly the air grew
piercingly cold. Carley had forgotten her gloves, and her pockets
had not been constructed to protect hands. Glenn drew her into
a sheltered nook where a rock jutted out from overhead and a
thicket of young pines helped break the onslaught of the wind.
There Carley sat on a cold rock, huddled up close to Glenn, and
wearing to a state she knew would be misery. Glenn not only
seemed content; he was happy. "This is great," he said. His coat
was open, his hands uncovered, and he watched the storm and
listened with manifest delight. Carley hated to betray what a
weakling she was, so she resigned herself to her fate, and imag-

ined she felt her fingers numbing into ice, and her sensitive nose slowly and painfully freezing.

The storm passed, however, before Carley sank into abject and open wretchedness. She managed to keep pace with Glenn until exercise warmed her blood. At every little ascent in the trail she found herself laboring to get her breath. There was assuredly evidence of abundance of air in this canyon, but somehow she could not get enough of it. Glenn detected this and said it was owing to the altitude. When they reached the cabin Carley was wet, stiff, cold, exhausted. How welcome the shelter, the open fireplace! Seeing the cabin in new light, Carley had the grace to acknowledge to herself that, after all, it was not so bad.

"Now for a good fire and then dinner," announced Glenn, with the air of one who knew his ground.

"Can I help?" queried Carley.

"Not today. I do not want you to spring any domestic science on me now." Carley was not averse to withholding her ignorance. She watched Glenn with surpassing curiosity and interest. First he threw a quantity of wood upon the smoldering fire.

"I have ham and mutton of my own raising," announced Glenn, with importance. "Which would you prefer?"

"Of your own raising. What do you mean?" queried Carley.

"My dear, you've been so steeped in the fog of the crowd that you are blind to the homely and necessary things of living. I mean I have here meat of both sheep and hog that I raised myself. That is to say, mutton and ham. Which do you like?"

"Ham!" cried Carley, incredulously.

Without more ado Glenn settled to brisk action, every move of which Carley watched with keen eyes. The usurping of a woman's province by a man was always an amusing thing. But for Glenn Kilbourne—what more would it be? He evidently knew what he wanted, for every movement was quick, decisive. One after another he placed bags, cans, sacks, pans, utensils on the table. Then he kicked at the roaring fire, settling some of the sticks. He strode outside to return with a bucket of water, a basin, towel, and soap. Then he took down two queer little iron pots with heavy lids. To each pot was attached a wire handle. He removed the lids, then set both the pots right on the fire or in it. Pouring water into the basin, he proceeded to wash his hands. Next he took a large pail, and from a sack he filled it half full of flour. To this he added baking powder and salt. It was instructive for Carley to see him run his skillful fingers all through that flour, as if searching for lumps. After this he knelt before the fire and, lifting off one of the iron pots with a forked stick, he proceeded to wipe out the inside of the pot and grease it with a piece of fat. His next move was to rake out a pile of the red coals, a feat he performed with the stick, and upon these he placed the pot. Also he removed the other pot from the fire, leaving it, however, quite close.

"Well, all eyes?" he bantered, suddenly staring at her. "Didn't I say I'd surprise you?"

"Don't mind me. This is about the happiest and most bewildered moment—of my life," replied Carley.

Returning to the table, Glenn dug at something in a large red can. He paused a moment to eye Carley.

"Girl, do you know how to make biscuits?" he queried.

"I might have known in my school days, but I've forgotten," she replied.

"Can you make apple pie?" he demanded, imperiously.

"No," rejoined Carley.

"How do you expect to please your husband?"

"Why—by marrying him, I suppose," answered Carley, as if weighing a problem.

"That has been the universal feminine point of view for a good many years," replied Glenn, flourishing a flour-whitened hand. "But it never served the women of the Revolution or the pioneers. And they were the builders of the nation. It will never serve the wives of the future, if we are to survive."

"Glenn, you rave!" ejaculated Carley, not knowing whether to laugh or be grave. "You were talking of humble housewifely things."

"Precisely. The humble things that were the foundation of the great nation of Americans. I meant work and children."

Carley could only stare at him. The look he flashed at her, the sudden intensity and passion of his ringing words, were as if he gave her a glimpse into the very depths of him. He might have begun in fun, but he had finished otherwise. She felt that she really did not know this man. Had he arraigned her in judgment? A flush, seemingly hot and cold, passed over her. Then it relieved her to see that he had returned to his task.

He mixed the shortening with the flour, and, adding water, he began a thorough kneading. When the consistency of the mixture appeared to satisfy him he took a handful of it, rolled it into a ball, patted and flattened it into a biscuit, and dropped it into the oven he had set aside on the hot coals. Swiftly he shaped eight or ten other biscuits and dropped them as the first. Then he put the heavy iron lid on the pot, and with a rude shovel, improvised from a flattened tin can, he shoveled red coals out of the fire, and covered the lid with them. His next move was to pare and slice potatoes, placing these aside in a pan. A small black coffee-pot half full of water, was set on a glowing part of the fire. Then he brought into use a huge, heavy knife, a murderous-looking implement it appeared to Carley, with which he cut slices of ham. These he dropped into the second pot, which he left uncovered. Next he removed the flour sack and other impedimenta from the table, and proceeded to set places for two—blue-enamel plate and cup, with plain, substantial-looking knives, forks, and spoons. He went outside, to return presently carrying a small crock of butter. Evidently he had kept the butter in or near the spring. It looked dewy and cold and hard. After that he peeped under the lid of the pot which contained the biscuits. The other pot was sizzling and smoking, giving forth a delicious savory odor that affected Carley most agreeably. The coffee-pot had begun to steam. With a long fork Glenn turned the slices of ham and stood a moment watching them. Next he placed cans of three sizes upon the table; and these Carley conjectured contained sugar, salt, and pepper. Carley might not have been present, for all the attention he paid to her. Again he peeped at the biscuits. At the edge of the hot embers he placed a tin plate, upon which he carefully deposited the slices of ham. Carley had not needed sight of them to know she was hungry; they made her simply ravenous. That done, he poured the pan of sliced potatoes into the pot. Carley judged the heat of that pot to be extreme. Next he removed the lid from the other pot, exposing biscuits slightly browned; and evidently satisfied with these, he removed them from the coals. He stirred the slices of potatoes round and round; he emptied two heaping tablespoonfuls of coffee into the coffee-pot.

"Carley," he said, at last turning to her with a warm smile, "out here in the West the cook usually yells, 'Come and get it.' Draw up your stool."

And presently Carley found herself seated across the crude table from Glenn, with the background of chinked logs in her sight, and the smart of wood smoke in her eyes. In years past she had sat with him in the soft, subdued, gold-green shadows of the Astor, or in the sumptuous atmosphere of the St. Regis. But this event was so different, so striking, that she felt it would have limitless significance. For one thing, the look of Glenn! When had he ever seemed like this, wonderfully happy to have her there, consciously proud of this dinner he had prepared in half an hour, strangely studying her as one on trial? This might have had its effect upon Carley's reaction to the situation, making it sweet, trenchant with meaning, but she was hungry enough and the dinner was good enough to make this hour memorable on that score alone. She ate until she was actually ashamed of herself. She laughed heartily, she talked, she made love to Glenn. Then suddenly an idea flashed into her quick mind.

"Glenn, did this girl Flo teach you to cook?" she queried, sharply.

"No. I always was handy in camp. Then out here I had the luck to fall in with an old fellow who was a wonderful cook. He lived with me for a while. . . . Why, what difference would it have made—had Flo taught me?"

Carley felt the heat of blood in her face. "I don't know that it would have made a difference. Only—I'm glad she didn't teach you. I'd rather no girl could teach you what I couldn't."

"You think I'm a pretty good cook, then?" he asked.

"I've enjoyed this dinner more than any I've ever eaten."

"Thanks, Carley. That'll help a lot," he said, gayly, but his eyes shone with earnest, glad light. "I hoped I'd surprise you. I've found out here that I want to do things well. The West stirs something in a man. It must be an unwritten law. You stand or fall by your own hands.

Back East you know meals are just occasions—to hurry through—to dress for—to meet somebody—to eat because you have to eat. But out here they are different. I don't know how. In the city, producers, merchants, waiters serve you for money. The meal is a transaction. It has no significance. It is money that keeps you from starvation. But in the West money doesn't mean much. You must work to live."

Carley leaned her elbows on the table and gazed at him curiously and admiringly. "Old fellow, you're a wonder. I can't tell you how proud I am of you. That you could come West weak and sick, and fight your way to health, and learn to be self-sufficient! It is a splendid achievement. It amazes me. I don't grasp it. I want to think. Nevertheless I—"

"What?" he queried, as she hesitated.

"Oh, never mind now," she replied, hastily, averting her eyes.

———

The day was far spent when Carley returned to the Lodge—and in spite of the discomfort of cold and sleet, and the bitter wind that beat in her face as she struggled up the trail—it was a day never to be forgotten. Nothing had been wanting in Glenn's attention or affection. He had been comrade, lover, all she craved for. And but for his few singular wordsabout work and children there had been no serious talk. Only a play day in his canyon and his cabin! Yet had she appeared at her best? Something vague and perplexing knocked at the gate of her consciousness.

CHAPTER FOUR

Two warm sunny days in early May inclined Mr. Hutter to the opinion that pleasant spring weather was at hand and that it would be a propitious time to climb up on the desert to look after his sheep interests. Glenn, of course, would accompany him.

"Carley and I will go too," asserted Flo.

"Reckon that'll be good," said Hutter, with approving nod.

His wife also agreed that it would be fine for Carley to see the beautiful desert country round Sunset Peak. But Glenn looked dubious.

"Carley, it'll be rather hard," he said. "You're soft, and riding and lying out will stove you up. You ought to break in gradually."

"I rode ten miles today," rejoined Carley. "And didn't mind it —much." This was a little deviation from stern veracity.

"Shore Carley's well and strong," protested Flo. "She'll get sore, but that won't kill her."

Glenn eyed Flo with rather penetrating glance. "I might drive Carley round about in the car," he said.

"But you can't drive over those lava flats, or go round, either. We'd have to send horses in some cases miles to meet you. It's horseback if you go at all."

"Shore we'll go horseback," spoke up Flo. "Carley has got it all over that Spencer girl who was here last summer."

"I think so, too. I am sure I hope so. Because you remember what the ride to Long Valley did to Miss Spencer," rejoined Glenn.

"What?" inquired Carley.

"Bad cold, peeled nose, skinned shin, saddle sores. She was in bed two days. She didn't show much pep the rest of her stay here, and she never got on another horse."

"Oh, is that all, Glenn?" returned Carley, in feigned surprise. "Why, I imagined from your tone that Miss Spencer's ride must have occasioned her discomfort. . . . See here, Glenn. I may be a tenderfoot, but I'm no mollycoddle."

"My dear, I surrender," replied Glenn, with a laugh. "Really, I'm delighted. But if anything happens—don't you blame me. I'm quite sure that a long horseback ride, in spring, on the desert, will show you a good many things about yourself."

That was how Carley came to find herself, the afternoon of the next day, astride a self-willed and unmanageable little mustang, riding in the rear of her friends, on the way through a cedar forest toward a place called Deep Lake.

Carley had not been able yet, during the several hours of their journey, to take any pleasure in the scenery or in her mount. For in the first place there was nothing to see but scrubby little gnarled cedars and drab-looking rocks; and in the second this Indian pony she rode had discovered she was not an adept horsewoman and had proceeded to take advantage of the fact. It did not help Carley's predicament to remember that Glenn had decidedly advised her against riding this particular mustang. To be sure, Flo had approved of Carley's choice, and Mr. Hutter, with a hearty laugh, had fallen in line: "Shore. Let her ride one of the broncs, if she wants." So this animal she bestrode must have been a bronc, for it did not take him long to elicit from Carley a muttered, "I don't know what bronc means, but it sounds like this pony acts."

Carley had inquired the animal's name from the young herder who had saddled him for her.

"Wal, I reckon he ain't got much of a name," replied the lad, with a grin, as he scratched his head. "For us boys always called him Spillbeans."

"Humph! What a beautiful cognomen!" ejaculated Carley, "But according to Shakespeare any name will serve. I'll ride him or—or—"

So far there had not really been any necessity for the completion of that sentence. But five miles of riding up into the cedar forest had convinced Carley that she might not have much farther to go. Spillbeans had ambled along well enough until he reached level ground where a long bleached grass waved in the wind. Here he manifested hunger, then a contrary nature, next insubordination, and finally direct hostility. Carley had urged, pulled, and commanded in vain. Then when she gave Spillbeans a kick in the flank he jumped stiff legged, propelling her up out of the saddle, and while she was descending he made the queer jump again, coming up to meet her. The jolt she got seemed to dislocate every bone in her body. Likewise it hurt. Moreover, along with her idea of what a spectacle she must have presented, it quickly decided Carley that Spillbeans was a horse that was not to be opposed. Whenever he wanted a mouthful of grass he stopped to get it. Therefore Carley was always in the rear, a fact which in itself did not displease her. Despite his contrariness, however, Spillbeans had apparently no intention of allowing the other horses to get completely out of sight.

Several times Flo waited for Carley to catch up. "He's loafing on you, Carley. You ought to have on a spur. Break off a switch and beat him some." Then she whipped the mustang across the flank with her bridle rein, which punishment caused Spillbeans meekly to trot on with alacrity. Carley had a positive belief that he would not do it for her. And after Flo's repeated efforts, assisted by chastisement from Glenn, had kept Spillbeans in a trot for a couple of miles Carley began to discover that the trotting of a horse was the most uncomfortable motion possible to imagine. It grew worse. It became painful. It gradually got unendurable. But pride made Carley endure it until suddenly she thought she had been stabbed in the side. This strange piercing pain must be what Glenn had called a "stitch" in the side, something common to novices on horseback. Carley could have screamed. She pulled the mustang to a walk and sagged in her saddle until the pain subsided. What a blessed relief! Carley had keen sense of the difference between riding in Central Park and in Arizona. She regretted her choice of horses. Spillbeans was attractive to look at, but the pleasure of riding him was a delusion. Flo had said his gait resembled the motion of a rocking chair. This Western girl, according to Charley, the sheep herder, was not above playing Arizona jokes. Be that as it might, Spillbeans now manifested a desire to remain with the other horses, and he broke out of a walk into a trot. Carley could not keep him from trotting. Hence her state soon wore into acute distress.

Her left ankle seemed broken. The stirrup was heavy, and as soon as she was tired she could no longer keep its weight from drawing her foot in. The inside of her right knee was as sore as a boil. Besides, she had other pains, just as severe, and she stood momentarily in mortal dread of that terrible stitch in her side. If it returned she knew she would fall off. But, fortunately, just when she was growing weak and dizzy, the horses ahead slowed to a walk on a descent. The road wound down into a wide deep canyon. Carley had a respite from her severest pains. Never before had she known what it meant to be so grateful for relief from anything.

The afternoon grew far advanced and the sunset was hazily shrouded in gray. Hutter did not like the looks of those clouds. "Reckon we're in for weather," he said. Carley did not care what happened. Weather or anything else that might make it possible to get off her horse! Glenn rode beside her, inquiring solicitously as to her pleasure. "Ride of my life!" she lied heroically. And it helped some to see that she both fooled and pleased him.

Beyond the canyon the cedared desert heaved higher and changed its aspect. The trees grew larger, bushier, greener, and closer together, with patches of bleached grass between, and russet-lichened rocks everywhere. Small cactus plants bristled sparsely in open places; and here and there bright red flowers— Indian paintbrush, Flo called them—added a touch of color to the gray. Glenn pointed to where dark banks of cloud had massed around the mountain peaks. The scene to the west was somber and compelling.

At last the men and the pack-horses ahead came to a halt in a level green forestland with no high trees. Far ahead a chain of soft gray round hills led up to the dark heaved mass of mountains. Carley saw the gleam of water through the trees. Probably her mustang saw or scented it, because he started to trot. Carley had reached a limit of strength, endurance, and patience. She hauled him up short. When Spillbeans evinced a stubborn intention to go on Carley gave him a kick. Then it happened.

She felt the reins jerked out of her hands and the saddle propel her upward. When she descended it was to meet that before-experienced jolt.

"Look!" cried Flo. "That bronc is going to pitch."

"Hold on, Carley!" yelled Glenn.

Desperately Carley essayed to do just that. But Spillbeans jolted her out of the saddle. She came down on his rump and began to slide back and down. Frightened and furious, Carley tried to hang to the saddle with her hands and to squeeze the mustang with her knees. But another jolt broke her hold, and then, helpless and bewildered, with her heart in her throat and a terrible sensation of weakness, she slid back at each upheave of the muscular rump until she slid off and to the ground in a heap. Whereupon Spillbeans trotted off toward the water.

Carley sat up before Glenn and Flo reached her. Manifestly they were concerned about her, but both were ready to burst with laughter. Carley knew she was not hurt and she was so glad to be off the mustang that, on the moment, she could almost have laughed herself.

"That beast is well named," she said. "He spilled me, all right. And I presume I resembled a sack of beans."

"Carley—you're—not hurt?" asked Glenn, choking, as he helped her up.

"Not physically. But my feelings are."

Then Glenn let out a hearty howl of mirth, which was seconded by a loud guffaw from Hutter. Flo, however, appeared to be able to restrain whatever she felt. To Carley she looked queer.

"Pitch! You called it that," said Carley.

"Oh, he didn't really pitch. He just humped up a few times," replied Flo, and then when she saw how Carley was going to take it she burst into a merry peal of laughter. Charley, the sheep herder was grinning, and some of the other men turned away with shaking shoulders.

"Laugh, you wild and woolly Westerners!" ejaculated Carley. "It must have been funny. I hope I can be a good sport. . . . But I bet you I ride him tomorrow."

"Shore you will," replied Flo.

Evidently the little incident drew the party closer together. Carley felt a warmth of good nature that overcame her first feeling of humiliation. They expected such things from her, and she should expect them, too, and take them, if not fearlessly or painlessly, at least without resentment.

Carley walked about to ease her swollen and sore joints, and while doing so she took stock of the camp ground and what was going on. At second glance the place had a certain attraction difficult for her to define. She could see far, and the view north toward those strange gray-colored symmetrical hills was one that fascinated while it repelled her. Near at hand the ground sloped down to a large rock-bound lake, perhaps a mile in circumference. In the distance, along the shore she saw a white conical tent, and blue smoke, and moving gray objects she took for sheep.

The men unpacked and unsaddled the horses, and, hobbling their forefeet together, turned them loose. Twilight had fallen and each man appeared to be briskly set upon his own task. Glenn was cutting around the foot of a thickly branched cedar where, he told Carley, he would make a bed for her and Flo. All that Carley could see that could be used for such purpose was a canvas-covered roll. Presently Glenn untied a rope from round this, unrolled it, and dragged it under the cedar. Then he spread down the outer layer of canvas, disclosing a considerable thickness of blankets. From under the top of these he pulled out two flat little pillows. These he placed in position, and turned back some of the blankets.

"Carley, you crawl in here, pile the blankets up, and the tarp over them," directed Glenn. "If it rains pull the tarp up over your head—and let it rain."

This direction sounded in Glenn's cheery voice a good deal more pleasurable than the possibilities suggested. Surely that cedar tree could not keep off rain or snow.

"Glenn, how about—about animals—and crawling things, you know?" queried Carley.

"Oh, there are a few tarantulas and centipedes, and sometimes a scorpion. But these don't crawl around much at night. The only thing to worry about are the hydrophobia skunks."

"What on earth are they?" asked Carley, quite aghast.

"Skunks are polecats, you know," replied Glenn, cheerfully. "Sometimes one gets bitten by a coyote that has rabies, and then he's a dangerous customer. He has no fear and he may run across you and bite you in the face. Queer how they generally bite your nose. Two men have been bitten since I've been here. One of them died, and the other had to go to the Pasteur Institute with a well-developed case of hydrophobia."

"Good heavens!" cried Carley, horrified.

"You needn't be afraid," said Glenn. "I'll tie one of the dogs near your bed."

Carley wondered whether Glenn's casual, easy tone had been adopted for her benefit or was merely an assimilation from this Western life. Not improbably Glenn himself might be capable of playing a trick on her. Carley endeavored to fortify herself against disaster, so that when it befell she might not be wholly ludicrous.

With the coming of twilight a cold, keen wind moaned through the cedars. Carley would have hovered close to the fire even if she had not been too tired to exert herself. Despite her aches, she did justice to the supper. It amazed her that appetite consumed her to the extent of overcoming a distaste for this strong, coarse cooking. Before the meal ended darkness had fallen, a windy raw darkness that enveloped heavily like a blanket. Presently Carley edged closer to the fire, and there she stayed, alternately turning back and front to the welcome heat. She seemingly roasted hands, face, and knees while her back froze. The wind blew the smoke in all directions. When she groped around with blurred, smarting eyes to escape the hot smoke, it followed her. The other members of the party sat comfortably on sacks or rocks, without much notice of the smoke that so exasperated Carley. Twice Glenn insisted that she take a seat he had fixed for her, but she preferred to stand and move around a little.

By and by the camp tasks of the men appeared to be ended, and all gathered near the fire to lounge and smoke and talk. Glenn and Hutter engaged in interested conversation with two Mexicans, evidently sheep herders. If the wind and cold had not made Carley so uncomfortable she might have found the scene picturesque. How black the night! She could scarcely distinguish the sky at all. The cedar branches swished in the wind, and from the gloom came a low sound of waves lapping a rocky shore. Presently Glenn held up a hand.

"Listen, Carley!" he said.

Then she heard strange wild yelps, staccato, piercing, somehow infinitely lonely. They made her shudder.

"Coyotes," said Glenn. "You'll come to love that chorus. Hear the dogs bark back."

Carley listened with interest, but she was inclined to doubt that she would ever become enamoured of such wild cries.

"Do coyotes come near camp?" she queried.

"Shore. Sometimes they pull your pillow out from under your head," replied Flo, laconically.

Carley did not ask any more questions. Natural history was not her favorite study and she was sure she could dispense with any first-hand knowledge of desert beasts. She thought, however, she heard one of the men say, "Big varmint prowlin' round the sheep." To which Hutter replied, "Reckon it was a bear." And Glenn said, "I saw his fresh track by the lake. Some bear!"

The heat from the fire made Carley so drowsy that she could scarcely hold up her head. She longed for bed even if it was out there in the open. Presently Flo called her: "Come. Let's walk a little before turning in."

So Carley permitted herself to be led to and fro down an open aisle between some cedars. The far end of that aisle, dark, gloomy, with the bushy secretive cedars all around, caused Carley apprehension she was ashamed to admit. Flo talked eloquently about the joys of camp life, and how the harder any outdoor task was and the more endurance and pain it required, the more pride and pleasure one had in remembering it. Carley was weighing the import of these words when suddenly Flo clutched her arm. "What's that?" she whispered, tensely.

Carley stood stockstill. They had reached the furthermost end of that aisle, but had turned to go back. The flare of the camp fire threw a wan light into the shadows before them. There came a rustling in the brush, a snapping of twigs. Cold tremors chased up and down Carley's back.

"Shore it's a varmint, all right. Let's hurry," whispered Flo.

Carley needed no urging. It appeared that Flo was not going

to run. She walked fast, peering back over her shoulder, and, hanging to Carley's arm, she rounded a large cedar that had obstructed some of the firelight. The gloom was not so thick here. And on the instant Carley espied a low, moving object, somehow furry, and gray in color. She gasped. She could not speak. Her heart gave a mighty throb and seemed to stop.

"What—do you see?" cried Flo, sharply, peering ahead. "Oh!. . . Come, Carley. *Run!*"

Flo's cry showed she must nearly be strangled with terror. But Carley was frozen in her tracks. Her eyes were riveted upon the gray furry object. It stopped. Then it came faster. It magnified. It was a huge beast. Carley had no control over mind, heart, voice, or muscle. Her legs gave way. She was sinking. A terrible panic, icy, sickening, rending, possessed her whole body.

The huge gray thing came at her. Into the rushing of her ears broke thudding sounds. The thing leaped up. A horrible petrifaction suddenly made stone of Carley. Then she saw a gray mantle-like object cast aside to disclose the dark form of a man. Glenn!

"Carley, dog-gone it! You don't scare worth a cent," he laughingly complained.

She collapsed into his arms. The liberating shock was as great as had been her terror. She began to tremble violently. Her hands got back a sense of strength to clutch. Heart and blood seemed released from that ice-banded vise.

"Say, I believe you were scared," went on Glenn, bending over her.

"Scar-ed!" she gasped. "Oh—there's no word—to tell—what I was!"

Flo came running back, giggling with joy. "Glenn, she shore took you for a bear. Why, I felt her go stiff as a post!. . . Ha! Ha! Ha! Carley, now how do you like the wild and woolly?"

"Oh! You put up a trick on me!" ejaculated Carley. "Glenn, how could you? . . . Such a terrible trick! I wouldn't have minded something reasonable. But that! Oh, I'll never forgive you!"

Glenn showed remorse, and kissed her before Flo in a way

that made some little amends. "Maybe I overdid it," he said. "But I thought you'd have a momentary start, you know, enough to make you yell, and then you'd see through it. I only had a sheepskin over my shoulders as I crawled on hands and knees."

"Glenn, for me you were a prehistoric monster—a dinosaur, or something," replied Carley.

It developed, upon their return to the campfire circle, that everybody had been in the joke; and they all derived hearty enjoyment from it.

"Reckon that makes you one of us," said Hutter, genially. "We've all had our scares."

Carley wondered if she were not so constituted that such trickery alienated her. Deep in her heart she resented being made to show her cowardice. But then she realized that no one had really seen any evidence of her state. It was fun to them.

Soon after this incident Hutter sounded what he called the roll-call for bed. Following Flo's instructions, Carley sat on their bed, pulled off her boots, folded coat and sweater at her head, and slid down under the blankets. How strange and hard a bed! Yet Carley had the most delicious sense of relief and rest she had ever experienced. She straightened out on her back with a feeling that she had never before appreciated the luxury of lying down.

Flo cuddled up to her in quite sisterly fashion, saying: "Now don't cover your head. If it rains I'll wake and pull up the tarp. Good night, Carley." And almost immediately she seemed to fall asleep.

For Carley, however, sleep did not soon come. She had too many aches; the aftermath of her shock of fright abided with her; and the blackness of night, the cold whip of wind over her face, and the unprotected helplessness she felt in this novel bed, were too entirely new and disturbing to be overcome at once. So she lay wide eyed, staring at the dense gray shadow, at the flickering lights upon the cedar. At length her mind formed a conclusion that this sort of thing might be worth the hardship once in a lifetime, anyway. What a concession to Glenn's West!

In the secret seclusion of her mind she had to confess that if her vanity had not been so assaulted and humiliated she might have enjoyed herself more. It seemed impossible, however, to have thrills and pleasures and exaltations in the face of discomfort, privation, and an uneasy half-acknowledged fear. No woman could have either a good or a profitable time when she was at her worst. Carley thought she would not be averse to getting Flo Hutter to New York, into an atmosphere wholly strange and difficult, and see how she met situation after situation unfamiliar to her. And so Carley's mind drifted on until at last she succumbed to drowsiness.

———

A voice pierced her dreams of home, of warmth and comfort. Something sharp, cold, and fragrant was scratching her eyes. She opened them. Glenn stood over her, pushing a sprig of cedar into her face.

"Carley, the day is far spent," he said, gayly. "We want to roll up your bedding. Will you get out of it?"

"Hello, Glenn! What time is it?" she replied.

"It's nearly six."

"What!. . . Do you expect me to get up at that ungodly hour?"

"We're all up. Flo's eating breakfast. It's going to be a bad day, I'm afraid. And we want to get packed and moving before it starts to rain."

"Why do girls leave home?" she asked, tragically.

"To make poor devils happy, of course," he replied, smiling down upon her.

That smile made up to Carley for all the clamoring sensations of stiff, sore muscles. It made her ashamed that she could not fling herself into this adventure with all her heart. Carley essayed to sit up. "Oh, I'm afraid my anatomy has become disconnected!. . . Glenn, do I look a sight?" She never would have asked him that if she had not known she could bear inspection at such an inopportune moment.

"You look great," he asserted, heartily. "You've got color. And as for your hair—I like to see it mussed that way. You were always one to have it dressed—just so. . . . Come, Carley, rustle now."

Thus adjured, Carley did her best under adverse circumstances. And she was gritting her teeth and complimenting herself when she arrived at the task of pulling on her boots. They were damp and her feet appeared to have swollen. Moreover, her ankles were sore. But she accomplished getting into them at the expense of much pain and sundry utterances more forcible than elegant. Glenn brought her warm water, a mitigating circumstance. The morning was cold and thought of that biting desert water had been trying.

"Shore you're doing fine," was Flo's greeting. "Come and get it before we throw it out."

Carley made haste to comply with the Western mandate, and was once again confronted with the singular fact that appetite did not wait upon the troubles of a tenderfoot. Glenn remarked that at least she would not starve to death on the trip.

"Come, climb the ridge with me," he invited. "I want you to take a look to the north and east."

He led her off through the cedars, up a slow red-earth slope, away from the lake. A green moundlike eminence topped with flat red rock appeared near at hand and not at all a hard climb. Nevertheless, her eyes deceived her, as she found to the cost of her breath. It was both far away and high.

"I like this location," said Glenn. "If I had the money I'd buy this section of land—six hundred and forty acres—and make a ranch of it. Just under this bluff is a fine open flat bench for a cabin. You could see away across the desert clear to Sunset Peak. There's a good spring of granite water. I'd run water from the lake down into the lower flats, and I'd sure raise some stock."

"What do you call this place?" asked Carley, curiously.

"Deep Lake. It's only a watering place for sheep and cattle. But there's fine grazing, and it's a wonder to me no one has ever settled here."

Looking down, Carley appreciated his wish to own the place; and immediately there followed in her a desire to get possession of this tract of land before anyone else discovered its advantages, and to hold it for Glenn. But this would surely conflict with her intention of persuading Glenn to go back East. As quickly as her impulse had been born it died.

Suddenly the scene gripped Carley. She looked from near to far, trying to grasp the illusive something. Wild lonely Arizona land! She saw ragged dumpy cedars of gray and green, lines of red earth, and a round space of water, gleaming pale under the lowering clouds; and in the distance isolated hills, strangely curved, wandering away to a black uplift of earth obscured in the sky.

These appeared to be mere steps leading her sight farther and higher to the cloud-navigated sky, where rosy and golden effulgence betokened the sun and the east. Carley held her breath. A transformation was going on before her eyes.

"Carley, it's a stormy sunrise," said Glenn.

His words explained, but they did not convince. Was this sudden-bursting glory only the sun rising behind storm clouds? She could see the clouds moving while they were being colored. The universal gray surrendered under some magic paint brush. The rifts widened, and the gloom of the pale-gray world seemed to vanish. Beyond the billowy, rolling, creamy edges of clouds, white and pink, shone the soft exquisite fresh blue sky. And a blaze of fire, a burst of molten gold, sheered up from behind the rim of cloud and suddenly poured a sea of sunlight from east to west. It transfigured the round foothills. They seemed bathed in ethereal light, and the silver mists that overhung them faded while Carley gazed, and a rosy flush crowned the symmetrical domes. Southward along the horizon line, down-dropping veils of rain, just touched with the sunrise tint, streamed in drifting slow movement from cloud to earth. To the north the range of foothills lifted toward the majestic dome of Sunset Peak, a volcanic upheaval of red and purple cinders, bare as rock, round as the lower hills, and wonderful in its color. Full in the blaze of the rising sun it flaunted an unchangeable front. Carley understood now what had been told her about this peak. Volcanic fires had thrown up a colossal mound of cinders burned forever to the hues of the setting sun. In every light and shade of day it held true to its name. Farther north rose the bold bulk of the San Francisco Peaks, that, half lost in the clouds, still dominated the desert scene. Then as Carley gazed the rifts began to close. Another transformation began, the reverse of what she watched. The golden radiance of sunrise vanished, and under a gray, lowering, coalescing pall of cloud the round hills returned to their bleak somberness, and the green desert took again its cold sheen.

"Wasn't it fine, Carley?" asked Glenn. "But nothing to what you will experience. I hope you stay till the weather gets warm. I want you to see a summer dawn on the Painted Desert, and a noon with the great white clouds rolling up from the horizon, and a sunset of massed purple and gold. If *they* do not get you then I'll give up."

Carley murmured something of her appreciation of what she had just seen. Part of his remark hung on her ear, thought-provoking and disturbing. He hoped she would stay until summer! That was kind of him. But her visit must be short and she now intended it to end with his return East with her. If she did not persuade him to go he might not want to go for a while, as he had written—"just yet." Carley grew troubled in mind. Such mental disturbance, however, lasted no longer than her return with Glenn to camp, where the mustang Spillbeans stood ready for her to mount. He appeared to put one ear up, the other down, and to look at her with mild surprise, as if to say: "What —hello—tenderfoot! Are you going to ride me again?"

Carley recalled that she had avowed she would ride him. There was no alternative, and her misgivings only made matters worse. Nevertheless, once in the saddle, she imagined she had the hallucination that to ride off so, with the long open miles ahead, was really thrilling. This remarkable state of mind lasted until Spillbeans began to trot, and then another day of misery beckoned to Carley with gray stretches of distance.

She was to learn that misery, as well as bliss, can swallow up the hours. She saw the monotony of cedar trees, but with blurred eyes; she saw the ground clearly enough, for she was always looking down, hoping for sandy places or rocky places where her mustang could not trot.

At noon the cavalcade ahead halted near a cabin and corral, which turned out to be a sheep ranch belonging to Hutter. Here Glenn was so busy that he had no time to devote to Carley. And Flo, who was more at home on a horse than on the ground, rode around everywhere with the men. Most assuredly Carley could not pass by the chance to get off Spillbeans and to walk a little. She found, however, that what she wanted most was to rest. The cabin was deserted, a dark, damp place with a rank odor. She did not stay long inside.

Rain and snow began to fall, adding to what Carley felt to be a disagreeable prospect. The immediate present, however, was cheered by a cup of hot soup and some bread and butter which the herder Charley brought her. By and by Glenn and Hutter returned with Flo, and all partook of some lunch.

All too soon Carley found herself astride the mustang again. Glenn helped her don the slicker, an abominable sticky rubber coat that bundled her up and tangled her feet round the stirrups. She was glad to find, though, that it served well indeed to protect her from raw wind and rain.

"Where do we go from here?" Carley inquired, ironically.

Glenn laughed in a way which proved to Carley that he knew

perfectly well how she felt. Again his smile caused her self-reproach. Plain indeed was it that he had really expected more of her in the way of complaint and less of fortitude. Carley bit her lips.

Thus began the afternoon ride. As it advanced the sky grew more threatening, the wind rawer, the cold keener, and the rain cut like little bits of sharp ice. It blew in Carley's face. Enough snow fell to whiten the open patches of ground. In an hour Carley realized that she had the hardest task of her life to ride to the end of the day's journey. No one could have guessed her plight. Glenn complimented her upon her adaptation to such unpleasant conditions. Flo evidently was on the lookout for the tenderfoot's troubles. But as Spillbeans, had taken to lagging at a walk, Carley was enabled to conceal all outward sign of her woes. It rained, hailed, sleeted, snowed, and grew colder all the time. Carley's feet became lumps of ice. Every step the mustang took sent acute pains ramifying from bruised and raw places all over her body.

Once, finding herself behind the others and out of sight in the cedars, she got off to walk awhile, leading the mustang. This would not do, however, because she fell too far in the rear. Mounting again, she rode on, beginning to feel that nothing mattered, that this trip would be the end of Carley Burch. How she hated that dreary, cold, flat land the road bisected without end. It felt as if she rode hours to cover a mile. In open stretches she saw the whole party straggling along, separated from one another, and each for himself. They certainly could not be enjoying themselves. Carley shut her eyes, clutched the pommel of the saddle, trying to support her weight. How could she endure another mile? Alas! there might be many miles. Suddenly a terrible shock seemed to rack her. But it was only that Spillbeans had once again taken to a trot. Frantically she pulled on the bridle. He was not to be thwarted. Opening her eyes, she saw a cabin far ahead which probably was the destination for the night. Carley knew she would never reach it, yet she clung on desperately. What she dreaded was the return of that stablike pain in her side. It came, and life seemed something abject and monstrous. She rode stiff legged, with her hands propping her stiffly above the pommel, but the stabbing pain went right on, and in deeper. When the mustang halted his trot beside the other horses Carley was in the last extremity. Yet as Glenn came to her, offering a hand, she still hid her agony. Then Flo called out gayly: "Carley, you've done twenty-five miles on as rotten a day as I remember. Shore we all hand it to you. And I'm confessing I didn't think you'd ever stay the ride out. Spillbeans is the meanest nag we've got and he has the hardest gait."

CHAPTER FIVE

Later Carley leaned back in a comfortable seat, before a blazing fire that happily sent its acrid smoke up the chimney, pondering ideas in her mind.

There could be a relation to familiar things that was astounding in its revelation. To get off a horse that had tortured her, to discover an almost insatiable appetite, to rest weary, aching body before the genial warmth of a beautiful fire—these were experiences which Carley found to have been hitherto unknown delights. It struck her suddenly and strangely that to know the real truth about anything in life might require infinite experience and understanding. How could one feel immense gratitude and relief, or the delight of satisfying acute hunger, or the sweet comfort of rest, unless there had been circumstances of extreme contrast? She had been compelled to suffer cruelly on horseback in order to make her appreciate how good it was to get down on the ground. Otherwise she never would have known. She wondered, then, how true that principle might be in all experience. It gave strong food for thought. There were things in the world never before dreamed of in her philosophy.

Carley was wondering if she were narrow and dense to

circumstances of life differing from her own when a remark of Flo's gave pause to her reflections.

"Shore the worst is yet to come." Flo had drawled.

Carley wondered if this distressing statement had to do in some way with the rest of the trip. She stifled her curiosity. Painful knowledge of that sort would come quickly enough.

"Flo, are you girls going to sleep here in the cabin?" inquired Glenn.

"Shore. It's cold and wet outside," replied Flo.

"Well, Felix, the Mexican herder, told me some Navajos had been bunking here."

"Navajos? You mean Indians?" interposed Carley, with interest.

"Shore do," said Flo. "I knew that. But don't mind Glenn. He's full of tricks, Carley. He'd give us a hunch to lie out in the wet."

Hutter burst into his hearty laugh. "Wal, I'd rather get some things any day than a bad cold."

"Shore I've had both," replied Flo, in her easy drawl, "and I'd prefer the cold. But for Carley's sake—"

"Pray don't consider me," said Carley. The rather crude drift of the conversation affronted her.

"Well, my dear," put in Glenn, "it's a bad night outside. We'll all make our beds here."

"Glenn, you shore are a nervy fellow," drawled Flo.

Long after everybody was in bed Carley lay awake in the blackness of the cabin, sensitively fidgeting and quivering over imaginative contact with creeping things. The fire had died out. A cold air passed through the room. On the roof pattered gusts of rain. Carley heard a rustling of mice. It did not seem possible that she could keep awake, yet she strove to do so. But her pangs of body, her extreme fatigue soon yielded to the quiet and rest of her bed, engendering a drowsiness that proved irresistible.

Morning brought fair weather and sunshine, which helped to sustain Carley in her effort to brave out her pains and woes.

Another disagreeable day would have forced her to humiliating defeat. Fortunately for her, the business of the men was concerned with the immediate neighborhood, in which they expected to stay all morning.

"Flo, after a while persuade Carley to ride with you to the top of this first foothill," said Glenn. "It's not far, and it's worth a good deal to see the Painted Desert from there. The day is clear and the air free from dust."

"Shore. Leave it to me. I want to get out of camp, anyhow. That conceited *hombre*, Lee Stanton, will be riding in here," answered Flo, laconically.

The slight knowing smile on Glenn's face and the grinning disbelief on Mr. Hutter's were facts not lost upon Carley. And when Charley, the herder, deliberately winked at Carley, she conceived the idea that Flo, like many women, only ran off to be pursued. In some manner Carley did not seek to analyze, the purported advent of this Lee Stanton pleased her. But she did admit to her consciousness that women, herself included, were both as deep and mysterious as the sea, yet as transparent as an inch of crystal water.

It happened that the expected newcomer rode into camp before anyone left. Before he dismounted he made a good impression on Carley, and as he stepped down in lazy, graceful action, a tall lithe figure, she thought him singularly handsome. He wore black sombrero, flannel shirt, blue jeans stuffed into high boots, and long, big-roweled spurs.

"How are you-all?" was his greeting.

From the talk that ensued between him and the men, Carley concluded that he must be overseer of the sheep hands. Carley knew that Hutter and Glenn were not interested in cattle raising. And in fact they were, especially Hutter, somewhat inimical to the dominance of the range land by cattle barons of Flagstaff.

"When's Ryan goin' to dip?" asked Hutter.

"Today or tomorrow," replied Stanton.

"Reckon we ought to ride over," went on Hutter. "Say, Glenn, do you reckon Miss Carley could stand a sheep-dip?"

This was spoken in a low tone, scarcely intended for Carley, but she had keen ears and heard distinctly. Not improbably this sheep-dip was what Flo meant as the worst to come. Carley adopted a listless posture to hide her keen desire to hear what Glenn would reply to Hutter.

"I should say not!" whispered Glenn, fiercely.

"Cut out that talk. She'll hear you and want to go."

Whereupon Carley felt mount in her breast an intense and rebellious determination to see a sheep-dip. She would astonish Glenn. What did he want, anyway? Had she not withstood the torturing trot of the hardest-gaited horse on the range? Carley realized she was going to place considerable store upon that feat. It grew on her.

When the consultation of the men ended, Lee Stanton turned to Flo. And Carley did not need to see the young man look twice to divine what ailed him. He was caught in the toils of love. But seeing through Flo Hutter was entirely another matter.

"Howdy, Lee!" she said, coolly, with her clear eyes on him. A tiny frown knitted her brow. She did not, at the moment, entirely approve of him.

"Shore am glad to see you, Flo," he said, with rather a heavy expulsion of breath. He wore a cheerful grin that in no wise deceived Flo, or Carley either. The young man had a furtive expression of eye.

"Ahuh!" returned Flo.

"I was shore sorry about—about that—" he floundered, in low voice.

"About what?"

"Aw, you know, Flo."

Carley strolled out of hearing, sure of two things—that she felt rather sorry for Stanton, and that his course of love did not augur well for smooth running. What queer creatures were women! Carley had seen several million coquettes, she believed; and assuredly Flo Hutter belonged to the species.

Upon Carley's return to the cabin she found Stanton and Flo waiting for her to accompany them on a ride up the foothill. She was so stiff and sore that she could hardly mount into the saddle; and the first mile of riding was something like a nightmare. She lagged behind Flo and Stanton, who apparently forgot her in their quarrel.

The riders soon struck the base of a long incline of rocky ground that led up to the slope of the foothill. Here rocks and gravel gave place to black cinders out of which grew a scant bleached grass. This desert verdure was what lent the soft gray shade to the foothill when seen from a distance. The slope was gentle, so that the ascent did not entail any hardship. Carley was amazed at the length of the slope, and also to see how high over the desert she was getting. She felt lifted out of a monotonous level. A green-gray league-long cedar forest extended down toward Oak Creek. Behind her the magnificent bulk of the mountains reached up into the stormy clouds, showing white slopes of snow under the gray pall.

The hoofs of the horses sank in the cinders. A fine choking dust assailed Carley's nostrils. Presently, when there appeared at least a third of the ascent still to be accomplished and Flo dismounted to walk, leading their horses. Carley had no choice but to do likewise. At first walking was a relief. Soon, however, the soft yielding cinders began to drag at her feet. At every step she slipped back a few inches, a very annoying feature of climbing. When her legs seemed to grow dead Carley paused for a little rest. The last of the ascent, over a few hundred yards of looser cinders, taxed her remaining strength to the limit. She grew hot and wet and out of breath. Her heart labored. An unreasonable antipathy seemed to attend her efforts. Only her ridiculous vanity held her to this task. She wanted to please Glenn, but not so earnestly that she would have kept on plodding up this ghastly bare mound of cinders. Carley did not mind

being a tenderfoot, but she hated the thought of these Westerners considering her a weakling. So she bore the pain of raw
blisters and the miserable sensation of staggering on under a
leaden weight.

Several times she noted that Flo and Stanton halted to face
each other in rather heated argument. At least Stanton's red face
and forceful gestures attested to heat on his part. Flo evidently
was weary of argument, and in answer to a sharp reproach she
retorted, "Shore I was different after he came." To which
Stanton responded by a quick passionate shrinking as if he had
been stung.

Carley had her own reaction to this speech she could not
help hearing; and inwardly, at least, her feeling must have been
similar to Stanton's. She forgot the object of this climb and
looked off to her right at the green level without really seeing it.
A vague sadness weighed upon her soul. Was there to be a tangle
of fates here, a conflict of wills, a crossing of loves? Flo's terse
confession could not be taken lightly. Did she mean that she
loved Glenn? Carley began to fear it. Only another reason why
she must persuade Glenn to go back East! But the closer Carley
came to what she divined must be an ordeal the more she
dreaded it. This raw, crude West might have confronted her with
a situation beyond her control. And as she dragged her weighted
feet through the cinders, kicking, up little puffs of black dust,
she felt what she admitted to be an unreasonable resentment
toward these Westerners and their barren, isolated, and boundless world.

"Carley," called Flo, "come—looksee, as the Indians say. Here
is Glenn's Painted Desert, and I reckon it's shore worth seeing."

To Carley's surprise, she found herself upon the knob of the
foothill. And when she looked out across a suddenly distinguish-
able void she seemed struck by the immensity of something she
was unable to grasp. She dropped her bridle; she gazed slowly, as
if drawn, hearing Flo's voice.

"That thin green line of cottonwoods down there is the Little

Colorado River," Flo was saying. "Reckon it's sixty miles, all down hill. The Painted Desert begins there and also the Navajo Reservation. You see the white strips, the red veins, the yellow bars, the black lines. They are all desert steps leading up and up for miles. That sharp black peak is called Wildcat. It's about a hundred miles. You see the desert stretching away to the right, growing dim—lost in distance? We don't know that country. But that north country we know as landmarks, anyway.

Look at that saw-tooth range. The Indians call it Echo Cliffs. At the far end it drops off into the Colorado River. Lee's Ferry is there—about one hundred and sixty miles. That ragged black rent is the Grand Canyon. Looks like a thread, doesn't it? But Carley, it's some hole, believe me. Away to the left you see the tremendous wall rising and turning to come this way. That's the north wall of the Canyon. It ends at the great bluff—Greenland Point. See the black fringe above the bar of gold. That's a belt of pine trees. It's about eighty miles across this ragged old stone washboard of a desert. . . . Now turn and look straight and strain your sight over Wildcat. See the rim purple dome. You must look hard. I'm glad it's clear and the sun is shining. We don't often get this view. . . . That purple dome is Navajo Mountain, two hundred miles and more away!"

Carley yielded to some strange drawing power and slowly walked forward until she stood at the extreme edge of the summit.

What was it that confounded her sight? Desert slope—down and down—color—distance—space! The wind that blew in her face seemed to have the openness of the whole world back of it. Cold, sweet, dry, exhilarating, it breathed of untainted vastness. Carley's memory pictures of the Adirondacks faded into pastorals; her vaunted images of European scenery changed to operetta settings. She had nothing with which to compare this illimitable space.

"Oh!—America!" was her unconscious tribute.

Stanton and Flo had come on to places beside her. The young

man laughed. "Wal, now Miss Carley, you couldn't say more. When I was in camp trainin' for service overseas I used to remember how this looked. An' it seemed one of the things I was goin' to fight for. Reckon I didn't the idea of the Germans havin' my Painted Desert. I didn't get across to fight for it, but I shore was willin'."

"You see, Carley, this is our America," said Flo, softly.

Carley had never understood the meaning of the word. The immensity of the West seemed flung at her. What her vision beheld, so far-reaching and boundless, was only a dot on the map.

"Does any one live—out there?" she asked, with slow sweep of hand.

"A few white traders and some Indian tribes," replied Stanton. "But you can ride all day an' next day an' never see a livin' soul."

What was the meaning of the gratification in his voice? Did Westerners court loneliness? Carley wrenched her gaze from the desert void to look at her companions. Stanton's eyes were narrowed; his expression had changed; lean and hard and still, his face resembled bronze. The careless humor was gone, as was the heated flush of his quarrel with Flo. The girl, too, had subtly changed, had responded to an influence that had subdued and softened her. She was mute; her eyes held a light, comprehensive and all-embracing; she was beautiful then. For Carley, quick to read emotion, caught a glimpse of a strong, steadfast soul that spiritualized the brown freckled face.

Carley wheeled to gaze out and down into this incomprehensible abyss, and on to the far up-flung heights, white and red and yellow, and so on to the wonderful mystic haze of distance. The significance of Flo's designation of miles could not be grasped by Carley. She could not estimate distance. But she did not need that to realize her perceptions were swallowed up by magnitude. Hitherto the power of her eyes had been unknown. How splendid to see afar! She could see—yes—but what did she see?

Space first, annihilating space, dwarfing her preconceived images, and then wondrous colors! What had she known of color? No wonder artists failed adequately and truly to paint mountains, let alone the desert space. The toiling millions of the crowded cities were ignorant of this terrible beauty and sublimity. Would it have helped them to see? But just to breathe that untainted air, just to see once the boundless open of colored sand and rock—to realize what the freedom of eagles meant would not that have helped anyone?

And with the thought there came to Carley's quickened and struggling mind a conception of freedom. She had not yet watched eagles, but she now gazed out into their domain. What then must be the effect of such environment on people whom it encompassed? The idea stunned Carley. Would such people grow in proportion to the nature with which they were in conflict? Hereditary influence could not be comparable to such environment in the shaping of character.

"Shore I could stand here all day," said Flo. "But it's beginning to cloud over and this high wind is cold. So we'd better go, Carley."

"I don't know what I am, but it's not cold," replied Carley.

"Wal, Miss Carley, I reckon you'll have to come again an' again before you get a comfortable feelin' here," said Stanton.

It surprised Carley to see that this young Westerner had hit upon the truth. He understood her. Indeed she was uncomfortable. She was oppressed, vaguely unhappy. But why? The thing there—the infinitude of open sand and rock—was beautiful, wonderful, even glorious. She looked again.

Steep black-cindered slope, with its soft gray patches of grass, sheered down and down, and out in rolling slope to merge upon a cedar-dotted level. Nothing moved below, but a red-tailed hawk sailed across her vision. How still—how gray the desert floor as it reached away, losing its black dots, and gaining bronze spots of stone! By plain and prairie it fell away, each inch of gray in her sight magnifying into its league-long roll. On and on, and down across dark lines that were steppes, and at last blocked and changed by the meandering green thread which was the verdure of a desert river. Beyond stretched the white sand, where whirl-winds of dust sent aloft their funnel-shaped spouts; and it led up to the horizon-wide ribs and ridges of red and walls of yellow and mountains of black, to the dim mound of purple so ethereal and mystic against the deep-blue cloud-curtained band of sky.

And on the moment the sun was obscured and that world of colorful flame went out, as if a blaze had died.

Deprived of its fire, the desert seemed to retreat, to fade coldly and gloomily, to lose its great landmarks in dim obscurity. Closer, around to the north, the canyon country yawned with innumerable gray jaws, ragged and hard, and the riven earth took on a different character. It had no shadows. It grew flat and, like the sea, seemed to mirror the vast gray cloud expanse. The sublime vanished, but the desolate remained. No warmth—no movement—no life! Dead stone it was, cut into a million ruts by ruthless ages. Carley felt that she was gazing down into chaos.

At this moment, as before, a hawk had crossed her vision, so now a raven sailed by, black as coal, uttering a hoarse croak.

"Quoth the raven—" murmured Carley, with a half-bitter laugh, as she turned away shuddering in spite of an effort of self-control. "Maybe he meant this wonderful and terrible West is never for such as I. . . . Come, let us go."

———

Carley rode all that afternoon in the rear of the caravan, gradually succumbing to the cold raw wind and the aches and pains to which she had subjected her flesh. Nevertheless, she finished the day's journey, and, sorely as she needed Glenn's kindly hand, she got off her horse without aid.

Camp was made at the edge of the devastated timber zone that Carley had found so dispiriting. A few melancholy pines were standing, and everywhere, as far as she could see southward, were blackened fallen trees and stumps. It was a dreary scene. The few cattle grazing on the bleached grass appeared as melancholy as the pines. The sun shone fitfully at sunset, and then sank, leaving the land to twilight and shadows.

Once in a comfortable seat beside the camp fire, Carley had no further desire to move. She was so far exhausted and weary that she could no longer appreciate the blessing of rest. Appetite, too, failed her this meal time. Darkness soon settled down. The wind moaned through the pines. She was indeed glad to crawl into bed, and not even the thought of skunks could keep her awake.

Morning disclosed the fact that gray clouds had been blown away. The sun shone bright upon a white-frosted land. The air was still. Carley labored at her task of rising, and brushing her hair, and pulling on her boots; and it appeared her former sufferings were as naught compared with the pangs of this morning. How she hated the cold, the bleak, denuded forest land, the emptiness, the roughness, the crudeness! If this sort of feeling grew any worse she thought she would hate Glenn. Yet she was nonetheless set upon going on, and seeing the sheep-dip, and riding that fiendish mustang until the trip was ended.

Getting in the saddle and on the way this morning was an ordeal that made Carley actually sick. Glenn and Flo both saw how it was with her, and they left her to herself. Carley was grateful for this understanding. It seemed to proclaim their respect. She found further matter for satisfaction in the astonishing circumstance that after the first dreadful quarter of an hour in the saddle she began to feel easier. And at the end of several hours of riding she was not suffering any particular pain, though she was weaker.

At length the cut-over land ended in a forest of straggling pines, through which the road wound southward, and eventually down into a wide shallow canyon. Through the trees Carley saw a stream of water, open fields of green, log fences and cabins, and blue smoke. She heard the chug of a gasoline engine and the baa-

baa of sheep. Glenn waited for her to catch up with him, and he
said: "Carley, this is one of Hutter's sheep camps. It's not a—a
very pleasant place. You won't care to see the sheep-dip. So I'm
suggesting you wait here—"

"Nothing doing, Glenn," she interrupted. "I'm going to see
what there is to see."

"But, dear—the men—the way they handle sheep—they'll—
really it's no sight for you," he floundered.

"Why not?" she inquired, eying him.

"Because, Carley—you know how you hate the—the seamy
side of things. And the stench—why, it'll make you sick!"

"Glenn, be on the level," she said. "Suppose it does. Wouldn't
you think more of me if I could stand it?"

"Why, yes," he replied, reluctantly, smiling at her, "I would.
But I wanted to spare you. This trip has been hard. I'm sure
proud of you. And, Carley—you can overdo it. Spunk is not
everything. You simply couldn't stand this."

"Glenn, how little you know a woman!" she exclaimed.
"Come along and show me your old sheep-dip."

They rode out of the woods into an open valley that might
have been picturesque if it had not been despoiled by the work
of man. A log fence ran along the edge of open ground and a
mud dam held back a pool of stagnant water, slimy and green. As
Carley rode on the baa-baa of sheep became so loud that she
could scarcely hear Glenn talking.

Several log cabins, rough hewn and gray with age, stood down
inside the inclosure; and beyond there were large corrals. From
the other side of these corrals came sounds of rough voices of
men, a trampling of hoofs, heavy splashes, the beat of an engine,
and the incessant baaing of the sheep.

At this point the members of Hutter's party dismounted and
tied their horses to the top log of the fence. When Carley
essayed to get off Glenn tried to stop her, saying she could see
well enough from there. But Carley got down and followed Flo.
She heard Hutter call to Glenn:

"Say, Ryan is short of men. We'll lend a hand for a couple of hours."

Presently Carley reached Flo's side and the first corral that contained sheep. They formed a compact woolly mass, rather white in color, with a tinge of pink. When Flo climbed up on the fence the flock plunged as one animal and with a trampling roar ran to the far side of the corral. Several old rams with wide curling horns faced around; and some of the ewes climbed up on the densely packed mass. Carley rather enjoyed watching them. She surely could not see anything amiss in this sight.

The next corral held a like number of sheep, and also several Mexicans who were evidently driving them into a narrow lane that led farther down. Carley saw the heads of men above other corral fences, and there was also a thick yellowish smoke rising from somewhere.

"Carley, are you game to see the dip?" asked Flo, with good nature that yet had a touch of taunt in it.

"That's my middle name," retorted Carley, flippantly.

Both Glenn and this girl seemed to be bent upon bringing out Carley's worst side, and they were succeeding. Flo laughed. The ready slang pleased her.

She led Carley along that log fence, through a huge open gate, and across a wide pen to another fence, which she scaled. Carley followed her, not particularly overanxious to look ahead. Some thick odor had begun to reach Carley's delicate nostrils. Flo led down a short lane and climbed another fence, and sat astride the top log. Carley hurried along to clamber up to her side, but stood erect with her feet on the second log of the fence.

Then a horrible stench struck Carley almost like a blow in the face, and before her confused sight there appeared to be drifting smoke and active men and running sheep, all against a background of mud. But at first it was the odor that caused Carley to close her eyes and press her knees hard against the upper log to keep from reeling. Never in her life had such a sick-

ening nausea assailed her. It appeared to attack her whole body.
The forerunning qualm of seasickness was as nothing to this.
Carley gave a gasp, pinched her nose between her fingers so she
could not smell, and opened her eyes.

Directly beneath her was a small pen open at one end into
which sheep were being driven from the larger corral. The
drivers were yelling. The sheep in the rear plunged into those
ahead of them, forcing them on. Two men worked in this small
pen. One was a brawny giant in undershirt and overalls that
appeared filthy. He held a cloth in his hand and strode toward
the nearest sheep. Folding the cloth round the neck of the
sheep, he dragged it forward, with an ease which showed great
strength, and threw it into a pit that yawned at the side. Souse
went the sheep into a murky, muddy pool and disappeared. But
suddenly its head came up and then its shoulders. And it began
half to walk and half swim down what appeared to be a narrow
boxlike ditch that contained other floundering sheep. Then
Carley saw men on each side of this ditch bending over with
poles that had crooks at the end, and their work was to press and
pull the sheep along to the end of the ditch, and drive them up a
boarded incline into another corral where many other sheep
huddled, now a dirty muddy color like the liquid into which they
had been emersed. Souse! Splash! In went sheep after sheep.
Occasionally one did not go under. And then a man would press
it under with the crook and quickly lift its head. The work went
on with precision and speed, in spite of the yells and trampling
and baa-baas, and the incessant action that gave an effect of
confusion.

Carley saw a pipe leading from a huge boiler to the ditch.
The dark fluid was running out of it. From a rusty old engine
with big smokestack poured the strangling smoke. A man broke
open a sack of yellow powder and dumped it into the ditch.
Then he poured an acid-like liquid after it.

"Sulphur and nicotine," yelled Flo up at Carley. "The dip's

poison. If a sheep opens his mouth he's usually a goner. But sometimes they save one."

Carley wanted to tear herself away from this disgusting spectacle. But it held her by some fascination. She saw Glenn and Hutter fall in line with the other men, and work like beavers. These two pacemakers in the small pen kept the sheep coming so fast that every worker below had a task cut out for him. Suddenly Flo squealed and pointed.

"There! that sheep didn't come up," she cried. "Shore he opened his mouth."

Then Carley saw Glenn energetically plunge his hooked pole in and out and around until he had located the submerged sheep. He lifted its head above the dip. The sheep showed no sign of life. Down on his knees dropped Glenn, to reach the sheep with strong brown hands, and to haul it up on the ground, where it flopped inert. Glenn pummeled it and pressed it, and worked on it much as Carley had seen a life-guard work over a half-drowned man. But the sheep did not respond to Glenn's active administrations.

"No use, Glenn," yelled Hutter, hoarsely. "That one's a goner."

Carley did not fail to note the state of Glenn's hands and arms and overalls when he returned to the ditch work. Then back and forth Carley's gaze went from one end to the other of that scene. And suddenly it was arrested and held by the huge fellow who handled the sheep so brutally. Every time he dragged one and threw it into the pit he yelled: "Ho! Ho!" Carley was impelled to look at his face, and she was amazed to meet the rawest and boldest stare from evil eyes that had ever been her misfortune to incite. She felt herself stiffen with a shock that was unfamiliar. This man was scarcely many years older than Glenn, yet he had grizzled hair, a seamed and scarred visage, coarse, thick lips, and beetling brows, from under which peered gleaming light eyes. At every turn he flashed them upon Carley's face, her neck, the swell of her bosom. It was instinct that caused her hastily to close her riding coat. She felt as if her flesh had been burned. Like a snake he fascinated her. The intelligence in his bold gaze made the beastliness of it all the harder to endure, all the stronger to arouse.

"Come, Carley, let's rustle out of this stinkin' mess," cried Flo.

Indeed, Carley needed Flo's assistance in clambering down out of the choking smoke and horrid odor.

"*Adios*, pretty eyes," called the big man from the pen.

"Well," ejaculated Flo, when they got out, "I'll bet I call Glenn good and hard for letting you go down there."

"It was—my—fault," panted Carley. "I said I'd stand it."

"Oh, you're game, all right. I didn't mean the dip. . . . That sheep-slinger is Haze Ruff, the toughest *hombre* on this range. Shore, now, wouldn't I like to take a shot at him?. . . I'm going to tell dad and Glenn."

"Please don't," returned Carley, appealingly.

"I shore am. Dad needs hands these days. That's why he's lenient. But Glenn will cowhide Ruff and I want to see him do it."

In Flo Hutter then Carley saw another and a different spirit of the West, a violence unrestrained and fierce that showed in the girl's even voice and in the piercing light of her eyes.

They went back to the horses, got their lunches from the saddlebags, and, finding comfortable seats in a sunny, protected place, they ate and talked. Carley had to force herself to swallow. It seemed that the horrid odor of dip and sheep had permeated everything. Glenn had known her better than she had known herself, and he had wished to spare her an unnecessary and disgusting experience. Yet so stubborn was Carley that she did not regret going through with it.

"Carley, I don't mind telling you that you've stuck it out better than any tenderfoot we ever had here," said Flo.

"Thank you. That from a Western girl is a compliment I'll not soon forget," replied Carley.

"I shore mean it. We've had rotten weather. And to end the little trip at this sheep-dip hole! Why, Glenn certainly wanted you to stack up against the real thing!"

"Flo, he did not want me to come on the trip, and especially here," protested Carley.

"Shore I know. But he *let* you."

"Neither Glenn nor any other man could prevent me from doing what I wanted to do."

"Well, if you'll excuse me," drawled Flo, "I'll differ with you. I reckon Glenn Kilbourne is not the man you knew before the war."

"No, he is not. But that does not alter the case."

"Carley, we're not well acquainted," went on Flo, more carefully feeling her way, "and I'm not your kind. I don't know your Eastern ways. But I know what the West does to a man. The war ruined your friend—both his body and mind. . . . How sorry mother and I were for Glenn, those days when it looked he'd sure 'go west,' for good!. . . Did you know he'd been gassed and that he had five hemorrhages?"

"Oh! I knew his lungs had been weakened by gas. But he never told me about having hemorrhages."

"Well, he shore had them. The last one I'll never forget. Every time he'd cough it would fetch the blood. I could tell!. . . Oh, it was awful. I begged him *not* to cough. He smiled—like a ghost smiling—and he whispered, 'I'll quit.'. . . And he did. The doctor came from Flagstaff and packed him in ice. Glenn sat propped up all night and never moved a muscle. Never coughed again! And the bleeding stopped. After that we put him out on the porch where he could breathe fresh air all the time. There's something wonderfully healing in Arizona air. It's from the dry desert and here it's full of cedar and pine. Anyway Glenn got well. And I think the West has cured his mind, too."

"Of what?" queried Carley, in an intense curiosity she could scarcely hide.

"Oh, God only knows!" exclaimed Flo, throwing up her

gloved hands. "I never could understand. But I *hated* what the war did to him."

Carley leaned back against the log, quite spent. Flo was unwittingly torturing her. Carley wanted passionately to give in to jealousy of this Western girl, but she could not do it. Flo Hutter deserved better than that. And Carley's baser nature seemed in conflict with all that was noble in her. The victory did not yet go to either side. This was a bad hour for Carley. Her strength had about played out, and her spirit was at low ebb.

"Carley, you're all in," declared Flo. "You needn't deny it. I'm shore you've made good with me as a tenderfoot who stayed the limit. But there's no sense in your killing yourself, nor in me letting you. So I'm going to tell dad we want to go home."

She left Carley there. The word home had struck strangely into Carley's mind and remained there. Suddenly she realized what it was to be homesick. The comfort, the ease, the luxury, the rest, the sweetness, the pleasure, the cleanliness, the gratification to eye and ear—to all the senses—how these thoughts came to haunt her! All of Carley's will power had been needed to sustain her on this trip to keep her from miserably failing. She had not failed. But contact with the West had affronted, disgusted, shocked, and alienated her. In that moment she could not be fair minded; she knew it; she did not care.

Carley gazed around her. Only one of the cabins was in sight from this position. Evidently it was a home for some of these men. On one side the peaked rough roof had been built out beyond the wall, evidently to serve as a kind of porch. On that wall hung the motliest assortment of things Carley had ever seen—utensils, sheep and cow hides, saddles, harness, leather clothes, ropes, old sombreros, shovels, stove pipe, and many other articles for which she could find no name. The most striking characteristic manifest in this collection was that of service. How they had been used! They had enabled people to live under primitive conditions. Somehow this fact inhibited Carley's sense of repulsion at their rude and uncouth appearance. Had any of her forefathers ever been pioneers? Carley did not know, but the thought was disturbing. It was thought-provoking. Many times at home, when she was dressing for dinner, she had gazed into the mirror at the graceful lines of her throat and arms, at the proud poise of her head, at the alabaster whiteness of her skin, and wonderingly she had asked of her image: "Can it be possible that I am a descendant of cavemen?" She had never been able to realize it, yet she knew it was true. Perhaps somewhere not far back along her line there had been a great-great-grandmother who had lived some kind of a primitive life, using such implements and necessaries as hung on this cabin wall, and thereby helped some man to conquer the wilderness, to live in it, and reproduce his kind. Like flashes Glenn's words came back to Carley—"Work and children!"

Some interpretation of his meaning and how it related to this hour held aloof from Carley. If she would ever be big enough to understand it and broad enough to accept it the time was far distant. Just now she was sore and sick physically, and therefore certainly not in a receptive state of mind. Yet how could she have keener impressions than these she was receiving? It was all a problem. She grew tired of thinking. But even then her mind pondered on, a stream of consciousness over which she had no control. This dreary woods was deserted. No birds, no squirrels, no creatures such as fancy anticipated! In another direction, across the canyon, she saw cattle, gaunt, ragged, lumbering, and stolid. And on the moment the scent of sheep came on the breeze. Time seemed to stand still here, and what Carley wanted most was for the hours and days to fly, so that she would be home again.

At last Flo returned with the men. One quick glance at Glenn convinced Carley that Flo had not yet told him about the sheep dipper, Haze Ruff.

"Carley, you're a real sport," declared Glenn, with the rare smile she loved. "It's a dreadful mess. And to think you stood it!.

. . Why, old Fifth Avenue, if you needed to make another hit with me you've done it!"

His warmth amazed and pleased Carley. She could not quite understand why it would have made any difference to him whether she had stood the ordeal or not. But then every day she seemed to drift a little farther from a real understanding of her lover. His praise gladdened her, and fortified her to face the rest of this ride back to Oak Creek.

Four hours later, in a twilight so shadowy that no one saw her distress, Carley half slipped and half fell from her horse and managed somehow to mount the steps and enter the bright living room. A cheerful red fire blazed on the hearth; Glenn's hound, Moze, trembled eagerly at sight of her and looked up with humble dark eyes; the white-clothed dinner table steamed with savory dishes. Flo stood before the blaze, warming her hands. Lee Stanton leaned against the mantel, with eyes on her, and every line of his lean, hard face expressed his devotion to her. Hutter was taking his seat at the head of the table. "Come an' get it—you-all," he called, heartily. Mrs. Hutter's face beamed with the spirit of that home. And lastly, Carley saw Glenn waiting for her, watching her come, true in this very moment to his stern hope for her and pride in her, as she dragged her weary, spent body toward him and the bright fire.

By these signs, or the effect of them, Carley vaguely realized that she was incalculably changing, that this Carley Burch had become a vastly bigger person in the sight of her friends, and strangely in her own a lesser creature.

CHAPTER SIX

If spring came at all to Oak Creek Canyon it warmed into summer before Carley had time to languish with the fever characteristic of early June in the East.

As if by magic it seemed the green grass sprang up, the green buds opened into leaves, the bluebells and primroses bloomed, the apple and peach blossoms burst exquisitely white and pink against the blue sky. Oak Creek fell to a transparent, beautiful brook, leisurely eddying in the stone walled nooks, hurrying with murmur and babble over the little falls. The mornings broke clear and fragrantly cool, the noon hours seemed to lag under a hot sun, the nights fell like dark mantles from the melancholy star-sown sky.

Carley had stubbornly kept on riding and climbing until she killed her secret doubt that she was really a thoroughbred, until she satisfied her own insistent vanity that she could train to a point where this outdoor life was not too much for her strength. She lost flesh despite increase of appetite; she lost her pallor for a complexion of gold-brown she knew her Eastern friends would admire; she wore out the blisters and aches and pains; she found herself growing firmer of muscle, lither of line, deeper of chest. And in addition to these physical manifestations there were

subtle intimations of a delight in a freedom of body she had
never before known, of an exhilaration in action that made her
hot and made her breathe, of a sloughing off of numberless petty
and fussy and luxurious little superficialities which she had
supposed were necessary to her happiness. What she had undertaken in vain conquest of Glenn's pride and Flo Hutter's Western
tolerance she had found to be a boomerang. She had won Glenn's
admiration; she had won the Western girl's recognition. But her
passionate, stubborn desire had been ignoble, and was proved so
by the rebound of her achievement, coming home to her with a
sweetness she had not the courage to accept. She forced it from
her. This West with its rawness, its ruggedness, she hated.

Nevertheless, the June days passed, growing dreamily swift,
growing more incomprehensibly full; and still she had not
broached to Glenn the main object of her visit—to take him
back East. Yet a little while longer! She hated his work and had
not talked of that. Yet an honest consciousness told her that as
time flew by she feared more and more to tell him that he was
wasting his life there and that she could not bear it. Still was he
wasting it? Once in a while a timid and unfamiliar Carley Burch
voiced a pregnant query. Perhaps what held Carley back most
was the happiness she achieved in her walks and rides with
Glenn. She lingered because of them. Every day she loved him
more, and yet—there was something. Was it in her or in him?
She had a woman's assurance of his love and sometimes she
caught her breath—so sweet and strong was the tumultuous
emotion it stirred. She preferred to enjoy while she could, to
dream instead of think. But it was not possible to hold a blank,
dreamy, lulled consciousness all the time. Thought would
return. And not always could she drive away a feeling that
Glenn would never be her slave. She divined something in his
mind that kept him gentle and kindly, restrained always, sometimes melancholy and aloof, as if he were an impassive destiny
waiting for the iron consequences he knew inevitably must fall.
What was this that he knew which she did not know? The idea

haunted her. Perhaps it was that which compelled her to use all her woman's wiles and charms on Glenn. Still, though it thrilled her to see she made him love her more as the days passed, she could not blind herself to the truth that no softness or allurement of hers changed this strange restraint in him. How that baffled her! Was it resistance or knowledge or nobility or doubt?

Flo Hutter's twentieth birthday came along the middle of June, and all the neighbors and range hands for miles around were invited to celebrate it.

For the second time during her visit Carley put on the white gown that had made Flo gasp with delight, and had stunned Mrs. Hutter, and had brought a reluctant compliment from Glenn. Carley liked to create a sensation. What were exquisite and expensive gowns for, if not that?

It was twilight on this particular June night when she was ready to go downstairs, and she tarried a while on the long porch. The evening star, so lonely and radiant, so cold and passionless in the dusky blue, had become an object she waited for and watched, the same as she had come to love the dreaming, murmuring melody of the waterfall. She lingered there. What had the sights and sounds and smells of this wild canyon come to mean to her? She could not say. But they had changed her immeasurably.

Her soft slippers made no sound on the porch, and as she turned the corner of the house, where shadows hovered thick, she heard Lee Stanton's voice: "But, Flo, you loved me before Kilbourne came."

The content, the pathos, of his voice chained Carley to the spot. Some situations, like fate, were beyond resisting.

"Shore I did," replied Flo, dreamily. This was the voice of a girl who was being confronted by happy and sad thoughts on her birthday.

"Don't you—love me—still?" he asked, huskily.

"Why, of course, Lee! *I* don't change," she said.

"But then, why—" There for the moment his utterance or courage failed.

"Lee, do you want the honest to God's truth?"

"I reckon—I do."

"Well, I love you just as I always did," replied Flo, earnestly. "But, Lee, I love—*him* more than you or anybody."

"My Heaven! Flo—you'll ruin us all!" he exclaimed, hoarsely.

"No, I won't either. You can't say I'm not level headed. I hated to tell you this, Lee, but you made me."

"Flo, you love me an' him—two men?" queried Stanton, incredulously.

"I shore do," she drawled, with a soft laugh. "And it's no fun."

"Reckon I don't cut much of a figure alongside Kilbourne," said Stanton, disconsolately.

"Lee, you could stand alongside any man," replied Flo, eloquently. "You're Western, and you're steady and loyal, and you'll—well, some day you'll be like dad. Could I say more?. . . But, Lee, this man is *different*. He is wonderful. I can't explain it, but I feel it. He has been through hell's fire. Oh! will I ever forget his ravings when he lay so ill? He means more to me than just *one* man. He's American. You're American, too, Lee, and you trained to be a soldier, and you would have made a grand one—if I know old Arizona. But you were not called to France. . . . Glenn Kilbourne went. God only knows what that means. But he *went*. And there's the difference. I saw the wreck of him. I did a little to save his life and his mind. I wouldn't be an American girl if I *didn't* love him. . . . Oh, Lee, can't you understand?"

"I reckon so. I'm not begrudging Glenn what—what you care. I'm only afraid I'll lose you."

"I never promised to marry you, did I?"

"Not in words. But kisses ought to—?"

"Yes, kisses mean a lot," she replied. "And so far I stand committed. I suppose I'll marry you some day and be blamed lucky. I'll be happy, too—don't you overlook that hunch. . . . You

needn't worry. Glenn is in love with Carley. She's beautiful, rich
—and of his class. How could he ever see me?"

"Flo, you can never tell," replied Stanton, thoughtfully. "I
didn't like her at first. But I'm comin' round. The thing is, Flo,
does she love him as you love him?"

"Oh, I think so—I hope so," answered Flo, as if in distress.

"I'm not so shore. But then I can't savvy her. Lord knows I
hope so, too. If she doesn't—if she goes back East an' leaves him
here—I reckon my case—"

"Hush! I know she's out here to take him back. Let's go
downstairs now."

"Aw, wait—Flo," he begged. "What's your hurry?. . . Come-
give me—"

"There! That's all you get, birthday or no birthday," replied
Flo, gayly.

Carley heard the soft kiss and Stanton's deep breath, and
then footsteps as they walked away in the gloom toward the
stairway. Carley leaned against the log wall. She felt the rough
wood—smelled the rusty pine rosin. Her other hand pressed her
bosom where her heart beat with unwonted vigor. Footsteps and
voices sounded beneath her. Twilight had deepened into night.
The low murmur of the waterfall and the babble of the brook
floated to her strained ears.

Listeners never heard good of themselves. But Stanton's
subtle doubt of any depth to her, though it hurt, was not so
conflicting as the ringing truth of Flo Hutter's love for Glenn.
This unsought knowledge powerfully affected Carley. She was
forewarned and forearmed now. It saddened her, yet did not
lessen her confidence in her hold on Glenn. But it stirred to
perplexing pitch her curiosity in regard to the mystery that
seemed to cling round Glenn's transformation of character. This
Western girl really knew more about Glenn than his fiancée
knew. Carley suffered a humiliating shock when she realized that
she had been thinking of herself, of her love, her life, her needs,
her wants instead of Glenn's. It took no keen intelligence or

insight into human nature to see that Glenn needed her more than she needed him.

Thus unwontedly stirred and upset and flung back upon pride of herself, Carley went downstairs to meet the assembled company. And never had she shown to greater contrast, never had circumstance and state of mind contrived to make her so radiant and gay and unbending. She heard many remarks not intended for her far-reaching ears. An old grizzled Westerner remarked to Hutter: "Wall, she's shore an unbroke filly." Another of the company—a woman—remarked: "Sweet an' pretty as a columbine. But I'd like her better if she was dressed decent." And a gaunt range rider, who stood with others at the porch door, looking on, asked a comrade: "Do you reckon that's style back East?" To which the other replied: "Mebbe, but I'd gamble they're short on silk back East an' likewise sheriffs."

Carley received some meed of gratification out of the sensation she created, but she did not carry her craving for it to the point of overshadowing Flo. On the contrary, she contrived to have Flo share the attention she received. She taught Flo to dance the fox-trot and got Glenn to dance with her. Then she taught it to Lee Stanton. And when Lee danced with Flo, to the infinite wonder and delight of the onlookers, Carley experienced her first sincere enjoyment of the evening.

Her moment came when she danced with Glenn. It reminded her of days long past and which she wanted to return again. Despite war tramping and Western labors Glenn retained something of his old grace and lightness. But just to dance with him was enough to swell her heart, and for once she grew oblivious to the spectators.

"Glenn, would you like to go to the Plaza with me again, and dance between dinner courses, as we used to?" she whispered up to him.

"Sure I would—unless Morrison knew you were to be there," he replied.

"Glenn!. . . I would not even see him."

"Any old time you wouldn't see Morrison!" he exclaimed, half mockingly.

His doubt, his tone grated upon her. Pressing closer to him, she said, "Come back and I'll prove it."

But he laughed and had no answer for her. At her own daring words Carley's heart had leaped to her lips. If he had responded, even teasingly, she could have burst out with her longing to take him back. But silence inhibited her, and the moment passed.

At the end of that dance Hutter claimed Glenn in the interest of neighboring sheep men. And Carley, crossing the big living room alone, passed close to one of the porch doors. Some one, indistinct in the shadow, spoke to her in low voice: "Hello, pretty eyes!"

Carley felt a little cold shock go tingling through her. But she gave no sign that she had heard. She recognized the voice and also the epithet. Passing to the other side of the room and joining the company there, Carley presently took a casual glance at the door. Several men were lounging there. One of them was the sheep dipper, Haze Ruff. His bold eyes were on her now, and his coarse face wore a slight, meaning smile, as if he understood something about her that was a secret to others. Carley dropped her eyes. But she could not shake off the feeling that wherever she moved this man's gaze followed her. The unpleasantness of this incident would have been nothing to Carley had she at once forgotten it. Most unaccountably, however, she could not make herself unaware of this ruffian's attention. It did no good for her to argue that she was merely the cynosure of all eyes. This Ruff's tone and look possessed something heretofore unknown to Carley. Once she was tempted to tell Glenn. But that would only cause a fight, so she kept her counsel. She danced again, and helped Flo entertain her guests, and passed that door often; and once stood before it, deliberately, with all the strange and contrary impulse so inscrutable in a woman, and never for a moment wholly lost the sense of the man's boldness. It dawned upon her, at length, that the singular thing about this boldness was its difference from any, which had ever before affronted her. The fool's smile meant that he thought she saw his attention, and, understanding it perfectly, had secret delight in it. Many and various had been the masculine egotisms which had come under her observation. But quite beyond Carley was this brawny sheep dipper, Haze Ruff. Once the party broke up and the guests had departed, she instantly forgot both man and incident.

Next day, late in the afternoon, when Carley came out on the porch, she was hailed by Flo, who had just ridden in from down the canyon.

"Hey Carley, come down. I shore have something to tell you," she called.

Carley did not use any time pattering down that rude porch stairway. Flo was dusty and hot, and her chaps carried the unmistakable scent of sheep-dip.

"Been over to Ryan's camp an' shore rode hard to beat Glenn home," drawled Flo.

"Why?" queried Carley, eagerly.

"Reckon I wanted to tell you something Glenn swore he wouldn't let me tell. . . . He makes me tired. He thinks you can't stand things."

"Oh! Has he been—hurt?"

"He's skinned an' bruised up some, but I reckon he's not hurt."

"Flo—what happened?" demanded Carley, anxiously.

"Carley, do you know Glenn can fight like the devil?" asked Flo.

"No, I don't. But I remember he used to be athletic. Flo, you make me nervous. Did Glenn fight?"

"I reckon he did," drawled Flo.

"With whom?"

"Nobody else but that big *hombre*, Haze Ruff."

"Oh!" gasped Carley, with a violent start. "That—that ruffian! Flo, did you see—were you there?"

"I shore was, an' next to a horse race I like a fight," replied the Western girl. "Carley, why didn't you tell me Haze Ruff insulted you last night?"

"Why, Flo—he only said, 'Hello, pretty eyes,' and I let it pass!" said Carley, lamely.

"You never want to let anything pass, out West. Because next time you'll get worse. This turn your other cheek doesn't go in Arizona. But we shore thought Ruff said worse than that. Though from him that's aplenty."

"How did you know?"

"Well, Charley told it. He was standing out here by the door last night an' he heard Ruff speak to you. Charley thinks a heap of you an' I reckon he hates Ruff. Besides, Charley stretches things. He shore riled Glenn, an' I want to say, my dear, you missed the best thing that's happened since you got here."

"Hurry—tell me," begged Carley, feeling the blood come to her face.

"I rode over to Ryan's place for dad, an' when I got there I knew nothing about what Ruff said to you," began Flo, and she took hold of Carley's hand. "Neither did dad. You see, Glenn hadn't got there yet. Well, just as the men had finished dipping a bunch of sheep Glenn came riding down, lickety cut."

"Now what the hell's wrong with Glenn?' said dad, getting up from where we sat.

"Shore I knew Glenn was mad, though I never before saw him that way. He looked sort of grim an' black. . . . Well, he rode right down on us an' piled off. Dad yelled at him an' so did I. But Glenn made for the sheep pen. You know where we watched Haze Ruff an' Lorenzo slinging the sheep into the dip. Ruff was just about to climb out over the fence when Glenn leaped up on it."

" 'Say, Ruff,' he said, sort of hard, 'Charley an' Ben tell me they heard you speak disrespectfully to Miss Burch last night.'"

"Dad an' I ran to the fence, but before we could catch hold of Glenn he'd jumped down into the pen."

" 'I'm not carin' much for what them herders say,' replied Ruff.

" 'Do you deny it?' demanded Glenn.

" 'I ain't denyin' nothin', Kilbourne,' growled Ruff. 'I might argue against me bein' disrespectful. That's a matter of opinion.'

" 'You'll apologize for speaking to Miss Burch or I'll beat you up an' have Hutter fire you.'

" 'Wal, Kilbourne, I never eat my words,' replied Ruff.

"Then Glenn knocked him flat. You ought to have heard that crack. Sounded like Charley hitting a steer with a club. Dad yelled: 'Look out, Glenn. He packs a gun!'—Ruff got up mad clear through I reckon. Then they mixed it. Ruff got in some swings, but he couldn't reach Glenn's face. An' Glenn batted him right an' left, every time in his ugly mug. Ruff got all bloody an' he cussed something awful. Glenn beat him against the fence an' then we all saw Ruff reach for a gun or knife. All the men yelled. An' shore I screamed. But Glenn saw as much as we saw. He got fiercer. He beat Ruff down to his knees an' swung on him hard. Deliberately knocked Ruff into the dip ditch. What a splash! It wet all of us. Ruff went out of sight. Then he rolled up like a huge hog. We were all scared now. That dip's rank poison, you know. Reckon Ruff knew that. He floundered along an' crawled up at the end. Anyone could see that he had mouth an' eyes tight shut. He began to grope an' feel around, trying to find the way to the pond. One of the men led him out. It was great to see him wade in the water an' wallow an' souse his head under. When he came out the men got in front of him any stopped him. He shore looked bad. . . . An' Glenn called to him, 'Ruff, that sheep-dip won't go through your tough hide, but a bullet will!'"

———

Not long after this incident Carley started out on her usual afternoon ride, having arranged with Glenn to meet her on his return from work.

Toward the end of June Carley had advanced in her horsemanship to a point where Flo lent her one of her own mustangs. This change might not have had all to do with a wonderful difference in riding, but it seemed so to Carley. There was as much difference in horses as in people. This mustang she had ridden of late was of Navajo stock, but he had been born and raised and broken at Oak Creek. Carley had not yet discovered any objection on his part to do as she wanted him to. He liked what she liked, and most of all he liked to go. His color resembled a pattern of calico, and in accordance with Western ways his name was therefore Calico. Left to choose his own gait, Calico always dropped into a gentle pace which was so easy and comfortable and swinging that Carley never tired of it. Moreover, he did not shy at things lying in the road or rabbits darting from bushes or at the upwhirring of birds. Carley had grown attached to Calico before she realized she was drifting into it; and for Carley to care for anything or anybody was a serious matter, because it did not happen often and it lasted. She was exceedingly tenacious of affection.

June had almost passed and summer lay upon the lonely land. Such perfect and wonderful weather had never before been Carley's experience. The dawns broke cool, fresh, fragrant, sweet, and rosy, with a breeze that seemed of heaven rather than earth, and the air seemed tremulously full of the murmur of falling water and the melody of mocking birds. At the solemn noontides the great white sun glared down hot—so hot that it burned the skin, yet strangely was a pleasant burn. The waning afternoons were Carley's especial torment, when it seemed the sounds and winds of the day were tiring, and all things were seeking repose, and life must soften to an unthinking happiness. These hours troubled Carley because she wanted them to last, and because she knew for her this changing and transforming time could not last. So long as she did not think she was satisfied.

Maples and sycamores and oaks were in full foliage, and their bright greens contrasted softly with the dark shine of the pines. Through the spaces between brown tree trunks and the white-spotted holes of the sycamores gleamed the amber water of the creek. Always there was murmur of little rills and the musical dash of little rapids. On the surface of still, shady pools trout broke to make ever-widening ripples. Indian paintbrush, so brightly carmine in color, lent touch of fire to the green banks, and under the oaks, in cool dark nooks where mossy bowlders lined the stream, there were stately nodding yellow columbines. And high on the rock ledges shot up the wonderful mescal stalks, beginning to blossom, some with tints of gold and others with tones of red.

Riding along down the canyon, under its looming walls, Carley wondered that if unawares to her these physical aspects of Arizona could have become more significant than she realized. The thought had confronted her before. Here, as always, she fought it and denied it by the simple defense of elimination. Yet refusing to think of a thing when it seemed ever present was not going to do forever. Insensibly and subtly it might get a hold on her, never to be broken. Yet it was infinitely easier to dream than to think.

But the thought encroached upon her that it was not a dreamful habit of mind she had fallen into of late. When she dreamed or mused she lived vaguely and sweetly over past happy hours or dwelt in enchanted fancy upon a possible future. Carley had been told by a Columbia professor that she was a type of the present age—a modern young woman of materialistic mind. Be that as it might, she knew many things seemed loosening from the narrowness and tightness of her character, sloughing away like scales, exposing a new and strange and susceptible softness of fiber. And this blank habit of mind, when she did not think, and now realized that she was not dreaming, seemed to be the body of Carley Burch, and her heart and soul stripped of a shell. Nerve and emotion and spirit received something from her surroundings. She absorbed her environment. She felt. It was a delightful state. But when her own consciousness caused it to elude her, then she both resented and regretted. Anything that approached permanent attachment to this crude and untenanted West Carley would not tolerate for a moment. Reluctantly she admitted it had bettered her health, quickened her blood, and quite relegated Florida and the Adirondacks, to little consideration.

"Well, as I told Glenn," soliloquized Carley, "every time I'm almost won over a little to Arizona she gives me a hard jolt. I'm getting near being mushy today. Now let's see what I'll get. I suppose that's my pessimism or materialism. Funny how Glenn keeps saying its the jolts, the hard knocks, the fights that are best to remember afterward. I don't get that at all."

Five miles below West Fork a road branched off and climbed the left side of the canyon. It was a rather steep road, long and zigzaging, and full of rocks and ruts. Carley did not enjoy ascending it, but she preferred the going up to coming down. It took half an hour to climb.

Once up on the flat cedar-dotted desert she was met, full in the face, by a hot dusty wind coming from the south. Carley searched her pockets for her goggles, only to ascertain that she had forgotten them. Nothing, except a freezing sleety wind, annoyed and punished Carley so much as a hard puffy wind, full of sand and dust. Somewhere along the first few miles of this road she was to meet Glenn. If she turned back for any cause he would be worried, and, what concerned her more vitally, he would think she had not the courage to face a little dust. So Carley rode on.

The wind appeared to be gusty. It would blow hard awhile, then lull for a few moments. On the whole, however, it increased in volume and persistence until she was riding against a gale. She had now come to a bare, flat, gravelly region, scant of cedars and brush, and far ahead she could see a dull yellow pall rising high into the sky. It was a duststorm and it was sweeping down on the wings of that gale. Carley remembered that somewhere along this flat there was a log cabin which had before provided shelter for her and Flo when they were caught in a rainstorm. It seemed unlikely that she had passed by this cabin.

Resolutely she faced the gale and knew she had a task to find that refuge. If there had been a big rock or bushy cedar to offer shelter she would have welcomed it. But there was nothing. When the hard dusty gusts hit her, she found it absolutely necessary to shut her eyes. At intervals less windy she opened them, and rode on, peering through the yellow gloom for the cabin. Thus she got her eyes full of dust—an alkali dust that made them sting and smart. The fiercer puffs of wind carried pebbles large enough to hurt severely. Then the dust clogged her nose and sand got between her teeth. Added to these annoyances was a heat like a blast from a furnace. Carley perspired freely and that caked the dust on her face. She rode on, gradually growing more uncomfortable and miserable. Yet even then she did not utterly lose a sort of thrilling zest in being thrown upon her own responsibility. She could hate an obstacle, yet feel something of pride in holding her own against it.

Another mile of buffeting this increasing gale so exhausted Carley and wrought upon her nerves that she became nearly panic-stricken. It grew harder and harder not to turn back. At last she was about to give up when right at hand through the flying dust she espied the cabin. Riding behind it, she dismounted and tied the mustang to a post. Then she ran around to the door and entered.

What a welcome refuge! She was all right now, and when Glenn came along she would have added to her already considerable list another feat for which he would commend her. With aid of her handkerchief, and the tears that flowed so copiously, Carley presently freed her eyes of the blinding dust. But when she essayed to remove it from her face she discovered she would need a towel and soap and hot water.

The cabin appeared to be enveloped in a soft, swishing, hollow sound. It seeped and rustled. Then the sound lulled, only to rise again. Carley went to the door, relieved and glad to see that the duststorm was blowing by. The great sky-high pall of yellow had moved on to the north. Puffs of dust were whipping along the road, but no longer in one continuous cloud. In the west, low down the sun was sinking, a dull magenta in hue, quite weird and remarkable.

"I knew I'd get the jolt all right," soliloquized Carley, wearily, as she walked to a rude couch of poles and sat down upon it. She had begun to cool off. And there, feeling dirty and tired, and slowly wearing to the old depression, she composed herself to wait.

Suddenly she heard the clip-clop of hoofs. "There! that's Glenn," she cried, gladly, and rising, she ran to the door.

She saw a big bay horse bearing a burly rider. He discovered her at the same instant, and pulled his horse.

"Ho! Ho! if it ain't Pretty Eyes!" he called out, in gay, coarse voice.

Carley recognized the voice, and then the epithet, before her sight established the man as Haze Ruff. A singular stultifying shock passed over her.

"Wal, by all thet's lucky!" he said, dismounting. "I knowed we'd meet some day. I can't say I just laid fer you, but I kept my eyes open."

Manifestly he knew she was alone, for he did not glance into the cabin.

"I'm waiting for—Glenn," she said, with lips she tried to make stiff.

"Shore I reckoned thet," he replied, genially. "But he won't be along yet awhile."

He spoke with a cheerful inflection of tone, as if the fact designated was one that would please her; and his swarthy, seamy face expanded into a good-humored, meaning smile. Then without any particular rudeness he pushed her back from the door, into the cabin, and stepped across the threshold.

"How dare—you!" cried Carley. A hot anger that stirred in

her seemed to be beaten down and smothered by a cold shaking internal commotion, threatening collapse. This man loomed over her, huge, somehow monstrous in his brawny uncouth presence. And his knowing smile, and the hard, glinting twinkle of his light eyes, devilishly intelligent and keen, in no wise lessened the sheer brutal force of him physically. Sight of his bulk was enough to terrorize Carley.

"Me! Aw, I'm a darin' *hombre* an' a devil with the wimmin," he said, with a guffaw.

Carley could not collect her wits. The instant of his pushing her back into the cabin and following her had shocked her and almost paralyzed her will. If she saw him now any the less fearful she could not so quickly rally her reason to any advantage.

"Let me out of here," she demanded.

"Nope. I'm a-goin' to make a little love to you," he said, and he reached for her with great hairy hands.

Carley saw in them the strength that had so easily swung the sheep. She saw, too, that they were dirty, greasy hands. And they made her flesh creep.

"Glenn will kill—you," she panted.

"What fer?" he queried, in real or pretended surprise. "Aw, I know wimmin. You'll never tell him."

"Yes, I will."

"Wal, mebbe. I reckon you're lyin', Pretty Eyes," he replied, with a grin. "Anyhow, I'll take a chance."

"I tell you—he'll kill you," repeated Carley, backing away until her weak knees came against the couch.

"What fer, I ask you?" he demanded.

"For this—this insult."

"Huh! I'd like to know who's insulted you. Can't a man take an invitation to kiss an' hug a girl—without insultin' her?"

"Invitation!. . . Are you crazy?" queried Carley, bewildered.

"Nope, I'm not crazy, an' I shore said invitation. . . . I meant thet white shimmy dress you wore the night of Flo's party. Thet's my invitation to get a little fresh with you, Pretty Eyes!"

Carley could only stare at him. His words seemed to have some peculiar, unanswerable power.

"Wal, if it wasn't an invitation, what was it?" he asked, with another step that brought him within reach of her. He waited for her answer, which was not forthcoming.

"Wal, you're gettin' kinda pale around the gills," he went on, derisively. "I reckoned you was a real sport. . . . Come here."

He fastened one of his great hands in the front of her coat and gave her a pull. So powerful was it that Carley came hard against him, almost knocking her breathless. There he held her a moment and then put his other arm round her. It seemed to crush both breath and sense out of her. Suddenly limp, she sank strengthless. She seemed reeling in darkness. Then she felt herself thrust away from him with violence. She sank on the couch and her head and shoulders struck the wall.

"Say, if you're a-goin' to keel over like thet I pass," declared Ruff, in disgust. "Can't you Eastern wimmin stand nothin?"

Carley's eyes opened and beheld this man in an attitude of supremely derisive protest.

"You look like a sick kitten," he added. "When I get me a sweetheart or wife I want her to be a wild cat."

His scorn and repudiation of her gave Carley intense relief. She sat up and endeavored to collect her shattered nerves. Ruff gazed down at her with great disapproval and even disappointment.

"Say, did you have some fool idee I was a-goin' to kill you?" he queried, gruffly.

"I'm afraid—I did," faltered Carley. Her relief was a release; it was so strange that it was gratefulness.

"Wal, I reckon I wouldn't have hurt you. None of these flop-over Janes for me!. . . An' I'll give you a hunch, Pretty Eyes. You might have run acrost a fellar thet was no gentleman!"

Of all the amazing statements that had ever been made to Carley, this one seemed the most remarkable.

"What'd you wear thet onnatural white dress fer?" he demanded, as if he had a right to be her judge.

"Unnatural?" echoed Carley.

"Shore. Thet's what I said. Any woman's dress without top or bottom is onnatural. It's not right. Why, you looked like—like"— here he floundered for adequate expression—"like one of the devil's angels. An' I want to hear why you wore it."

"For the same reason I'd wear any dress," she felt forced to reply.

"Pretty Eyes, thet's a lie. An' you know it's a lie. You wore thet white dress to knock the daylights out of men. Only you ain't honest enough to say so. . . . Even me or my kind! Even us, who're dirt under your little feet. But all the same we're men, an' mebbe better men than you think. If you had to put that dress on, why didn't you stay in your room? Naw, you had to come down an' strut around an' show off your beauty. An' I ask you—if you're a nice girl like Flo Hutter—what'd you wear it fer?"

Carley not only was mute; she felt rise and burn in her a singular shame and surprise.

"I'm only a sheep dipper," went on Ruff, "but I ain't no fool. A fellar doesn't have to live East an' wear swell clothes to have sense. Mebbe you'll learn thet the West is bigger'n you think. A man's a man East or West. But if your Eastern men stand for such dresses as thet white one they'd do well to come out West awhile, like your lover, Glenn Kilbourne. I've been rustlin' round here ten years, an' I never before seen a dress like yours—an' I never heerd of a girl bein' insulted, either. Mebbe you think I insulted you. Wal, I didn't. Fer I reckon *nothin*' could insult you in thet dress. . . . An' my last hunch is this, Pretty Eyes. You're not what a *hombre* like me calls either square or game. *Adios*."

His bulky figure darkened the doorway, passed out, and the light of the sky streamed into the cabin again. Carley sat staring. She heard Ruff's spurs tinkle, then the ring of steel on stirrup, a sodden leathery sound as he mounted, and after that a rapid pound of hoofs, quickly dying away.

He was gone. She had escaped something raw and violent. Dazedly she realized it, with unutterable relief. And she sat there slowly gathering the nervous force that had been shattered. Every word that he had uttered was stamped in startling characters upon her consciousness.

But she was still under the deadening influence of shock. This raw experience was the worst the West had yet dealt her. It brought back former states of revulsion and formed them in one whole irrefutable and damning judgment that seemed to blot out the vaguely dawning and growing happy susceptibilities. It was, perhaps, just as well to have her mind reverted to realistic fact. The presence of Haze Ruff, the astounding truth of the contact with his huge sheep-defiled hands, had been profanation and degradation under which she sickened with fear and shame. Yet hovering back of her shame and rising anger seemed to be a pale, monstrous, and indefinable thought, insistent and accusing, with which she must sooner or later reckon. It might have been the voice of the new side of her nature, but at that moment of outraged womanhood, and of revolt against the West, she would not listen. It might, too, have been the still small voice of conscience. But decision of mind and energy coming to her then, she threw off the burden of emotion and perplexity, and forced herself into composure before the arrival of Glenn.

The dust had ceased to blow, although the wind had by no means died away. Sunset marked the west in old rose and gold, a vast flare. Carley espied a horseman far down the road, and presently recognized both rider and steed. He was coming fast. She went out and, mounting her mustang, she rode out to meet Glenn. It did not appeal to her to wait for him at the cabin; besides hoof tracks other than those made by her mustang might have been noticed by Glenn. Presently he came up to her and pulled his loping horse.

"Hello! I sure was worried," was his greeting, as his gloved hand went out to her. "Did you run into that sandstorm?"

"It ran into me, Glenn, and buried me," she laughed.

His fine eyes lingered on her face with glad and warm glance, and the keen, apprehensive penetration of a lover.

"Well, under all that dust you look scared," he said.

"Scared! I was worse than that. When I first ran into the flying dirt I was only afraid I'd lose my way—and my complexion. But when the worst of the storm hit me—then I feared I'd lose my breath."

"Did you face that sand and ride through it all?" he queried.

"No, not all. But enough. I went through the worst of it before I reached the cabin," she replied.

"Wasn't it great?"

"Yes—great bother and annoyance," she said, laconically.

Whereupon he reached with long, arm and wrapped it round her as they rocked side by side. Demonstrations of this nature were infrequent with Glenn. Despite losing one foot out of a stirrup and her seat in the saddle Carley rather encouraged it. He kissed her dusty face, and then set her back.

"By George! Carley, sometimes I think you've changed since you've been here," he said, with warmth. "To go through that sandstorm without one kick—one knock at my West!"

"Glenn, I always think of what Flo says—the worst is yet to come," replied Carley, trying to hide her unreasonable and tumultuous pleasure at words of praise from him.

"Carley Burch, you don't know yourself," he declared, enigmatically.

"What woman knows herself? But do you know me?"

"Not I. Yet sometimes I see depths in you—wonderful possibilities—submerged under your poise—under your fixed, complacent idle attitude toward life."

This seemed for Carley to be dangerously skating near thin ice, but she could not resist a retort:

"Depths in me? Why I am a shallow, transparent stream like your West Fork! . . . And as for possibilities—may I ask what of them you imagine you see?"

"As a girl, before you were claimed by the world, you were

earnest at heart. You had big hopes and dreams. And you had intellect, too. But you have wasted your talents, Carley. Having money, and spending it, living for pleasure, you have not realized your powers. . . . Now, don't look hurt. I'm not censuring you. It's just the way of modern life. And most of your friends have been more careless, thoughtless, useless than you. The aim of their existence is to be comfortable, free from work, worry, pain. They want pleasure, luxury. And what a pity it is! The best of you girls regard marriage as an escape, instead of responsibility. You don't marry to get your shoulders square against the old wheel of American progress—to help some man make good—to bring a troop of healthy American kids into the world. You bare your shoulders to the gaze of the multitude and like it best if you are strung with pearls."

"Glenn, you distress me when you talk like this," replied Carley, soberly. "You did not use to talk so. It seems to me you are bitter against women."

"Oh no, Carley! I am only sad," he said. "I only see where once I was blind. American women are the finest on earth, but as a race, if they don't change, they're doomed to extinction."

"How can you say such things?" demanded Carley, with spirit.

"I say them because they are true. Carley, on the level now, tell me how many of your immediate friends have children."

Put to a test, Carley rapidly went over in mind her circle of friends, with the result that she was somewhat shocked and amazed to realize how few of them were even married, and how the babies of her acquaintance were limited to three. It was not easy to admit this to Glenn.

"My dear," replied he, "if that does not show you the handwriting on the wall, nothing ever will."

"A girl has to find a husband, doesn't she?" asked Carley, roused to defense of her sex. "And if she's anybody she has to find one in her set. Well, husbands are not plentiful. Marriage certainly is not the end of existence these days. We have to get along somehow. The high cost of living is no inconsderable

factor today. Do you know that most of the better-class apartment houses in New York will not take children? Women are not
all to blame. Take the speed mania. Men must have automobiles.
I know one girl who wanted a baby, but her husband wanted a
car. They couldn't afford both."

"Carley, I'm not blaming women more than men," returned
Glenn. "I don't know that I blame them as a class. But in my
own mind I have worked it all out. Every man or woman who is
genuinely American should read the signs of the times, realize
the crisis, and meet it in an American way. Otherwise we are
done as a race. Money is God in the older countries. But it
should never become God in America. If it does we will make
the fall of Rome pale into insignificance."

"Glenn, let's put off the argument," appealed Carley. "I'm not
—just up to fighting you today. Oh—you needn't smile. I'm not
showing a yellow streak, as Flo puts it. I'll fight you some other
time."

"You're right, Carley," he assented. "Here we are loafing six or
seven miles from home. Let's rustle along."

Riding fast with Glenn was something Carley had only of late
added to her achievements. She had greatest pride in it. So she
urged her mustang to keep pace with Glenn's horse and gave
herself up to the thrill of the motion and feel of wind and sense
of flying along. At a good swinging lope Calico covered ground
swiftly and did not tire. Carley rode the two miles to the rim of
the canyon, keeping alongside of Glenn all the way. Indeed, for
one long level stretch she and Glenn held hands. When they
arrived at the descent, which necessitated slow and careful
riding, she was hot and tingling and breathless, worked by the
action into an exuberance of pleasure. Glenn complimented her
riding as well as her rosy cheeks. There was indeed a sweetness
in working at a task as she had worked to learn to ride in
Western fashion. Every turn of her mind seemed to confront her
with sobering antitheses of thought. Why had she come to love
to ride down a lonely desert road, through ragged cedars where

the wind whipped her face with fragrant wild breath, if at the same time she hated the West? Could she hate a country, however barren and rough, if it had saved the health and happiness of her future husband? Verily there were problems for Carley to solve.

Early twilight purple lay low in the hollows and clefts of the canyon. Over the western rim a pale ghost of the evening star seemed to smile at Carley, to bid her look and look. Like a strain of distant music, the dreamy hum of falling water, the murmur and melody of the stream, came again to Carley's sensitive ear.

"Do you love this?" asked Glenn, when they reached the green-forested canyon floor, with the yellow road winding away into the purple shadows.

"Yes, both the ride—and you," flashed Carley, contrarily. She knew he had meant the deep-walled canyon with its brooding solitude.

"But I want you to love Arizona," he said.

"Glenn, I'm a faithful creature. You should be glad of that. I love New York."

"Very well, then. Arizona to New York," he said, lightly brushing her cheek with his lips. And swerving back into his saddle, he spurred his horse and called back over his shoulder: "That mustang and Flo have beaten me many a time. Come on."

It was not so much his words as his tone and look that roused Carley. Had he resented her loyalty to the city of her nativity? Always there was a little rift in the lute. Had his tone and look meant that Flo might catch him if Carley could not? Absurd as the idea was, it spurred her to recklessness. Her mustang did not need any more than to know she wanted him to run. The road was of soft yellow earth flanked with green foliage and overspread by pines. In a moment she was racing at a speed she had never before half attained on a horse. Down the winding road

Glenn's big steed sped, his head low, his stride tremendous, his action beautiful. But Carley saw the distance between them diminishing. Calico was overtaking the bay. She cried out in the thrilling excitement of the moment. Glenn saw her gaining and pressed his mount to greater speed. Still he could not draw away from Calico. Slowly the little mustang gained. It seemed to Carley that riding him required no effort at all. And at such fast pace, with the wind roaring in her ears, the walls of green vague and continuous in her sight, the sting of pine tips on cheek and neck, the yellow road streaming toward her, under her, there rose out of the depths of her, out of the tumult of her breast, a sense of glorious exultation. She closed in on Glenn. From the flying hoofs of his horse shot up showers of damp sand and gravel that covered Carley's riding habit and spattered in her face. She had to hold up a hand before her eyes. Perhaps this caused her to lose something of her confidence, or her swing in the saddle, for suddenly she realized she was not riding well. The pace was too fast for her inexperience. But nothing could have stopped her then. No fear or awkwardness of hers should be allowed to hamper that thoroughbred mustang. Carley felt that Calico understood the situation; or at least he knew he could catch and pass this big bay horse, and he intended to do it. Carley was hard put to it to hang on and keep the flying sand from blinding her.

When Calico drew alongside the bay horse and brought Carley breast to breast with Glenn, and then inch by inch forged ahead of him, Carley pealed out an exultant cry. Either it frightened Calico or inspired him, for he shot right ahead of Glenn's horse. Then he lost the smooth, wonderful action. He seemed hurtling through space at the expense of tremendous muscular action. Carley could feel it. She lost her equilibrium. She seemed rushing through a blurred green and black aisle of the forest with a gale in her face. Then, with a sharp jolt, a break, Calico plunged to the sand. Carley felt herself propelled forward out of the saddle into the air, and down to strike with a sliding, stunning force that ended in sudden dark oblivion.

Upon recovering consciousness she first felt a sensation of

oppression in her chest and a dull numbness of her whole body. When she opened her eyes she saw Glenn bending over her, holding her head on his knee. A wet, cold, reviving sensation evidently came from the handkerchief with which he was mopping her face.

"Carley, you can't be hurt—really!" he was ejaculating, in eager hope. "It was some spill. But you lit on the sand and slid. You can't be hurt."

The look of his eyes, the tone of his voice, the feel of his hands were such that Carley chose for a moment to pretend to be very badly hurt indeed. It was worth taking a header to get so much from Glenn Kilbourne. But she believed she had suffered no more than a severe bruising and scraping.

"Glenn—dear," she whispered, very low and very eloquently. "I think—my back—is broken. . . . You'll be free— soon."

Glenn gave a terrible start and his face turned a deathly white. He burst out with quavering, inarticulate speech.

Carley gazed up at him and then closed her eyes. She could not look at him while carrying on such deceit. Yet the sight of him and the feel of him then were inexpressibly blissful to her. What she needed most was assurance of his love. She had it. Beyond doubt, beyond morbid fancy, the truth had proclaimed itself, filling her heart with joy.

Suddenly she flung her arms up around his neck. "Oh— Glenn! It was too good a chance to miss!. . . I'm not hurt a bit."

CHAPTER SEVEN

The day came when Carley asked Mrs. Hutter: "Will you please put up a nice lunch for Glenn and me? I'm going to walk down to his farm where he's working, and surprise him."

"That's a downright fine idea," declared Mrs. Hutter, and forthwith bustled away to comply with Carley's request.

So presently Carley found herself carrying a bountiful basket on her arm, faring forth on an adventure that both thrilled and depressed her. Long before this hour something about Glenn's work had quickened her pulse and given rise to an inexplicable admiration. That he was big and strong enough to do such labor made her proud; that he might want to go on doing it made her ponder and brood.

The morning resembled one of the rare Eastern days in June, when the air appeared flooded by rich thick amber light. Only the sun here was hotter and the shade cooler.

Carley took to the trail below where West Fork emptied its golden-green waters into Oak Creek. The red walls seemed to dream and wait under the blaze of the sun; the heat lay like a blanket over the still foliage; the birds were quiet; only the murmuring stream broke the silence of the canyon. Never had Carley felt more the isolation and solitude of Oak Creek

Canyon. Far indeed from the madding crowd! Only Carley's stubbornness kept her from acknowledging the sense of peace that enveloped her—that and the consciousness of her own discontent. Whatwould it be like to come to this canyon—to give up to its enchantments? That, like many another disturbing thought, had to go unanswered, to be driven into the closed chambers of Carley's mind, there to germinate subconsciously, and stalk forth some day to overwhelm her.

The trail led along the creek, threading a maze of bowlders, passing into the shade of cottonwoods, and crossing sun-flecked patches of sand. Carley's every step seemed to become slower. Regrets were assailing her. Long indeed had she overstayed her visit to the West. She must not linger there indefinitely. And mingled with misgiving was a surprise that she had not tired of Oak Creek. In spite of all, and of the dislike she vaunted to herself, the truth stared at her—she was not tired.

The long-delayed visit to see Glenn working on his own farm must result in her talking to him about his work; and in a way not quite clear she regretted the necessity for it. To disapprove of Glenn! She received faint intimations of wavering, of uncertainty, of vague doubt. But these were cried down by the dominant and habitable voice of her personality.

Presently through the shaded and shadowed breadth of the belt of forest she saw gleams of a sunlit clearing. And crossing this space to the border of trees she peered forth, hoping to espy Glenn at his labors. She saw an old shack, and irregular lines of rude fence built of polesof all sizes and shapes, and several plots of bare yellow ground, leading up toward the west side of the canyon wall. Could this clearing be Glenn's farm? Surely she had missed it or had not gone far enough. This was not a farm, but a slash in the forested level of the canyon floor, bare and somehow hideous. Dead trees were standing in the lots. They had been ringed deeply at the base by an ax, to kill them, and so prevent their foliage from shading the soil. Carley saw a long pile of rocks that evidently had been carried from the plowed ground. There was no neatness, no regularity, although there was abundant evidence of toil. To clear that rugged space, to fence it, and plow it, appeared at once to Carley an extremely strenuous and useless task. Carley persuaded herself that this must be the plot of ground belonging to the herder Charley, and she was about to turn on down the creek when far up under the bluff she espied a man. He was stalking along and bending down, stalking along and bending down. She recognized Glenn. He was planting something in the yellow soil.

Curiously Carley watched him, and did not allow her mind to become concerned with a somewhat painful swell of her heart. What a stride he had! How vigorous he looked, and earnest! He was as intent upon this job as if he had been a rustic. He might have been failing to do it well, but he most certainly was doing it conscientiously. Once he had said to her that a man should never be judged by the result of his labors, but by the nature of his effort. A man might strive with all his heart and strength, yet fail. Carley watched him striding along and bending down, absorbed in his task, unmindful of the glaring hot sun, and somehow to her singularly detached from the life wherein he had once moved and to which she yearned to take him back. Suddenly an unaccountable flashing query assailed her conscience: How dare she want to take him back? She seemed as shocked as if some stranger had accosted her. What was this dimming of her eye, this inward tremulousness; this dammed tide beating at an unknown and riveted gate of her intelligence? She felt more then than she dared to face. She struggled against something in herself. The old habit of mind instinctively resisted the new, the strange. But she did not come off wholly victorious. The Carley Burch whom she recognized as of old, passionately hated this life and work of Glenn Kilbourne's, but the rebel self, an unaccountable and defiant Carley, loved him all the better for them.

Carley drew a long deep breath before she called Glenn. This meeting would be momentous and she felt no absolute surety of herself.

Manifestly he was surprised to hear her call, and, dropping his sack and implement, he hurried across the tilled ground, sending up puffs of dust. He vaulted the rude fence of poles, and upon sight of her called out lustily. How big and virile he looked! Yet he was gaunt and strained. It struck Carley that he had not looked so upon her arrival at Oak Creek. Had she worried him? The query gave her a pang.

"Sir Tiller of the Fields," said Carley, gayly, "see, your dinner! *I* brought it and *I* am going to share it."

"You old darling!" he replied, and gave her an embrace that left her cheek moist with the sweat of his. He smelled of dust and earth and his body was hot. "I wish to God it could be true for always!"

His loving, bearish onslaught and his words quite silenced Carley. How at critical moments he always said the thing that hurt her or inhibited her! She essayed a smile as she drew back from him.

"It's sure good of you," he said, taking the basket. "I was thinking I'd be through work sooner today, and was sorry I had not made a date with you. Come, we'll find a place to sit."

Whereupon he led her back under the trees to a half-sunny, half-shady bench of rock overhanging the stream. Great pines overshadowed a still, eddying pool. A number of brown butter-flies hovered over the water, and small trout floated like spotted feathers just under the surface. Drowsy summer enfolded the sylvan scene.

Glenn knelt at the edge of the brook, and, plunging his hands in, he splashed like a huge dog and bathed his hot face and head, and then turned to Carley with gay words and laughter, while he wiped himself dry with a large red scarf. Carley was not proof against the virility of him then, and at the moment, no matter what it was that had made him the man he looked, she loved it.

"I'll sit in the sun," he said, designating a place. "When you're hot you mustn't rest in the shade, unless you've coat or sweater. But you sit here in the shade."

"Glenn, that'll put us too far apart," complained Carley. "I'll sit in the sun with you."

The delightful simplicity and happiness of the ensuing hour was something Carley believed she would never forget.

"There! we've licked the platter clean," she said. "What starved bears we were!. . . I wonder if I shall enjoy eating—when I get home. I used to be so finnicky and picky."

"Carley, don't talk about home," said Glenn, appealingly.

"You dear old farmer, I'd love to stay here and just dream—forever," replied Carley, earnestly. "But I came on purpose to talk seriously."

"Oh, you did! About what?" he returned, with some quick, indefinable change of tone and expression.

"Well, first about your work. I know I hurt your feelings when I wouldn't listen. But I wasn't ready. I wanted to—to just be gay with you for a while. Don't think I wasn't interested. I was. And now, I'm ready to hear all about it—and everything."

She smiled at him bravely, and she knew that unless some unforeseen shock upset her composure, she would be able to conceal from him anything which might hurt his feelings.

"You do look serious," he said, with keen eyes on her.

"Just what are your business relations with Hutter?" she inquired.

"I'm simply working for him," replied Glenn. "My aim is to get an interest in his sheep, and I expect to, some day. We have some plans. And one of them is the development of that Deep Lake section. You remember—you were with us. The day Spillbeans spilled you?"

"Yes, I remember. It was a pretty place," she replied.

Carley did not tell him that for a month past she had owned the Deep Lake section of six hundred and forty acres. She had, in fact, instructed Hutter to purchase it, and to keep the transaction a secret for the present. Carley had never been able to understand the impulse that prompted her to do it. But as Hutter had assured her it was a remarkably good investment on very little capital, she had tried to persuade herself of its advantages. Back of it all had been an irresistible desire to be able some day to present to Glenn this ranch site he loved. She had concluded he would never wholly dissociate himself from this West; and as he would visit it now and then, she had already begun forming plans of her own. She could stand a month in Arizona at long intervals.

"Hutter and I will go into cattle raising some day," went on Glenn. "And that Deep Lake place is what I want for myself."

"What work are you doing for Hutter?" asked Carley.

"Anything from building fence to cutting timber," laughed Glenn. "I've not yet the experience to be a foreman like Lee Stanton. Besides, I have a little business all my own. I put all my money in that."

"You mean here—this—this farm?"

"Yes. And the stock I'm raisin'. You see I have to feed corn. And believe me, Carley, those cornfields represent some job."

"I can well believe that," replied Carley. "You—you looked it."

"Oh, the hard work is over. All I have to do now it to plant and keep the weeds out."

"Glenn, do sheep eat corn?"

"I plant corn to feed my hogs."

"Hogs?" she echoed, vaguely.

"Yes, hogs," he said, with quiet gravity. "The first day you visited my cabin I told you I raised hogs, and I fried my own ham for your dinner."

"Is that what you—put your money in?"

"Yes. And Hutter says I've done well."

"*Hogs!*" ejaculated Carley, aghast.

"My dear, are you growin' dull of comprehension?" retorted Glenn. "H-o-g-s." He spelled the word out. "I'm in the hog-raising business, and pretty blamed well pleased over my success so far."

Carley caught herself in time to quell outwardly a shock of amaze and revulsion. She laughed, and exclaimed against her stupidity. The look of Glenn was no less astounding than the content of his words. He was actually proud of his work. Moreover, he showed not the least sign that he had any idea such information might be startlingly obnoxious to his fiancée.

"Glenn! It's so—so queer," she ejaculated. "That you—Glenn Kilbourne-should ever go in for—for hogs!. . . It's unbelievable. How'd you ever—ever happen to do it?"

"By Heaven! you're hard on me!" he burst out, in sudden dark, fierce passion. "How'd I ever happen to do it?. . . *What* was there left for me? I gave my soul and heart and body to the government—to fight for my country. I came home a wreck. *What* did my government do for me? *What* did my employers do for me? *What* did the people I fought for do for me?. . . Nothing —so help me God—*nothing!*. . . I got a ribbon and a bouquet—a little applause for an hour—and then the sight of me sickened my countrymen. I was broken and used. I was absolutely forgotten. . . . But my body, my life, my soul meant *all* to me. My future was ruined, but I wanted to live. I had killed men who never harmed me—I was not fit to die. . . . I *tried* to live. So I fought out my battle alone. Alone!. . . No one understood. No one cared. I came West to keep from dying of consumption in sight of the indifferent mob for whom I had sacrificed myself. I chose to die on my feet away off alone somewhere. . . . But I got well. And what *made* me well—and *saved* my soul—was the first work that offered. *Raising and tending hogs!*"

The dead whiteness of Glenn's face, the lightning scorn of his eyes, the grim, stark strangeness of him then had for Carley a terrible harmony with this passionate denunciation of her, of her kind, of the America for whom he had lost all.

"Oh, Glenn!—forgive—me!" she faltered. "I was only—talking. What do I know? Oh, I am blind—blind and little!"

She could not bear to face him for a moment, and she hung her head. Her intelligence seemed concentrating swift, wild thoughts round the shock to her consciousness. By that terrible expression of his face, by those thundering words of scorn, would she come to realize the mighty truth of his descent into the abyss and his rise to the heights. Vaguely she began to see. An awful sense of her deadness, of her soul-blighting selfishness, began to dawn upon her as something monstrous out of dim, gray obscurity. She trembled under the reality of thoughts that were not new. How she had babbled about Glenn and the crippled soldiers! How she had imagined she sympathized! But she had only been a vain, worldly, complacent, effusive little fool. She had here the shock of her life, and she sensed a greater one, impossible to grasp.

"Carley, that was coming to you," said Glenn, presently, with deep, heavy expulsion of breath.

"I only know I love you—more—more," she cried, wildly, looking up and wanting desperately to throw herself in his arms.

"I guess you do—a little," he replied. "Sometimes I feel you are a kid. Then again you represent the world—your world with its age-old custom—its unalterable. . . . But, Carley, let's get back to my work."

"Yes—yes," exclaimed Carley, gladly. "I'm ready to—to go pet your hogs—anything."

"By George! I'll take you up," he declared. "I'll bet you won't go near one of my hogpens."

"Lead me to it!" she replied, with a hilarity that was only a nervous reversion of her state.

"Well, maybe I'd better hedge on the bet," he said, laughing again. "You have more in you than I suspect. You sure fooled me when you stood for the sheep-dip. But, come on, I'll take you anyway."

So that was how Carley found herself walking arm in arm with Glenn down the canyon trail. A few moments of action gave her at least an appearance of outward composure. And the state of her emotion was so strained and intense that her slightest show of interest must deceive

Glenn into thinking her eager, responsive, enthusiastic. It certainly appeared to loosen his tongue. But Carley knew she was farther from normal than ever before in her life, and that the subtle, inscrutable woman's intuition of her presaged another shock. Just as she had seemed to change, so had the aspects of the canyon undergone some illusive transformation. The beauty of green foliage and amber stream and brown tree trunks and gray rocks and red walls was there; and the summer drowsiness and languor lay as deep; and the loneliness and solitude brooded with its same eternal significance. But some nameless enchantment, perhaps of hope, seemed no longer to encompass her. A blow had fallen upon her, the nature of which only time could divulge.

Glenn led her around the clearing and up to the base of the west wall, where against a shelving portion of the cliff had been constructed a rude fence of poles. It formed three sides of a pen, and the fourth side was solid rock. A bushy cedar tree stood in the center. Water flowed from under the cliff, which accounted for the boggy condition of the red earth. This pen was occupied by a huge sow and a litter of pigs.

Carley climbed on the fence and sat there while Glenn leaned over the top pole and began to wax eloquent on a subject evidently dear to his heart. Today of all days Carley made an inspiring listener. Even the shiny, muddy, suspicious old sow in no wise daunted her fictitious courage. That filthy pen of mud a foot deep, and of odor rancid, had no terrors for her. With an arm round Glenn's shoulder she watched the rooting and squealing little pigs, and was amused and interested, as if they were far removed from the vital issue of the hour. But all the time as she looked and laughed, and encouraged Glenn to talk, there seemed to be a strange, solemn, oppressive knocking at her heart. Was it only the beat-beat-beat of blood?

"There were twelve pigs in that litter," Glenn was saying, "and now you see there are only nine. I've lost three. Mountain lions, bears, coyotes, wild cats are all likely to steal a pig. And at first I was sure one of these varmints had been robbing me. But as I could not find any tracks, I knew I had to lay the blame on something else. So I kept watch pretty closely in daytime, and at night I shut the pigs up in the corner there, where you see I've built a pen. Yesterday I heard squealing—and, by George! I saw an eagle flying off with one of my pigs. Say, I was mad. A great old bald-headed eagle—the regal bird you see with America's stars and stripes had degraded himself to the level of a coyote. I ran for my rifle, and I took some quick shots at him as he flew up. Tried to hit him, too, but I failed. And the old rascal hung on to my pig. I watched him carry it to that sharp crag way up there on the rim."

"Poor little piggy!" exclaimed Carley. "To think of our American emblem—our stately bird of noble warlike mien—our symbol of lonely grandeur and freedom of the heights—think of him being a robber of pigpens!—Glenn, I begin to appreciate the many-sidedness of things. Even my hide-bound narrowness is susceptible to change. It's never too late to learn. This should apply to the Society for the Preservation of the American Eagle."

Glenn led her along the base of the wall to three other pens, in each of which was a fat old sow with a litter. And at the last enclosure, that owing to dry soil was not so dirty, Glenn picked up a little pig and held it squealing out to Carley as she leaned over the fence. It was fairly white and clean, a little pink and fuzzy, and certainly cute with its curled tall.

"Carley Burch, take it in your hands," commanded Glenn.

The feat seemed monstrous and impossible of accomplishment for Carley. Yet such was her temper at the moment that she would have undertaken anything.

"Why, shore I will, as Flo says," replied Carley, extending her ungloved hands. "Come here, piggy. I christen you Pinky." And hiding an almost insupportable squeamishness from Glenn, she took the pig in her hands and fondled it.

"By George!" exclaimed Glenn, in huge delight. "I wouldn't have believed it. Carley, I hope you tell your fastidious and immaculate Morrison that you held one of my pigs in your beautiful hands."

"Wouldn't it please you more to tell him yourself?" asked Carley.

"Yes, it would," declared Glenn, grimly.

This incident inspired Glenn to a Homeric narration of his hog-raising experience. In spite of herself the content of his talk interested her. And as for the effect upon her of his singular enthusiasm, it was deep and compelling. The little-boned Berkshire razorback hogs grew so large and fat and heavy that their bones broke under their weight. The Duroc jerseys were the best breed in that latitude, owing to their larger and stronger bones, that enabled them to stand up under the greatest accumulation of fat.

Glenn told of his droves of pigs running wild in the canyon below. In summertime they fed upon vegetation, and at other seasons on acorns, roots, bugs, and grubs. Acorns, particularly, were good and fattening feed. They ate cedar and juniper berries, and pinyon nuts. And therefore they lived off the land, at little or no expense to the owner. The only loss was from beasts and birds of prey. Glenn showed Carley how a profitable business could soon be established. He meant to fence off side canyons and to segregate droves of his hogs, and to raise abundance of corn for winter feed. At that time there was a splendid market for hogs, a condition Hutter claimed would continue indefinitely in a growing country. In conclusion Glenn eloquently told how in his necessity he had accepted gratefully the humblest of labors, to find in the hard pursuit of it a rejuvenation of body and mind, and a promise of independence and prosperity.

When he had finished, and excused himself to go repair a

weak place in the corral fence, Carley sat silent, wrapped in strange meditation.

Whither had faded the vulgarity and ignominy she had attached to Glenn's raising of hogs? Gone—like other miasmas of her narrow mind! Partly she understood him now. She shirked consideration of his sacrifice to his country. That must wait. But she thought of his work, and the more she thought the less she wondered.

First he had labored with his hands. What infinite meaning lay unfolding to her vision! Somewhere out of it all came the conception that man was intended to earn his bread by the sweat of his brow. But there was more to it than that. By that toil and sweat, by the friction of horny palms, by the expansion and contraction of muscle, by the acceleration of blood, something great and enduring, something physical and spiritual, came to a man. She understood then why she would have wanted to surrender herself to a man made manly by toil; she understood how a woman instinctively leaned toward the protection of a man who had used his hands—who had strength and red blood and virility who could fight like the progenitors of the race. Any toil was splendid that served this end for any man. It all went back to the survival of the fittest. And suddenly Carley thought of Morrison. He could dance and dangle attendance upon her, and amuse her—but how would he have acquitted himself in a moment of peril? She had her doubts. Most assuredly he could not have beaten down for her a ruffian like Haze Ruff. What then should be the significance of a man for a woman?

Carley's querying and answering mind reverted to Glenn. He had found a secret in this seeking for something through the labor of hands. All development of body must come through exercise of muscles. The virility of cell in tissue and bone depended upon that. Thus he had found in toil the pleasure and reward athletes had in their desultory training. But when a man learned this secret the need of work must become permanent.

Did this explain the law of the Persians that every man was required to sweat every day?

Carley tried to picture to herself Glenn's attitude of mind when he had first gone to work here in the West. Resolutely she now denied her shrinking, cowardly sensitiveness. She would go to the root of this matter, if she had intelligence enough. Crippled, ruined in health, wrecked and broken by an inexplicable war, soul-blighted by the heartless, callous neglect of government and public, on the verge of madness at the insupportable facts, he had yet been wonderful enough, true enough to himself and God, to fight for life with the instinct of a man, to fight for his mind with a noble and unquenchable faith. Alone indeed he had been alone! And by some miracle beyond the power of understanding he had found day by day in his painful efforts some hope and strength to go on. He could not have had any illusions. For Glenn Kilbourne the health and happiness and success most men held so dear must have seemed impossible. His slow, daily, tragic, and terrible task must have been something he owed himself. Not for Carley Burch! She like all the others had failed him. How Carley shuddered in confession of that! Not for the country which had used him and cast him off!

Carley divined now, as if by a flash of lightning, the meaning of Glenn's strange, cold, scornful, and aloof manner when he had encountered young men of his station, as capable and as strong as he, who had escaped the service of the army. For him these men did not exist. They were less than nothing. They had waxed fat on lucrative jobs; they had basked in the presence of girls whose brothers and lovers were in the trenches or on the turbulent sea, exposed to the ceaseless dread and almost ceaseless toil of war. If Glenn's spirit had lifted him to endurance of war for the sake of others, how then could it fail him in a precious duty of fidelity to himself? Carley could see him day by day toiling in his lonely canyon—plodding to his lonely cabin. He had been playing the game—fighting it out alone as surely he knew his brothers of like misfortune were fighting.

So Glenn Kilbourne loomed heroically in Carley's transfigured sight. He was one of Carlyle's battle-scarred warriors. Out of his travail he had climbed on stepping-stones of his dead self. *Resurgam*! That had been his unquenchable cry. Who had heard it? Only the solitude of his lonely canyon, only the waiting, dreaming, watching walls, only the silent midnight shadows, only the white, blinking, passionless stars, only the wild creatures of his haunts, only the moaning wind in the pines—only these had been with him in his agony. How near were these things to God?

Carley's heart seemed full to bursting. Not another single moment could her mounting love abide in a heart that held a double purpose. How bitter the assurance that she had not come West to help him! It was self, self, all self that had actuated her. Unworthy indeed was she of the love of this man. Only a lifetime of devotion to him could acquit her in the eyes of her better self. Sweetly and madly raced the thrill and tumult of her blood. There must be only one outcome to her romance. Yet the next instant there came a dull throbbing—an oppression which was pain—an impondering vague thought of catastrophe. Only the fearfulness of love perhaps!

She saw him complete his task and wipe his brown moist face and stride toward her, coming nearer, tall and erect with something added to his soldierly bearing, with a light in his eyes she could no longer bear.

The moment for which she had waited more than two months had come at last.

"Glenn—when will you go back East?" she asked, tensely and low.

The instant the words were spent upon her lips she realized that he had always been waiting and prepared for this question that had been so terrible for her to ask.

"Carley," he replied gently, though his voice rang, "I am never going back East."

An inward quivering hindered her articulation.

"*Never?*" she whispered.

"Never to live, or stay any while," he went on. "I might go some time for a little visit. . . . But never to live."

"Oh—Glenn!" she gasped, and her hands fluttered out to him. The shock was driving home. No amaze, no incredulity succeeded her reception of the fact. It was a slow stab. Carley felt the cold blanch of her skin. "Then—this is it—the something I felt strange between us?"

"Yes, I knew—and you never asked me," he replied.

"That was it? All the time you knew," she whispered, huskily. "You knew. . . . *I'd never—marry you—never live out here?*"

"Yes, Carley, I knew you'd never be woman enough—*American enough*—to help me reconstruct my broken life out here in the West," he replied, with a sad and bitter smile.

That flayed her. An insupportable shame and wounded vanity and clamoring love contended for dominance of her emotions. Love beat down all else.

"Dearest—I beg of you—don't break my heart," she implored.

"I love you, Carley," he answered, steadily, with piercing eyes on hers.

"Then come back—home—home with me."

"No. If you love me you will be my wife."

"Love you! Glenn, I worship you," she broke out, passionately. "But I could not live here—*I could not.*"

"Carley, did you ever read of the woman who said, 'Whither thou goest, there will I go'. . ."

"Oh, don't be ruthless! Don't judge me. . . . I never dreamed of this. I came West to take you back."

"My dear, it was a mistake," he said, gently, softening to her distress. "I'm sorry I did not write you more plainly. But, Carley, I could not ask you to share this—this wilderness home with me. I don't ask it now. I always knew you couldn't do it. Yet you've changed so—that I hoped against hope. Love makes us blind even to what we see."

"Don't try to spare me. I'm slight and miserable. I stand

abased in my own eyes. I thought I loved you. But I must love best the crowd—people—luxury—fashion—the damned round of things I was born to."

"Carley, you will realize their insufficiency too late," he replied, earnestly. "The things you were born to are love, work, children, happiness."

"Don't! don't!. . . they are hollow mockery for me," she cried, passionately. "Glenn, it is the end. It must come—quickly. . . . You are free."

"I do not ask to be free. Wait. Go home and look at it again with different eyes. Think things over. Remember what came to me out of the West. I will always love you—and I will be here—hoping—"

"I—I cannot listen," she returned, brokenly, and she clenched her hands tightly to keep from wringing them. "I—I cannot face you. . . . Here is—your ring. . . . You—are—free. . . . Don't stop me—don't come. . . . Oh, Glenn, good-by!"

With breaking heart she whirled away from him and hurried down the slope toward the trail. The shade of the forest enveloped her. Peering back through the trees, she saw Glenn standing where she had left him, as if already stricken by the loneliness that must be his lot. A sob broke from Carley's throat. She hated herself. She was in a terrible state of conflict. Decision had been wrenched from her, but she sensed unending strife. She dared not look back again. Stumbling and breathless, she hurried on. How changed the atmosphere and sunlight and shadow of the canyon! The looming walls had pitiless eyes for her flight. When she crossed the mouth of West Fork an almost irresistible force breathed to her from under the stately pines.

An hour later she had bidden farewell to the weeping Mrs. Hutter, and to the white-faced Flo, and Lolomi Lodge, and the murmuring waterfall, and the haunting loneliness of Oak Creek Canyon.

CHAPTER EIGHT

At Flagstaff, where Carley arrived a few minutes before train time, she was too busily engaged with tickets and baggage to think of herself or of the significance of leaving Arizona. But as she walked into the Pullman she overheard a passenger remark, "Regular old Arizona sunset," and that shook her heart. Suddenly she realized she had come to love the colorful sunsets, to watch and wait for them. And bitterly she thought how that was her way to learn the value of something when it was gone.

The jerk and start of the train affected her with singular depressing shock. She had burned her last bridge behind her. Had she unconsciously hoped for some incredible reversion of Glenn's mind or of her own? A sense of irreparable loss flooded over her—the first check to shame and humiliation.

From her window she looked out to the southwest. Somewhere across the cedar and pine-greened uplands lay Oak Creek Canyon, going to sleep in its purple and gold shadows of sunset. Banks of broken clouds hung to the horizon, like continents and islands and reefs set in a turquoise sea. Shafts of sunlight streaked down through creamy-edged and purple-centered clouds. Vast flare of gold dominated the sunset background.

When the train rounded a curve Carley's strained vision

became filled with the upheaved bulk of the San Francisco Mountains. Ragged gray grass slopes and green forests on end, and black fringed sky lines, all pointed to the sharp clear peaks spearing the sky. And as she watched, the peaks slowly flushed with sunset hues, and the sky flared golden, and the strength of the eternal mountains stood out in sculptured sublimity. Every day for two months and more Carley had watched these peaks, at all hours, in every mood; and they had unconsciously become a part of her thought. The train was relentlessly whirling her eastward. Soon they must become a memory. Tears blurred her sight. Poignant regret seemed added to the anguish she was suffering. Why had she not learned sooner to see the glory of the mountains, to appreciate the beauty and solitude? Why had she not understood herself?

The next day through New Mexico she followed magnificent ranges and valleys—so different from the country she had seen coming West—so supremely beautiful that she wondered if she had only acquired the harvest of a seeing eye.

But it was at sunset of the following day, when the train was speeding down the continental slope of prairie land beyond the Rockies, that the West took its ruthless revenge.

Masses of strange cloud and singular light upon the green prairie, and a luminosity in the sky, drew Carley to the platform of her car, which was the last of the train. There she stood, gripping the iron gate, feeling the wind whip her hair and the iron-tracked ground speed from under her, spellbound and stricken at the sheer wonder and glory of the firmament, and the mountain range that it canopied so exquisitely.

A rich and mellow light, singularly clear, seemed to flood out of some unknown source. For the sun was hidden. The clouds just above Carley hung low, and they were like thick, heavy smoke, mushrooming, coalescing, forming and massing, of strange yellow cast of nature. It shaded westward into heliotrope and this into a purple so royal, so matchless and rare that Carley understood why the purple of the heavens could never be reproduced in paint. Here the cloud mass thinned and paled, and a tint of rose began to flush the billowy, flowery, creamy white. Then came the surpassing splendor of this cloud pageant—a vast canopy of shell pink, a sun-fired surface like an opal sea, rippled and webbed, with the exquisite texture of an Oriental fabric, pure, delicate, lovely—as no work of human hands could be. It mirrored all the warm, pearly tints of the inside whorl of the tropic nautilus. And it ended abruptly, a rounded depth of bank, on a broad stream of clear sky, intensely blue, transparently blue, as if through the lambent depths shone the infinite firmament. The lower edge of this stream took the golden lightning of the sunset and was notched for all its horizon-long length by the wondrous white glistening-peaked range of the Rockies. Far to the north, standing aloof from the range, loomed up the grand black bulk and noble white dome of Pikes Peak.

Carley watched the sunset transfiguration of cloud and sky and mountain until all were cold and gray. And then she returned to her seat, thoughtful and sad, feeling that the West had mockingly flung at her one of its transient moments of loveliness.

Nor had the West wholly finished with her. Next day the mellow gold of the Kansas wheat fields, endless and boundless as a sunny sea, rich, waving in the wind, stretched away before her aching eyes for hours and hours. Here was the promise fulfilled, the bountiful harvest of the land, the strength of the West. The great middle state had a heart of gold.

East of Chicago Carley began to feel that the long days and nights of riding, the ceaseless turning of the wheels, the constant and wearing stress of emotion, had removed her an immeasurable distance of miles and time and feeling from the scene of her catastrophe. Many days seemed to have passed. Many had been the hours of her bitter regret and anguish.

Indiana and Ohio, with their green pastoral farms, and numberless villages, and thriving cities, denoted a country far removed and different from the West, and an approach to the populous East. Carley felt like a wanderer coming home. She was restlessly and impatiently glad. But her weariness of body and mind, and the close atmosphere of the car, rendered her extreme discomfort. Summer had laid its hot hand on the low country east of the Mississippi.

Carley had wired her aunt and two of her intimate friends to meet her at the Grand Central Station. This reunion soon to come affected Carley in recurrent emotions of relief, gladness, and shame. She did not sleep well, and arose early, and when the train reached Albany she felt that she could hardly endure the tedious hours. The majestic Hudson and the palatial mansions on the wooded bluffs proclaimed to Carley that she was back in the East. How long a time seemed to have passed! Either she was not the same or the aspect of everything had changed. But she believed that as soon as she got over the ordeal of meeting her friends, and was home again, she would soon see things rationally.

At last the train sheered away from the broad Hudson and entered the environs of New York. Carley sat perfectly still, to all outward appearances a calm, superbly-poised New York woman returning home, but inwardly raging with contending tides. In her own sight she was a disgraceful failure, a prodigal sneaking back to the ease and protection of loyal friends who did not know her truly. Every familiar landmark in the approach to the city gave her a thrill, yet a vague unsatisfied something lingered after each sensation.

Then the train with rush and roar crossed the Harlem River to enter New York City. As one waking from a dream Carley saw the blocks and squares of gray apartment houses and red buildings, the miles of roofs and chimneys, the long hot glaring streets full of playing children and cars. Then above the roar of the train sounded the high notes of a hurdy-gurdy. Indeed she was home. Next to startle her was the dark tunnel, and then the slowing of the train to a stop. As she walked behind a porter up the long incline toward the station gate her legs seemed to be dead.

In the circle of expectant faces beyond the gate she saw her

aunt's, eager and agitated, then the handsome pale face of
Eleanor Harmon, and beside her the sweet thin one of Beatrice
Lovell. As they saw her how quick the change from expectancy
to joy! It seemed they all rushed upon her, and embraced her,
and exclaimed over her together. Carley never recalled what she
said. But her heart was full.

"Oh, how perfectly stunning you look!" cried Eleanor,
backing away from Carley and gazing with glad, surprised eyes.

"Carley!" gasped Beatrice. "You wonderful golden-skinned
goddess! . . . You're *young* again, like you were in our school days."

It was before Aunt Mary's shrewd, penetrating, loving gaze
that Carley quailed.

"Yes, Carley, you look well—better than I ever saw you, but—
but—"

"But I don't look happy," interrupted Carley. "I am happy to
get home—to see you all. . . But—my—my heart is broken!"

A little shocked silence ensued, then Carley found herself
being led across the lower level and up the wide stairway. As she
mounted to the vast-domed cathedral-like chamber of the
station a strange sensation pierced her with a pang. Not the old
thrill of leaving New York or returning! Nor was it the welcome
sight of the hurrying, well-dressed throng of travelers and
commuters, nor the stately beauty of the station. Carley shut her
eyes, and then she knew. The dim light of vast space above, the
looming gray walls, shadowy with tracery of figures, the lofty
dome like the blue sky, brought back to her the walls of Oak
Creek Canyon and the great caverns under the ramparts. As
suddenly as she had shut her eyes Carley opened them to face
her friends.

"Let me get it over—quickly," she burst out, with hot blood
surging to her face. "I—I hated the West. It was so raw—so
violent—so big. I think I hate it more—now. . . . But it changed
me—made me over physically—and did something to my soul—
God knows what. . . . And it has saved Glenn. Oh! he is wonderful! You would never know him. . . . For long I had not the

courage to tell him I came to bring him back East. I kept putting it off. And I rode, I climbed, I camped, I lived outdoors. At first it nearly killed me. Then it grew bearable, and easier, until I forgot. I wouldn't be honest if I didn't admit now that somehow I had a wonderful time, in spite of all. . . . Glenn's business is raising hogs. He has a hog ranch. Doesn't it sound sordid? But things are not always what they sound—or seem. Glenn is absorbed in his work. I hated it—I expected to ridicule it. But I ended by infinitely respecting him. I learned through his hog-raising the real nobility of work. . . . Well, at last I found courage to ask him when he was coming back to New York. He said 'never!'. . . I realized then my blindness, my selfishness. I could not be his wife and live there. I could not. I was too small, too miserable, too comfort-loving—too spoiled. And all the time he knew this—*knew* I'd never be big enough to marry him. . . . That broke my heart. I left him free—and here I am. . . . I beg you—don't ask me any more—and never to mention it to me—so I can forget."

The tender unspoken sympathy of women who loved her proved comforting in that trying hour. With the confession ruthlessly made the hard compression in Carley's breast subsided, and her eyes cleared of a hateful dimness. When they reached the taxi stand outside the station Carley felt a rush of hot devitalized air from the street. She seemed not to be able to get air into her lungs.

"Isn't it dreadfully hot?" she asked.

"This is a cool spell to what we had last week," replied Eleanor.

"Cool!" exclaimed Carley, as she wiped her moist face. "I wonder if you Easterners know the real significance of words."

Then they entered a taxi, to be whisked away apparently through a labyrinthine maze of cars and streets, where pedestrians had to run and jump for their lives. A congestion of traffic at Fifth Avenue and Forty-second Street halted their taxi for a few moments, and here in the thick of it Carley had full assurance that she was back in the metropolis. Her sore heart eased somewhat at sight of the streams of people passing to and fro. How they rushed! Where were they going? What was their story? And all the while her aunt held her hand, and Beatrice and Eleanor talked as fast as their tongues could wag. Then the taxi clattered on up the Avenue, to turn down a side street and presently stop at Carley's home. It was a modest three-story brownstone house. Carley had been so benumbed by sensations that she did not imagine she could experience a new one. But peering out of the taxi, she gazed dubiously at the brownish-red stone steps and front of her home.

"I'm going to have it painted," she muttered, as if to herself.

Her aunt and her friends laughed, glad and relieved to hear such a practical remark from Carley. How were they to divine that this brownish-red stone was the color of desert rocks and canyon walls?

In a few more moments Carley was inside the house, feeling a sense of protection in the familiar rooms that had been her home for seventeen years. Once in the sanctity of her room, which was exactly as she had left it, her first action was to look in the mirror at her weary, dusty, heated face. Neither the brownness of it nor the shadow appeared to harmonize with the image of her that haunted the mirror.

"Now!" she whispered low. "It's done. I'm home. The old life —or a new life? How to meet either. Now!"

Thus she challenged her spirit. And her intelligence rang at her the imperative necessity for action, for excitement, for effort that left no time for rest or memory or wakefulness. She accepted the issue. She was glad of the stern fight ahead of her. She set her will and steeled her heart with all the pride and vanity and fury of a woman who had been defeated but who scorned defeat. She was what birth and breeding and circumstance had made her. She would seek what the old life held.

What with unpacking and chatting and telephoning and lunching, the day soon passed. Carley went to dinner with friends and later to a roof garden. The color and light, the gayety and music, the news of acquaintances, the humor of the actors—all, in fact, except the unaccustomed heat and noise, were most welcome and diverting. That night she slept the sleep of weariness.

Awakening early, she inaugurated a habit of getting up at once, instead of lolling in bed, and breakfasting there, and reading her mail, as had been her wont before going West. Then she went over business matters with her aunt, called on her lawyer and banker, took lunch with Rose Maynard, and spent the afternoon shopping. Strong as she was, the unaccustomed heat and the hard pavements and the jostle of shoppers and the continual rush of sensations wore her out so completely that she did not want any dinner. She talked to her aunt a while, then went to bed.

Next day Carley motored through Central Park, and out of town into Westchester County, finding some relief from the stifling heat. But she seemed to look at the dusty trees and the worn greens without really seeing them. In the afternoon she called on friends, and had dinner at home with her aunt, and then went to a theatre. The musical comedy was good, but the almost unbearable heat and the vitiated air spoiled her enjoyment. That night upon arriving home at midnight she stepped out of the taxi, and involuntarily, without thought, looked up to see the stars. But there were no stars. A murky yellow-tinged blackness hung low over the city. Carley recollected that stars, and sunrises and sunsets, and untainted air, and silence were not for city dwellers. She checked any continuation of the thought.

A few days sufficed to swing her into the old life. Many of Carley's friends had neither the leisure nor the means to go away from the city during the summer. Some there were who might have afforded that if they had seen fit to live in less showy apart-ments, or to dispense with cars. Other of her best friends were on their summer outings in the Adirondacks. Carley decided to go with her aunt to Lake Placid about the first of August. Meanwhile she would keep going and doing.

She had been a week in town before Morrison telephoned her and added his welcome. Despite the gay gladness of his voice, it irritated her. Really, she scarcely wanted to see him. But a meeting was inevitable, and besides, going out with him was in accordance with the plan she had adopted. So she made an engagement to meet him at the Plaza for dinner. When with slow and pondering action she hung up the receiver it occurred to her that she resented the idea of going to the Plaza. She did not dwell on the reason why.

When Carley went into the reception room of the Plaza that night Morrison was waiting for her—the same slim, fastidious, elegant, sallow-faced Morrison whose image she had in mind, yet somehow different. He had what Carley called the New York masculine face, blasé and lined, with eyes that gleamed, yet had no fire. But at sight of her his face lighted up.

"By Jove! but you've come back a peach!" he exclaimed, clasping her extended hand. "Eleanor told me you looked great. It's worth missing you to see you like this."

"Thanks, Larry," she replied. "I must look pretty well to win that compliment from you. And how are you feeling? You don't seem robust for a golfer and horseman. But then I'm used to husky Westerners."

"Oh, I'm fagged with the daily grind," he said. "I'll be glad to get up in the mountains next month. Let's go down to dinner."

They descended the spiral stairway to the grillroom, where an orchestra was playing jazz, and dancers gyrated on a polished floor, and diners in evening dress looked on over their cigarettes.

"Well, Carley, are you still finicky about the eats?" he queried, consulting the menu.

"No. But I prefer plain food," she replied.

"Have a cigarette," he said, holding out his silver monogrammed case.

"Thanks, Larry. I—I guess I'll not take up smoking again. You see, while I was West I got out of the habit."

"Yes, they told me you had changed," he returned. "How about drinking?"

"Why, I thought New York had gone dry!" she said, forcing a laugh.

"Only on the surface. Underneath it's wetter than ever."

"Well, I'll obey the law."

He ordered a rather elaborate dinner, and then turning his attention to Carley, gave her closer scrutiny. Carley knew then that he had become acquainted with the fact of her broken engagement. It was a relief not to need to tell him.

"How's that big stiff, Kilbourne?" asked Morrison, suddenly. "Is it true he got well?"

"Oh—yes! He's fine," replied Carley with eyes cast down. A hot knot seemed to form deep within her and threatened to break and steal along her veins. "But if you please—I do not care to talk of him."

"Naturally. But I must tell you that one man's loss is another's gain."

Carley had rather expected renewed courtship from Morrison. She had not, however, been prepared for the beat of her pulse, the quiver of her nerves, the uprising of hot resentment at the mere mention of Kilbourne. It was only natural that Glenn's former rivals should speak of him, and perhaps disparagingly. But from this man Carley could not bear even a casual reference. Morrison had escaped the army service. He had been given a high-salaried post at the ship-yards—the duties of which, if there had been any, he performed wherever he happened to be. Morrison's father had made a fortune in leather during the war. And Carley remembered Glenn telling her he had seen two whole blocks in Paris piled twenty feet deep with leather army goods that were never used and probably had never been intended to be used. Morrison represented the not inconsiderable number of young men in New York who had gained at the expense of the valiant legion who had lost. But what had Morrison gained? Carley raised her eyes to gaze steadily at him. He looked well-fed, indolent, rich, effete, and supremely self-satisfied. She could not see that he had gained anything. She would rather have been a crippled ruined soldier.

"Larry, I fear gain and loss are mere words," she said. "The thing that counts with me is what you *are*."

He stared in well-bred surprise, and presently talked of a new dance which had lately come into vogue. And from that he passed on to gossip of the theatres. Once between courses of the dinner he asked Carley to dance, and she complied. The music would have stimulated an Egyptian mummy, Carley thought, and the subdued rose lights, the murmur of gay voices, the glide and grace and distortion of the dancers, were exciting and pleasurable. Morrison had the suppleness and skill of a dancing-master. But he held Carley too tightly, and so she told him, and added, "I imbibed some fresh pure air while I was out West—something you haven't here—and I don't want it all squeezed out of me."

————

The latter days of July Carley made busy—so busy that she lost her tan and appetite, and something of her splendid resistance to the dragging heat and late hours. Seldom was she without some of her friends. She accepted almost any kind of an invitation, and went even to Coney Island, to baseball games, to the motion pictures, which were three forms of amusement not customary with her. At Coney Island, which she visited with two of her younger girl friends, she had the best time since her arrival home. What had put her in accord with ordinary people? The baseball games, likewise pleased her. The running of the players and the screaming of the spectators amused and excited her. But she hated the motion pictures with their salacious and absurd misrepresentations of life, in some cases capably acted by skillful actors, and in others a silly series of scenes featuring some doll-faced girl.

But she refused to go horseback riding in Central Park. She refused to go to the Plaza. And these refusals she made deliberately, without asking herself why.

On August 1st she accompanied her aunt and several friends to Lake Placid, where they established themselves at a hotel. How welcome to Carley's strained eyes were the green of mountains, the soft gleam of amber water! How sweet and refreshing a breath of cool pure air! The change from New York's glare and heat and dirt, and iron-red insulating walls, and thronging millions of people, and ceaseless roar and rush, was tremendously relieving to Carley. She had burned the candle at both ends. But the beauty of the hills and vales, the quiet of the forest, the sight of the stars, made it harder to forget. She had to rest. And when she rested she could not always converse, or read, or write.

For the most part her days held variety and pleasure. The place was beautiful, the weather pleasant, the people congenial. She motored over the forest roads, she canoed along the margin of the lake, she played golf and tennis. She wore exquisite gowns to dinner and danced during the evenings. But she seldom walked anywhere on the trails and, never alone, and she never climbed the mountains and never rode a horse.

Morrison arrived and added his attentions to those of other men. Carley neither accepted nor repelled them. She favored the association with married couples and older people, and rather shunned the pairing off peculiar to vacationists at summer hotels. She had always loved to play and romp with children, but here she found herself growing to avoid them, somehow hurt by sound of pattering feet and joyous laughter. She filled the days as best she could, and usually earned quick slumber at night. She staked all on present occupation and the truth of flying time.

CHAPTER NINE

The latter part of September Carley returned to New York.

Soon after her arrival she received by letter a formal proposal of marriage from Elbert Harrington, who had been quietly attentive to her during her sojourn at Lake Placid. He was a lawyer of distinction, somewhat older than most of her friends, and a man of means and fine family. Carley was quite surprised. Harrington was really one of the few of her acquaintances whom she regarded as somewhat behind the times, and liked him the better for that. But she could not marry him, and replied to his letter in as kindly a manner as possible. Then he called personally.

"Carley, I've come to ask you to reconsider," he said, with a smile in his gray eyes. He was not a tall or handsome man, but he had what women called a nice strong face.

"Elbert, you embarrass me," she replied, trying to laugh it out. "Indeed I feel honored, and I thank you. But I can't marry you."

"Why not?" he asked, quietly.

"Because I don't love you," she replied.

"I did not expect you to," he said. "I hoped in time you might come to care. I've known you a good many years, Carley. Forgive me if I tell you I see you are breaking—wearing yourself down. Maybe it is not a husband you need so much now, but you do need a home and children. You are wasting your life."

"All you say may be true, my friend," replied Carley, with a helpless little upflinging of hands. "Yet it does not alter my feelings."

"But you will marry sooner or later?" he queried, persistently.

This straightforward question struck Carley as singularly as if it was one she might never have encountered. It forced her to think of things she had buried.

"I don't believe I ever will," she answered, thoughtfully.

"That is nonsense, Carley," he went on. "You'll have to marry. What else can you do? With all due respect to your feelings— that affair with Kilbourne is ended—and you're not the wishy-washy heartbreak kind of a girl."

"You can never tell what a woman will do," she said, some-what coldly.

"Certainly not. That's why I refuse to take no. Carley, be reasonable. You like me—respect me, do you not?"

"Why, of course I do!"

"I'm only thirty-five, and I could give you all any sensible woman wants," he said. "Let's make a real American home. Have you thought at all about that, Carley? Something is wrong today. Men are not marrying. Wives are not having children. Of all the friends I have, not one has a real American home. Why, it is a terrible fact! But, Carley, you are not a sentimentalist, or a melancholiac. Nor are you a waster. You have fine qualities. You need something to do, some one to care for."

"Pray do not think me ungrateful, Elbert," she replied, "nor insensible to the truth of what you say. But my answer is no!"

When Harrington had gone Carley went to her room, and precisely as upon her return from Arizona she faced her mirror skeptically and relentlessly. "I am such a liar that I'll do well to look at myself," she meditated. "Here I am again. Now! The world expects me to marry. But *what* do I expect?"

There was a raw unheated wound in Carley's heart. Seldom had she permitted herself to think about it, let alone to probe it with hard materialistic queries. But custom to her was as inexorable as life. If she chose to live in the world she must conform to its customs. For a woman marriage was the aim and the end and the all of existence. Nevertheless, for Carley it could not be without love. Before she had gone West she might have had many of the conventional modern ideas about women and marriage. But because out there in the wilds her love and perception had broadened, now her arraignment of herself and her sex was bigger, sterner, more exacting. The months she had been home seemed fuller than all the months of her life. She had tried to forget and enjoy; she had not succeeded; but she had looked with far-seeing eyes at her world. Glenn Kilbourne's tragic fate had opened her eyes.

Either the world was all wrong or the people in it were. But if that were an extravagant and erroneous supposition, there certainly was proof positive that her own small individual world was wrong. The women did not do any real work; they did not bear children; they lived on excitement and luxury. They had no ideals. How greatly were men to blame? Carley doubted her judgment here. But as men could not live without the smiles and comradeship and love of women, it was only natural that they should give the women what they wanted. Indeed, they had no choice. It was give or go without. How much of real love entered into the marriages among her acquaintances? Before marriage Carley wanted a girl to be sweet, proud, aloof, with a heart of golden fire. Not attainable except through love! It would be better that no children be born at all unless born of such beautiful love. Perhaps that was why so few children were born. Nature's balance and revenge! In Arizona Carley had learned something of the ruthlessness and inevitableness of nature. She was finding out she had learned this with many other staggering facts.

"I love Glenn still," she whispered, passionately, with trembling lips, as she faced the tragic-eyed image of herself in the mirror. "I love him more—more. Oh, my God! If I were honest I'd cry out the truth! It is terrible. . . . I will always love him. How then could I marry any other man? I would be a lie, a cheat. If I could only forget him—only kill that love. Then I might love another man— and if I did love him—no matter what I had felt or done before, I would be worthy. I could feel worthy. I could give him just as much. But without such love I'd give only a husk—a body without soul."

Love, then, was the sacred and holy flame of life that sanctioned the begetting of children. Marriage might be a necessity of modern time, but it was not the vital issue. Carley's anguish revealed strange and hidden truths. In some inexplicable way Nature struck a terrible balance—revenged herself upon a people who had no children, or who brought into the world children not created by the divinity of love, unyearned for, and therefore somehow doomed to carry on the blunders and burdens of life.

Carley realized how right and true it might be for her to throw herself away upon an inferior man, even a fool or a knave, if she loved him with that great and natural love of woman; likewise it dawned upon her how false and wrong and sinful it would be to marry the greatest or the richest or the noblest man unless she had that supreme love to give him, and knew it was reciprocated.

"What am I going to do with my life?" she asked, bitterly and aghast. "I have been—I am a waster. I've lived for nothing but pleasurable sensation. I'm utterly useless. I do absolutely no good on earth."

Thus she saw how Harrington's words rang true—how they had precipitated a crisis for which her unconscious brooding had long made preparation.

"Why not give up ideals and be like the rest of my kind?" she soliloquized.

That was one of the things which seemed wrong with modern life. She thrust the thought from her with passionate scorn. If poor, broken, ruined Glenn Kilbourne could cling to an ideal and fight for it, could not she, who had all the world esteemed worth while, be woman enough to do the same? The direction of her thought seemed to have changed. She had been ready for rebellion. Three months of the old life had shown her that for her it was empty, vain, farcical, without one redeeming feature. The naked truth was brutal, but it cut clean to wholesome consciousness. Such so-called social life as she had plunged into deliberately to forget her unhappiness had failed her utterly. If she had been shallow and frivolous it might have done otherwise. Stripped of all guise, her actions must have been construed by a penetrating and impartial judge as a mere parading of her decorated person before a number of males with the purpose of ultimate selection.

"I've got to find some work," she muttered, soberly.

At the moment she heard the postman's whistle outside; and a little later the servant brought up her mail. The first letter, large, soiled, thick, bore the postmark Flagstaff, and her address in Glenn Kilbourne's writing.

Carley stared at it. Her heart gave a great leap. Her hand shook. She sat down suddenly as if the strength of her legs was inadequate to uphold her.

"Glenn has—written me!" she whispered, in slow, halting realization. "For what? Oh, why?"

The other letters fell off her lap, to lie unnoticed. This big thick envelope fascinated her. It was one of the stamped envelopes she had seen in his cabin. It contained a letter that had been written on his rude table, before the open fire, in the light of the doorway, in that little log-cabin under the spreading pines of West Ford Canyon. Dared she read it? The shock to her heart passed; and with mounting swell, seemingly too full for her breast, it began to beat and throb a wild gladness through all her being. She tore the envelope apart and read:

DEAR CARLEY:

I'm surely glad for a good excuse to write you.

Once in a blue moon I get a letter, and today Hutter brought me one from a soldier pard of mine who was with me in the Argonne. His name is Virgil Rust—queer name, don't you think?—and he's from Wisconsin. Just a rough-diamond sort of chap, but fairly well educated. He and I were in some pretty hot places, and it was he who pulled me out of a shell crater. I'd "gone west" sure then if it hadn't been for Rust.

Well, he did all sorts of big things during the war. Was down several times with wounds. He liked to fight and he was a holy terror. We all thought he'd get medals and promotion. But he didn't get either. These much-desired things did not always go where they were best deserved.

Rust is now lying in a hospital in Bedford Park. His letter is pretty blue. All he says about why he's there is that he's knocked out. But he wrote a heap about his girl. It seems he was in love with a girl in his home town—a pretty, big-eyed lass whose picture I've seen—and while he was overseas she married one of the chaps who got out of fighting. Evidently Rust is deeply hurt. He wrote: "I'd not care so. . . if she'd thrown me down to marry an old man or a boy who couldn't have gone to war." You see, Carley, service men feel queer about that sort of thing.

It's something we got over there, and none of us will ever outlive it. Now, the point of this is that I am asking you to go see Rust, and cheer him up, and do what you can for the poor devil. It's a good deal to ask of you, I know, especially as Rust saw your picture many a time and knows you were my girl. But you needn't tell him that you—we couldn't make a go of it.

And, as I am writing this to you, I see no reason why I shouldn't go on in behalf of myself.

The fact is, Carley, I miss writing to you more than I miss anything of my old life. I'll bet you have a trunkful of letters from me —unless you've destroyed them. I'm not going to say how I miss your letters. But I will say you wrote the most charming and fascinating letters of anyone I ever knew, quite aside from any sentiment. You knew, of course, that I had no other girl correspondent. Well, I got along fairly well before you came West, but I'd be an awful liar if I denied I didn't get lonely for you and your letters. It's different now that you've been to Oak Creek. I'm alone most of the time and I dream a lot, and I'm afraid I see you here in my cabin, and along the brook, and under the pines, and riding Calico—which you came to do well—and on my hogpen fence—and, oh, everywhere! I don't want you to think I'm down in the mouth, for I'm not. I'll take my medicine. But, Carley, you spoiled me, and I miss hearing from you, and I don't see why it wouldn't be all right for you to send me a friendly letter occasionally.

It is autumn now. I wish you could see Arizona canyons in their gorgeous colors. We have had frost right along and the mornings are great. There's a broad zigzag belt of gold halfway up the San Francisco peaks, and that is the aspen thickets taking on their fall coat. Here in the canyon you'd think there was blazing fire everywhere. The vines and the maples are red, scarlet, carmine, cerise, magenta, all the hues of flame. The oak leaves are turning russet gold, and the sycamores are yellow green. Up on the desert the other day I rode across a patch of asters, lilac and lavender, almost purple. I had to get off and pluck a handful. And then what do you think? I dug up the whole bunch, roots and all, and planted them on the sunny side of my cabin. I rather guess your love of flowers engendered this remarkable susceptibility in me.

I'm home early most every afternoon now, and I like the couple of hours loafing around. Guess it's bad for me, though. You know I seldom hunt, and the trout in the pool here are so tame now they'll almost eat out of my hand. I haven't the heart to fish for them. The squirrels, too, have grown tame and friendly. There's a red squirrel that climbs up on my table. And there's a chipmunk who lives in my cabin and runs over my bed. I've a new pet—the little pig you christened Pinky. After he had the wonderful good fortune to be caressed and named by you I couldn't think of letting him grow up in an ordinary piglike manner. So I fetched him home. My dog, Moze, was jealous at first and did not like this intrusion, *but now they are good friends and sleep together. Flo has a kitten she's going to give me, and then, as Hutter says, I'll be "Jake."*

My occupation during these leisure hours perhaps would strike my old friends East as idle, silly, mawkish. But I believe you will understand me.

I have the pleasure of doing nothing, and of catching now and then a glimpse of supreme joy in the strange state of thinking nothing. Tennyson came close to this in his "Lotus Eaters." Only to see—only to feel is enough!

Sprawled on the warm sweet pine needles, I breathe through them the breath of the earth and am somehow no longer lonely. I cannot, of course, see the sunset, but I watch for its coming on the eastern wall of the canyon. I see the shadow slowly creep up, driving the gold before it, until at last the canyon rim and pines are turned to golden fire. I watch the sailing eagles as they streak across the gold, and swoop up into the blue, and pass out of sight. I watch the golden flush fade to gray, and then, the canyon slowly fills with purple shadows. This hour of twilight is the silent and melancholy one. Seldom is there any sound save the soft rush of the water over the stones, and that seems to die away. For a moment, perhaps, I am Hiawatha alone in his forest home, or a more primitive savage, feeling the great, silent pulse of nature, happy in unconsciousness, like a beast of the wild. But only for an instant do I ever catch this fleeting state. Next I am Glenn Kilbourne of West Fork, doomed and haunted by memories of the past. The great looming walls then become no longer blank. They are vast pages of the history of my life, with its past and present, and, alas! its future. Everything time does is written on the stones. And my stream seems to murmur the sad and ceaseless flow of human life, with its music and its misery.

Then, descending from the sublime to the humdrum and necessary, I heave a sigh, and pull myself together, and go in to make biscuits and fry ham. But I should not forget to tell you that before I do go in, very often my looming, wonderful walls and crags weave in strange shadowy characters the beautiful and unforgettable face of Carley Burch!

I append what little news Oak Creek affords.

That blamed old bald eagle stole another of my pigs.

*I am doing so well with my hog-raising that Hutter wants to come
in with me, giving me an interest in his sheep.*

*It is rumored some one has bought the Deep Lake section I wanted
for a ranch. I don't know who. Hutter was rather noncommittal.*

*Charley, the herder, had one of his queer spells the other day, and
swore to me he had a letter from you. He told the blamed lie with a
sincere and placid eye, and even a smile of pride. Queer guy, that
Charley!*

*Flo and Lee Stanton had another quarrel—the worst yet, Lee tells
me. Flo asked a girl friend out from Flag and threw her in Lee's way, so
to speak, and when Lee retaliated by making love to the girl Flo got
mad. Funny creatures, you girls! Flo rode with me from High Falls to
West Fork, and never showed the slightest sign of trouble. In fact she was
delightfully gay. She rode Calico, and beat me bad in a race.*

Adios, Carley. Won't you write me?

GLENN

No sooner had Carley read the letter through to the end than
she began it all over again, and on this second perusal she
lingered over passages—only to reread them. That suggestion of
her face sculptured by shadows on the canyon walls seemed to
thrill her very soul.

She leaped up from the reading to cry out something that
was unutterable. All the intervening weeks of shame and anguish
and fury and strife and pathos, and the endless striving to forget,
were as if by the magic of a letter made nothing but vain
oblations.

"He loves me still!" she whispered, and pressed her breast
with clenching hands, and laughed in wild exultance, and paced
her room like a caged lioness. It was as if she had just awakened
to the assurance she was beloved. That was the shibboleth—the
cry by which she sounded the closed depths of her love and
called to the stricken life of a woman's insatiate vanity.

Then she snatched up the letter, to scan it again, and,

suddenly grasping the import of Glenn's request, she hurried to the telephone to find the number of the hospital in Bedford Park. A nurse informed her that visitors were received at certain hours and that any attention to disabled soldiers was most welcome.

Carley motored out there to find the hospital merely a long one-story frame structure, a barracks hastily thrown up for the care of invalided men of the service. The chauffeur informed her that it had been used for that purpose during the training period of the army, and later when injured soldiers began to arrive from France.

A nurse admitted Carley into a small bare anteroom. Carley made known her errand.

"I'm glad it's Rust you want to see," replied the nurse. "Some of these boys are going to die. And some will be worse off if they live. But Rust may get well if he'll only behave. You are a relative —or friend?"

"I don't know him," answered Carley. "But I have a friend who was with him in France."

The nurse led Carley into a long narrow room with a line of single beds down each side, a stove at each end, and a few chairs. Each bed appeared to have an occupant and those nearest Carley lay singularly quiet. At the far end of the room were soldiers on crutches, wearing bandages on their beads, carrying their arms in slings. Their merry voices contrasted discordantly with their sad appearance.

Presently Carley stood beside a bed and looked down upon a gaunt, haggard young man who lay propped up on pillows.

"Rust—a lady to see you," announced the nurse.

Carley had difficulty in introducing herself. Had Glenn ever looked like this? What a face! It's healed scar only emphasized the pallor and furrows of pain that assuredly came from present wounds. He had unnaturally bright dark eyes, and a flush of fever in his hollow cheeks.

"How do!" he said, with a wan smile. "Who're you?"

"I'm Glenn Kilbourne's fiancée," she replied, holding out her hand.

"Say, I ought to've known you," he said, eagerly, and a warmth of light changed the gray shade of his face. "You're the girl Carley! You're almost like my—my own girl. By golly! You're some looker! It was good of you to come. Tell me about Glenn."

Carley took the chair brought by the nurse, and pulling it close to the bed, she smiled down upon him and said: "I'll be glad to tell you all I know—presently. But first you tell me about yourself. Are you in pain? What is your trouble? You must let me do everything I can for you, and these other men."

Carley spent a poignant and depth-stirring hour at the bedside of Glenn's comrade. At last she learned from loyal lips the nature of Glenn Kilbourne's service to his country. How Carley clasped to her sore heart the praise of the man she loved—the simple proofs of his noble disregard of self! Rust said little about his own service to country or to comrade. But Carley saw enough in his face. He had been like Glenn. By these two Carley grasped the compelling truth of the spirit and sacrifice of the legion of boys who had upheld American traditions. Their children and their children's children, as the years rolled by into the future, would hold their heads higher and prouder. Some things could never die in the hearts and the blood of a race. These boys, and the girls who had the supreme glory of being loved by them, must be the ones to revive the Americanism of their forefathers. Nature and God would take care of the slackers, the cowards who cloaked their shame with bland excuses of home service, of disability, and of dependence.

Carley saw two forces in life—the destructive and constructive. On the one side greed, selfishness, materialism: on the other generosity, sacrifice, and idealism. Which of them builded for the future? She saw men as wolves, sharks, snakes, vermin, and opposed to them men as lions and eagles. She saw women who did not inspire men to fare forth to seek, to imagine, to dream, to hope, to work, to fight. She began to have a glimmering of what a woman might be.

———

That night she wrote swiftly and feverishly, page after page, to Glenn, only to destroy what she had written. She could not keep her heart out of her words, nor a hint of what was becoming a sleepless and eternal regret. She wrote until a late hour, and at last composed a letter she knew did not ring true, so stilted and restrained was it in all passages save those concerning news of Glenn's comrade and of her own friends. "I'll never—never write him again," she averred with stiff lips, and next moment could have laughed in mockery at the bitter truth. If she had ever had any courage, Glenn's letter had destroyed it. But had it not been a kind of selfish, false courage, roused to hide her hurt, to save her own future? Courage should have a thought of others. Yet shamed one moment at the consciousness she would write Glenn again and again, and exultant the next with the clamouring love, she seemed to have climbed beyond the self that had striven to forget. She would remember and think though she died of longing.

Carley, like a drowning woman, caught at straws. What a relief and joy to give up that endless nagging at her mind! For months she had kept ceaselessly active, by associations which were of no help to her and which did not make her happy, in her determination to forget. Suddenly then she gave up to remembrance. She would cease trying to get over her love for Glenn, and think of him and dream about him as much as memory dictated. This must constitute the only happiness she could have.

The change from strife to surrender was so novel and sweet that for days she felt renewed. It was augmented by her visits to the hospital in Bedford Park. Through her bountiful presence Virgil Rust and his comrades had many dull hours of pain and weariness alleviated and brightened. Interesting herself in the condition of the seriously disabled soldiers and possibility of their future took time and work Carley gave willingly and gladly. At first she endeavored to get acquaintances with means and leisure to help the boys, but these overtures met with such little success that she quit wasting valuable time she could herself devote to their interests.

Thus several weeks swiftly passed by. Several soldiers who had been more seriously injured than Rust improved to the extent that they were discharged. But Rust gained little or nothing. The nurse and doctor both informed Carley that Rust brightened for her, but when she was gone he lapsed into somber indifference. He did not care whether he ate or not, or whether he got well or died.

"If I do pull out, where'll I go and what'll I do?" he once asked the nurse.

Carley knew that Rust's hurt was more than loss of a leg, and she decided to talk earnestly to him and try to win him to hope and effort. He had come to have a sort of reverence for her. So, biding her time, she at length found opportunity to approach his bed while his comrades were asleep or out of hearing. He endeavored to laugh her off, and then tried subterfuge, and lastly he cast off his mask and let her see his naked soul.

"Carley, I don't want your money or that of your kind friends —whoever they are—you say will help me to get into business," he said. "God knows I thank you and it warms me inside to find *some one* who appreciates what I've given. But I don't want charity. . . . And I guess

I'm pretty sick of the game. I'm sorry the Boches didn't do the job right."

"Rust, that is morbid talk," replied Carley. "You're ill and you just can't see any hope. You must cheer up—fight *yourself;* and look at the brighter side. It's a horrible pity you must be a cripple, but Rust, indeed life can be worth living if you make it so."

"How could there be a brighter side when a man's only half a man—" he queried, bitterly.

"You can be just as much a man as ever," persisted Carley, trying to smile when she wanted to cry.

"Could you care for a man with only one leg?" he asked, deliberately.

"What a question! Why, of course I could!"

"Well, maybe you are different. Glenn always swore even if he was killed no slacker or no rich guy left at home could ever get you. Maybe you haven't any idea how much it means to us fellows to know there *are* true and faithful girls. But I'll tell you, Carley, we fellows who went across got to see things strange when we came home. The good old U. S. needs a lot of faithful girls just now, believe me."

"Indeed that's true," replied Carley. "It's a hard time for everybody, and particularly you boys who have lost so—so much."

"I lost *all*, except my life—and I wish to God I'd lost that," he replied, gloomily.

"Oh, don't talk so!" implored Carley in distress. "Forgive me, Rust, if I hurt you. But I must tell you—that—that Glenn wrote me—you'd lost your girl. Oh, I'm sorry! It is dreadful for you now. But if you got well—and went to work—and took up life where you left it—why soon your pain would grow easier. And you'd find some happiness yet."

"Never for me in this world."

"But why, Rust, *why?* You're no—no—Oh! I mean you have intelligence and courage. Why isn't there anything left for you?"

"Because something here's been killed," he replied, and put his hand to his heart.

"Your faith? Your love of—of everything? Did the war kill it?"

"I'd gotten over that, maybe," he said, drearily, with his somber eyes on space that seemed lettered for him. "But *she* half murdered it—and *they* did the rest."

"They? Whom do you mean, Rust?"

"Why, Carley, I mean the people I lost my leg for!" he replied, with terrible softness.

"The British? The French?" she queried, in bewilderment.

"*No!*" he cried, and turned his face to the wall.

Carley dared not ask him more. She was shocked. How helplessly impotent all her earnest sympathy! No longer could she feel an impersonal, however kindly, interest in this man. His last ringing word had linked her also to his misfortune and his suffering. Suddenly he turned away from the wall. She saw him swallow laboriously. How tragic that thin, shadowed face of agony! Carley saw it differently. But for the beautiful softness of light in his eyes, she would have been unable to endure gazing longer.

"Carley, I'm bitter," he said, "but I'm not rancorous and callous, like some of the boys. I know if you'd been my girl you'd have stuck to me."

"Yes," Carley whispered.

"That makes a difference," he went on, with a sad smile. "You see, we soldiers all had feelings. And in one thing we all felt alike. That was we were going to fight for our homes and our women. I should say women first. No matter what we read or heard about standing by our allies, fighting for liberty or civilization, the truth was we all felt the same, even if we never breathed it. . . . Glenn fought for you. I fought for Nell. . . . We were not going to let the Huns treat you as they treated French and Belgian girls. . . . And think! Nell was engaged to me—she *loved* me—and, by God! She married a slacker when I lay half dead on the battlefield!"

"She was not worth loving or fighting for," said Carley, with agitation.

"Ah! now you've said something," he declared. "If I can only hold to that truth! What does one girl amount to? *I* do not count. It is the sum that counts. We love America—our homes—our women!. . . Carley, I've had comfort and strength come to me through you. Glenn will have his reward in your love. Somehow I seem to share it, a little. Poor Glenn! He got his, too. Why, Carley, that guy wouldn't *let* you do what he could do *for you*. He was cut to pieces—"

"Please—Rust—don't say any more. I am unstrung," she pleaded.

"Why not? It's due you to know how splendid Glenn was. . . . I tell you, Carley, all the boys here love you for the way you've stuck to Glenn. Some of them knew him, and I've told the rest. We thought he'd never pull through. But he has, and we know how you helped. Going West to see him! He didn't write it to me, but I know. . . . I'm wise. I'm happy for him—the lucky dog. Next time you go West—"

"Hush!" cried Carley. She could endure no more. She could no longer be a lie.

"You're white—you're shaking," exclaimed Rust, in concern. "Oh, I—what did I say? Forgive me—"

"Rust, I am no more worth loving and fighting for than your Nell."

"What!" he ejaculated.

"I have not told you the truth," she said, swiftly. "I have let you believe a lie. . . . I shall never marry Glenn. I broke my engagement to him."

Slowly Rust sank back upon the pillow, his large luminous eyes piercingly fixed upon her, as if he would read her soul.

"I went West—yes—" continued Carley. "But it was selfishly. I wanted Glenn to come back here. . . . He had suffered as you have. He nearly died. But he fought—he fought—Oh! he went through hell! And after a long, slow, horrible struggle he began to mend. He worked. He went to raising hogs. He lived alone. He worked harder and harder. . . . The West and his work saved him, body and soul. . . . He had learned to love both the West and his work. I did not blame him. But I could not live out there. He needed me. But I was too little—too selfish. I could not marry him. I gave him up. . . . I left—him—alone!"

Carley shrank under the scorn in Rust's eyes.

"And there's another man," he said, "a clean, straight, unscarred fellow who wouldn't fight!"

"Oh, no—I—I swear there's not," whispered Carley.

"You, too," he replied, thickly. Then slowly he turned that worn dark face to the wall. His frail breast heaved. And his lean hand made her a slight gesture of dismissal, significant and imperious.

Carley fled. She could scarcely see to find the car. All her internal being seemed convulsed, and a deadly faintness made her sick and cold.

CHAPTER TEN

Carley's edifice of hopes, dreams, aspirations, and struggles fell in ruins about her. It had been built upon false sands. It had no ideal for foundation. It had to fall.

Something inevitable had forced her confession to Rust. Dissimulation had been a habit of her mind; it was more a habit of her class than sincerity. But she had reached a point in her mental strife where she could not stand before Rust and let him believe she was noble and faithful when she knew she was neither. Would not the next step in this painful metamorphosis of her character be a fierce and passionate repudiation of herself and all she represented?

She went home and locked herself in her room, deaf to telephone and servants. There she gave up to her shame. Scorned—despised—dismissed by that poor crippled flame-spirited Virgil Rust! He had reverenced her, and the truth had earned his hate. Would she ever forget his look—incredulous—shocked—bitter—and blazing with unutterable contempt? Carley Burch was only another Nell—a jilt—a mocker of the manhood of soldiers! Would she ever cease to shudder at memory of Rust's slight movement of hand? Go! Get out of my sight! Leave me to my agony as you left Glenn Kilbourne alone to fight his! Men such as I am do not want the smile of your face, the touch of your hand! We gave for womanhood! Pass on to lesser men who loved the fleshpots and who would buy your charms! So Carley interpreted that slight gesture, and writhed in her abasement.

Rust threw a white, illuminating light upon her desertion of Glenn. She had betrayed him. She had left him alone. Dwarfed and stunted was her narrow soul! To a man who had given all for her she had returned nothing. Stone for bread! Betrayal for love! Cowardice for courage!

The hours of contending passions gave birth to vague, slow-forming revolt.

She became haunted by memory pictures and sounds and smells of Oak Creek Canyon. As from afar she saw the great sculptured rent in the earth, green and red and brown, with its shining, flashing ribbons of waterfalls and streams. The mighty pines stood up magnificent and stately. The walls loomed high, shadowed under the shelves, gleaming in the sunlight, and they seemed dreaming, waiting, watching. For what? For her return to their serene fastnesses—to the little gray log cabin. The thought stormed Carley's soul.

Vivid and intense shone the images before her shut eyes. She saw the winding forest floor, green with grass and fern, colorful with flower and rock. A thousand aisles, glades, nooks, and caverns called her to come. Nature was every woman's mother. The populated city was a delusion. Disease and death and corruption stalked in the shadows of the streets. But her canyon promised hard work, playful hours, dreaming idleness, beauty, health, fragrance, loneliness, peace, wisdom, love, children, and long life. In the hateful shut-in isolation of her room Carley stretched forth her arms as if to embrace the vision. Pale close walls, gleaming placid stretches of brook, churning amber and white rapids, mossy banks and pine-matted ledges, the towers and turrets and ramparts where the eagles wheeled—she saw them all as beloved images lost to her save in anguished memory.

She heard the murmur of flowing water, soft, low, now loud,

and again lulling, hollow and eager, tinkling over rocks, bellowing into the deep pools, washing with silky seep of wind-swept waves the hanging willows. Shrill and piercing and far-aloft pealed the scream of the eagle. And she seemed to listen to a mocking bird while he mocked her with his melody of many birds. The bees hummed, the wind moaned, the leaves rustled, the waterfall murmured. Then came the sharp rare note of a canyon swift, most mysterious of birds, significant of the heights.

A breath of fragrance seemed to blow with her shifting senses. The dry, sweet, tangy canyon smells returned to her—of fresh-cut timber, of wood smoke, of the cabin fire with its steaming pots, of flowers and earth, and of the wet stones, of the redolent pines and the pungent cedars.

And suddenly, clearly, amazingly, Carley beheld in her mind's sight the hard features, the bold eyes, the slight smile, the coarse face of Haze Ruff. She had forgotten him. But he now returned. And with memory of him flashed a revelation as to his meaning in her life. He had appeared merely a clout, a ruffian, an animal with man's shape and intelligence. But he was the embodiment of the raw, crude violence of the West. He was the eyes of the natural primitive man, believing what he saw. He had seen in Carley Burch the paraded charm, the unashamed and serene front, the woman seeking man. Haze Ruff had been neither vile nor base nor unnatural. It had been her subjection to the deca-dence of feminine dress that had been unnatural. But Ruff had found her a lie. She invited what she did not want. And his scorn had been commensurate with the falsehood of her. So might any man have been justified in his insult to her, in his rejection of her. Haze Ruff had found her unfit for his idea of dalliance. Virgil Rust had found her false to the ideals of womanhood for which he had sacrificed all but life itself. What then had Glenn Kilbourne found her? He possessed the greatness of noble love. He had loved her before the dark and changeful tide of war had come between them. How had he judged her? That last sight of him standing alone, leaning with head bowed, a solitary figure trenchant with suggestion of tragic resignation and strength, returned to flay Carley. He had loved, trusted, and hoped. She saw now what his hope had been—that she would have instilled into her blood the subtle, red, and revivifying essence of calling life in the open, the strength of the wives of earlier years, an emanation from canyon, desert, mountain, forest, of health, of spirit, of forward-gazing natural love, of the mysterious saving instinct he had gotten out of the West. And she had been too little too steeped in the indulgence of luxurious life too slight-natured and pale-blooded! And suddenly there pierced into the black storm of Carley's mind a blazing, white-streaked thought —she had left Glenn to the Western girl, Flo Hutter. Humiliated, and abased in her own sight, Carley fell prey to a fury of jealousy.

———

She went back to the old life. But it was in a bitter, restless, critical spirit, conscious of the fact that she could derive neither forgetfulness nor pleasure from it, nor see any release from the habit of years.

One afternoon, late in the fall, she motored out to a Long Island club where the last of the season's golf was being enjoyed by some of her most intimate friends. Carley did not play. Aimlessly she walked around the grounds, finding the autumn colors subdued and drab, like her mind.

The air held a promise of early winter. She thought that she would go South before the cold came. Always trying to escape anything rigorous, hard, painful, or disagreeable! Later she returned to the clubhouse to find her party assembled on an inclosed porch, chatting and partaking of refreshment. Morrison was there. He had not taken kindly to her late habit of denying herself to him.

During a lull in the idle conversation Morrison addressed

Carley pointedly. "Well, Carley, how's your Arizona hog-raiser?" he queried, with a little gleam in his usually lusterless eyes.

"I have not heard lately," she replied, coldly.

The assembled company suddenly quieted with a portent inimical to their leisurely content of the moment. Carley felt them all looking at her, and underneath the exterior she preserved with extreme difficulty, there burned so fierce an anger that she seemed to have swelling veins of fire.

"Queer how Kilbourne went into raising hogs," observed Morrison. "Such a low-down sort of work, you know."

"He had no choice," replied Carley. "Glenn didn't have a father who made tainted millions out of the war. He had to work. And I must differ with you about its being low-down. No honest work is that. It is idleness that is low down."

"But so foolish of Glenn when he might have married money," rejoined Morrison, sarcastically.

"The honor of soldiers is beyond your ken, Mr. Morrison." He flushed darkly and bit his lip.

"You women make a man sick with this rot about soldiers," he said, the gleam in his eye growing ugly. "A uniform goes to a woman's head no matter what's inside it. I don't see where your vaunted honor of soldiers comes in considering how they accepted the let-down of women during and after the war."

"How could you see when you stayed comfortably at home?" retorted Carley.

"All I could see was women falling into soldiers' arms," he said, sullenly.

"Certainly. Could an American girl desire any greater happiness—or opportunity to prove her gratitude?" flashed Carley, with proud uplift of head.

"It didn't look like gratitude to me," returned Morrison.

"Well, it *was* gratitude," declared Carley, ringingly. "If women of America did throw themselves at soldiers it was not owing to the moral lapse of the day. It was woman's instinct to save the race! Always, in every war, women have sacrificed themselves to the future. Not vile, but noble!. . . You insult both soldiers and women, Mr. Morrison. I wonder—did any American girls throw themselves at *you?*"

Morrison turned a dead white, and his mouth twisted to a distorted checking of speech, disagreeable to see.

"No, you were a slacker," went on Carley, with scathing scorn. "You let the other men go fight for American girls. Do you imagine one of them will ever *marry* you?. . . All your life, Mr. Morrison, you will be a marked man—outside the pale of friendship with real American men and the respect of real American girls."

Morrison leaped up, almost knocking the table over, and he glared at Carley as he gathered up his hat and cane. She turned her back upon him. From that moment he ceased to exist for Carley. She never spoke to him again.

———

Next day Carley called upon her dearest friend, whom she had not seen for some time.

"Carley dear, you don't look so very well," said Eleanor, after greetings had been exchanged.

"Oh, what does it matter how I look?" queried Carley, impatiently.

"You were so wonderful when you got home from Arizona."

"If I was wonderful and am now commonplace you can thank your old New York for it."

"Carley, don't you care for New York any more?" asked Eleanor.

"Oh, New York is all right, I suppose. It's I who am wrong."

"My dear, you puzzle me these days. You've changed. I'm sorry. I'm afraid you're unhappy."

"Me? Oh, impossible! I'm in a seventh heaven," replied Carley, with a hard little laugh. "What 're you doing this afternoon? Let's go out—riding—or somewhere."

"I'm expecting the dressmaker."

"Where are you going to-night?"

"Dinner and theater. It's a party, or I'd ask you."

"What did you do yesterday and the day before, and the days before that?"

Eleanor laughed indulgently, and acquainted Carley with a record of her social wanderings during the last few days.

"The same old things—over and over again! Eleanor don't you get sick of it?" queried Carley.

"Oh yes, to tell the truth," returned Eleanor, thoughtfully. "But there's nothing else to do."

"Eleanor, I'm no better than you," said Carley, with disdain. "I'm as useless and idle. But I'm beginning to see myself—and you—and all this rotten crowd of ours. We're no good. But you're married, Eleanor. You're settled in life. You ought to *do* *something*. I'm single and at loose ends. Oh, I'm in revolt!. . . Think, Eleanor, just think. Your husband works hard to keep you in this expensive apartment. You have a car. He dresses you in silks and satins. You wear diamonds. You eat your breakfast in bed. You loll around in a pink dressing gown all morning. You dress for lunch or tea. You ride or golf or worse than waste your time on some lounge lizard, dancing till time to come home to dress for dinner. You let other men make love to you. Oh, don't get sore. You do. . . . And so goes the round of your life. What good on earth are you, anyhow? You're just a—a gratification to the senses of your husband. And at that you don't see much of *him*."

"Carley, how you rave!" exclaimed her friend. "What has gotten into you lately? Why, everybody tells me you're—you're queer! The way you insulted Morrison—how unlike you, Carley!"

"I'm glad I found the nerve to do it. What do you think, Eleanor?"

"Oh, I despise him. But you can't say the things you feel."

"You'd be bigger and truer if you did. Some day I'll break out and flay you and your friends alive."

"But, Carley, you're my friend and you're just exactly like we are. Or you were, quite recently."

"Of course, I'm your friend. I've always loved you, Eleanor," went on Carley, earnestly. "I'm as deep in this—this damned stagnant muck as you, or anyone. But I'm no longer *blind.* There's something terribly wrong with us women, and it's not what Morrison hinted."

"Carley, the only thing wrong with you is that you jilted poor Glenn—and are breaking your heart over him still."

"Don't—don't!" cried Carley, shrinking. "God knows that is true. But there's more wrong with me than a blighted love affair."

"Yes, you mean the modern feminine unrest?"

"Eleanor, I positively hate that phrase 'modern feminine unrest!' It smacks of ultra—ultra—Oh! I don't know what. That phrase ought to be translated by a Western acquaintance of mine —one Haze Ruff. I'd not like to hurt your sensitive feelings with what he'd say. But this unrest means speed-mad, excitement-mad, fad-mad, dress-mad, or I should say *un*dress-mad, culture-mad, and Heaven only knows what else. The women of our set are idle, luxurious, selfish, pleasure-craving, lazy, useless, work-and-children shirking, absolutely no good."

"Well, if we are, who's to blame?" rejoined Eleanor, spiritedly. "Now, Carley Burch, you listen to me. I think the twentieth-century girl in America is the most wonderful female creation of all the ages of the universe. I admit it. That is why we are a prey to the evils attending greatness. Listen. Here is a crying sin—an infernal paradox. Take this twentieth-century girl, this American girl who is the finest creation of the ages. A young and healthy girl, the most perfect type of culture possible to the freest and greatest city on earth—New York! She holds absolutely an unreal, untrue position in the scheme of existence. Surrounded by parents, relatives, friends, suitors, and instructive schools of every kind, colleges, institutions, is she really happy, is she really living?"

"Eleanor," interrupted Carley, earnestly, "she is *not*. . . . And I've been trying to tell you why."

"My dear, let me get a word in, will you," complained Eleanor. "You don't know it all. There are as many different points of view as there are people. . . . Well, if this girl happened to have a new frock, and a new beau to show it to, she'd say, 'I'm the happiest girl in the world.' But she is nothing of the kind. Only she doesn't know that. She approaches marriage, or, for that matter, a more matured life, having had too much, having been too well taken care of, *knowing too much*. Her masculine satellites —father, brothers, uncles, friends, lovers—all utterly spoil her. Mind you, I mean, girls like us, of the middle class—which is to say the largest and best class of Americans. We are spoiled. . . . This girl marries. And life goes on smoothly, as if its aim was to exclude friction and effort. Her husband makes it too easy for her. She is an ornament, or a toy, to be kept in a luxurious cage. To soil her pretty hands would be disgraceful! Even if she can't afford a maid, the modern devices of science make the care of her four-room apartment a farce. Electric dish-washer, clothes-washer, vacuum-cleaner, and the near-by delicatessen and the caterer simply rob a young wife of her housewifely heritage. If she has a baby—which happens occasionally, Carley, in spite of your assertion—it very soon goes to the kindergarten. Then what does she find to do with hours and hours? If she is not married, what on earth *can* she find to do?"

"She can work," replied Carley, bluntly.

"Oh yes, she can, but she doesn't," went on Eleanor. "*You* don't work. I never did. We both hated the idea. You're calling spades spades, Carley, but you seem to be riding a morbid, impractical thesis. Well, our young American girl or bride goes in for being rushed or she goes in for fads, the ultra stuff you mentioned. New York City gets all the great artists, lecturers, and surely the great fakirs. The New York women support them. The men laugh, but they furnish the money. They take the women to the theaters, but they cut out the reception to a

Polish princess, a lecture by an Indian magician and mystic, or a benefit luncheon for a Home for Friendless Cats. The truth is most of our young girls or brides have a wonderful enthusiasm worthy of a better cause. What is to become of their surplus energy, the bottled-lightning spirit so characteristic of modern girls? Where is the outlet for intense feelings? What use can they make of education or of gifts? They just can't, that's all. I'm not taking into consideration the new-woman species, the faddist or the reformer. I mean normal girls like you and me. Just think, Carley. A girl's every wish, every need, is almost instantly satisfied without the slightest effort on her part to obtain it. No struggle, let alone work! If women crave to achieve something outside of the arts, you know, something universal and helpful which will make men acknowledge her worth, if not the equality, where is the opportunity?"

"Opportunities should be *made*," replied Carley.

"There are a million sides to this question of the modern young woman—the *fin-de-siècle* girl. I'm for her!"

"How about the extreme of style in dress for this remarkably-to-be-pitied American girl you champion so eloquently?" queried Carley, sarcastically.

"Immoral!" exclaimed Eleanor with frank disgust.

"You admit it?"

"To my shame, I do."

"Why do women wear extreme clothes? Why do you and I wear open-work silk stockings, skirts to our knees, gowns without sleeves or bodices?"

"We're slaves to fashion," replied Eleanor, "That's the popular excuse."

"Bah!" exclaimed Carley.

Eleanor laughed in spite of being half nettled. "Are you going to stop wearing what all the other women wear—and be looked at askance? Are you going to be dowdy and frumpy and old-fashioned?"

"No. But I'll never wear anything again that can be called

immoral. I want to be able to say *why* I wear a dress. You haven't answered my question yet. Why do you wear what you frankly admit is disgusting?"

"I don't know, Carley," replied Eleanor, helplessly. "How you harp on things! We must dress to make other women jealous and to attract men. To be a sensation! Perhaps the word 'immoral' is not what I mean. A woman will be shocking in her obsession to attract, but hardly more than that, if she knows it."

"Ah! So few women realize how they actually do look. Haze Ruff could tell them."

"Haze Ruff. Who in the world is he or she?" asked Eleanor.

"Haze Ruff is a he, all right," replied Carley, grimly.

"Well, who is he?"

"A sheep-dipper in Arizona," answered Carley, dreamily.

"Humph! And what can Mr. Ruff tell us?"

"He told *me* I looked like one of the devil's angels—and that I dressed to knock the daylights out of men."

"Well, Carley Burch, if that isn't rich!" exclaimed Eleanor, with a peal of laughter. "I dare say you appreciate that as an original compliment."

"No. . . . I wonder what Ruff would say about jazz—I just wonder," murmured Carley.

"Well, I wouldn't care what he said, and I don't care what *you* say," returned Eleanor. "The preachers and reformers and bishops and rabbis make me sick. They rave about jazz. Jazz— the discordant note of our decadence! Jazz—the harmonious expression of our musicless, mindless, soulless materialism!— The idiots! If they could be women for a while they would realize the error of their ways. But they will never, never abolish jazz— *never*, for it is the grandest, the most wonderful, the most absolutely necessary thing for women in this terrible age of smotheration."

"All right, Eleanor, we understand each other, even if we do not agree," said Carley. "You leave the future of women to chance, to life, to materialism, not to their own conscious efforts. I want to leave it to free will and idealism."

"Carley, you are getting a little beyond me," declared Eleanor, dubiously.

"What are you going to *do?* It all comes home to each individual woman. Her attitude toward life."

"I'll drift along with the current, Carley, and be a good sport," replied Eleanor, smiling.

"You don't care about the women and children of the future? You'll not deny yourself now, and think and work, and suffer a little, in the interest of future humanity?"

"How you put things, Carley!" exclaimed Eleanor, wearily. "Of course I care—when you make me think of such things. But what have *I* to do with the lives of people in the years to come?"

"Everything. America for Americans! While you dawdle, the life blood is being sucked out of our great nation. It is a man's job to fight; it is a woman's to save. . . . I think you've made your choice, though you don't realize it. I'm praying to God that I'll rise to mine."

———

Carley had a visitor one morning earlier than the usual or conventional time for calls.

"He wouldn't give no name," said the maid. "He wears soldier clothes, ma'am, and he's pale, and walks with a cane."

"Tell him I'll be right down," replied Carley.

Her hands trembled while she hurriedly dressed. Could this caller be Virgil Rust? She hoped so, but she doubted. As she entered the parlor a tall young man in worn khaki rose to meet her. At first glance she could not name him, though she recognized the pale face and light-blue eyes, direct and steady.

"Good morning, Miss Burch," he said. "I hope you'll excuse so early a call. You remember me, don't you? I'm George Burton, who had the bunk next to Rust's."

"Surely I remember you, Mr. Burton, and I'm glad to see you," replied Carley, shaking hands with him. "Please sit down. Your being here must mean you're discharged from the hospital."

"Yes, I was discharged, all right," he said.

"Which means you're well again. That is fine. I'm very glad."

"I was put out to make room for a fellow in bad shape. I'm still shaky and weak," he replied. "But I'm glad to go. I've pulled through pretty good, and it'll not be long until I'm strong again. It was the 'flu' that kept me down."

"You must be careful. May I ask where you're going and what you expect to do?"

"Yes, that's what I came to tell you," he replied, frankly. "I want you to help me a little. I'm from Illinois and my people aren't so badly off. But I don't want to go back to my home town down and out, you know. Besides, the winters are cold there. The doctor advises me to go to a little milder climate. You see, I was gassed, and got the 'flu' afterward. But I know I'll be all right if I'm careful. . . . Well, I've always had a leaning toward agriculture, and I want to go to Kansas. Southern Kansas. I want to travel around till I find a place I like, and there I'll get a job. Not too hard a job at first—that's why I'll need a little money. I know what to do. I want to lose myself in the wheat country and forget the—the war. I'll not be afraid of work, presently. . . . Now, Miss Burch, you've been so kind—I'm going to ask you to lend me a little money. I'll pay it back. I can't promise just when. But some day. Will you?"

"Assuredly I will," she replied, heartily. "I'm happy to have the opportunity to help you. How much will you need for immediate use? Five hundred dollars?"

"Oh no, not so much as that," he replied. "Just railroad fare home, and then to Kansas, and to pay board while I get well, you know, and look around."

"We'll make it five hundred, anyway," she replied, and, rising, she went toward the library. "Excuse me a moment." She wrote the check and, returning, gave it to him.

"You're very good," he said, rather low.

"Not at all," replied Carley. "You have no idea how much it means to me to be permitted to help you. Before I forget, I must ask you, can you cash that check here in New York?"

"Not unless you identify me," he said, ruefully, "I don't know anyone I could ask."

"Well, when you leave here go at once to my bank—it's on Thirty-fourth Street—and I'll telephone the cashier. So you'll not have any difficulty. Will you leave New York at once?"

"I surely will. It's an awful place. Two years ago when I came here with my company I thought it was grand. But I guess I lost something over there. . . . I want to be where it's quiet. Where I won't see many people."

"I think I understand," returned Carley. "Then I suppose you're in a hurry to get home? Of course you have a girl you're just dying to see?"

"No, I'm sorry to say I haven't," he replied, simply. "I was glad I didn't have to leave a sweetheart behind, when I went to France. But it wouldn't be so bad to have one to go back to now."

"Don't you worry!" exclaimed Carley. "You can take your choice presently. You have the open sesame to every real American girl's heart."

"And what is that?" he asked, with a blush.

"Your service to your country," she said, gravely.

"Well," he said, with a singular bluntness, "considering I didn't get any medals or bonuses, I'd like to draw a nice girl."

"You will," replied Carley, and made haste to change the subject. "By the way, did you meet Glenn Kilbourne in France?"

"Not that I remember," rejoined Burton, as he got up, rising rather stiffly by aid of his cane. "I must go, Miss Burch. Really I can't thank you enough. And I'll never forget it."

"Will you write me how you are getting along?" asked Carley, offering her hand.

"Yes."

Carley moved with him out into the hall and to the door.

There was a question she wanted to ask, but found it strangely difficult of utterance. At the door Burton fixed a rather penetrating gaze upon her.

"You didn't ask me about Rust," he said.

"No, I—I didn't think of him—until now, in fact," Carley lied.

"Of course then you couldn't have heard about him. I was wondering."

"I have heard nothing."

"It was Rust who told me to come to you," said Burton. "We were talking one day, and he—well, he thought you were true blue. He said he knew you'd trust me and lend me money. I couldn't have asked you but for him."

"True blue! He believed that. I'm glad. . . . Has he spoken of me to you since I was last at the hospital?"

"Hardly," replied Burton, with the straight, strange glance on her again.

Carley met this glance and suddenly a coldness seemed to envelop her. It did not seem to come from within though her heart stopped beating. Burton had not changed—the warmth, the gratitude still lingered about him. But the light of his eyes! Carley had seen it in Glenn's, in Rust's—a strange, questioning, far-off light, infinitely aloof and unutterably sad. Then there came a lift of her heart that released a pang. She whispered with dread, with a tremor, with an instinct of calamity.

"How about—Rust?"

"He's dead."

———

The winter came, with its bleak sea winds and cold rains and blizzards of snow. Carley did not go South. She read and brooded, and gradually avoided all save those true friends who tolerated her.

She went to the theater a good deal, showing preference for

the drama of strife, and she did not go anywhere for amusement. Distraction and amusement seemed to be dead issues for her. But she could become absorbed in any argument on the good or evil of the present day.

Socialism reached into her mind, to be rejected. She had never understood it clearly, but it seemed to her a state of mind where dissatisfied men and women wanted to share what harder working or more gifted people possessed. There were a few who had too much of the world's goods and many who had too little. A readjustment of such inequality and injustice must come, but Carley did not see the remedy in Socialism.

She devoured books on the war with a morbid curiosity and hope that she would find some illuminating truth as to the uselessness of sacrificing young men in the glory and prime of their lives. To her war appeared a matter of human nature rather than politics. Hate really was an effect of war. In her judgment future wars could be avoided only in two ways—by men becoming honest and just or by women refusing to have children to be sacrificed. As there seemed no indication whatever of the former, she wondered how soon all women of all races would meet on a common height, with the mounting spirit that consumed her own heart. Such time must come. She granted every argument for war and flung against it one ringing passionate truth—agony of mangled soldiers and agony of women and children. There was no justification for offensive war. It was monstrous and hideous. If nature and evolution proved the absolute need of strife, war, blood, and death in the progress of animal and man toward perfection, then it would be better to abandon this Christless code and let the race of man die out.

All through these weeks she longed for a letter from Glenn. But it did not come. Had he finally roused to the sweetness and worth and love of the western girl, Flo Hutter? Carley knew absolutely, through both intelligence and intuition, that Glenn Kilbourne would never love Flo.

Yet such was her intensity and stress at times, especially in the darkness of waking hours, that jealousy overcame her and insidiously worked its havoc. Peace and a strange kind of joy came to her in dreams of her walks and rides and climbs in Arizona, of the lonely canyon where it always seemed afternoon, of the tremendous colored vastness of that Painted Desert. But she resisted these dreams now because when she awoke from them she suffered such a yearning that it became unbearable. Then she knew the feeling of the loneliness and solitude of the hills. Then she knew the sweetness of the murmur of falling water, the wind in the pines, the song of birds, the white radiance of the stars, the break of day and its gold-flushed close. But she had not yet divined their meaning. It was not all love for Glenn Kilbourne. Had city life palled upon her solely because of the absence of her lover? So Carley plodded on, like one groping in the night, fighting shadows.

One day she received a card from an old schoolmate, a girl who had married out of Carley's set, and had been ostracized. She was living down on Long Island, at a little country place named Wading River. Her husband was an electrician—something of an inventor. He worked hard. A baby boy had just come to them. Would not Carley run down on the train to see the youngster?

That was a strong and trenchant call. Carley went. She found indeed a country village, and on the outskirts of it a little cottage that must have been pretty in summer, when the green was on vines and trees. Her old schoolmate was rosy, plump, bright-eyed, and happy. She saw in Carley no change—a fact that somehow rebounded sweetly on Carley's consciousness. Elsie prattled of herself and her husband and how they had worked to earn this little home, and then the baby.

When Carley saw the adorable dark-eyed, pink-toed, curly-fisted baby she understood Elsie's happiness and reveled in it. When she felt the soft, warm, living little body in her arms, against her breast, then she absorbed some incalculable and mysterious strength. What were the trivial, sordid, and selfish feelings that kept her in tumult compared to this welling emotion? Had she the secret in her arms? Babies and Carley had never become closely acquainted in those infrequent meetings that were usually the result of chance. But Elsie's baby nestled to her breast and cooed to her and clung to her finger. When at length the youngster was laid in his crib it seemed to Carley that the fragrance and the soul of him remained with her.

"A real American boy!" she murmured.

"You can just bet he is," replied Elsie. "Carley, you ought to see his dad."

"I'd like to meet him," said Carley, thoughtfully. "Elsie, was he in the service?"

"Yes. He was on one of the navy transports that took munitions to France. Think of me, carrying this baby, with my husband on a boat full of explosives and with German submarines roaming the ocean! Oh, it was horrible!"

"But he came back, and now all's well with you," said Carley, with a smile of earnestness. "I'm very glad, Elsie."

"Yes—but I shudder when I think of a possible war in the future. I'm going to raise boys, and girls, too, I hope—and the thought of war is torturing."

Carley found her return train somewhat late, and she took advantage of the delay to walk out to the wooded headlands above the Sound.

It was a raw March day, with a steely sun going down in a pale-gray sky. Patches of snow lingered in sheltered brushy places. This bit of woodland had a floor of soft sand that dragged at Carley's feet. There were sere and brown leaves still fluttering on the scrub-oaks. At length Carley came out on the edge of the bluff with the gray expanse of sea beneath her, and a long wandering shore line, ragged with wreckage or driftwood. The surge of water rolled in—a long, low, white, creeping line that softly roared on the beach and dragged the pebbles gratingly back. There was neither boat nor living creature in sight.

Carley felt the scene ease a clutching hand within her breast. Here was loneliness and solitude vastly different from that of Oak Creek Canyon, yet it held the same intangible power to soothe. The swish of the surf, the moan of the wind in the evergreens, were voices that called to her. How many more miles of lonely land than peopled cities! Then the sea—how vast! And over that the illimitable and infinite sky, and beyond, the endless realms of space. It helped her somehow to see and hear and feel the eternal presence of nature. In communion with nature the significance of life might be realized. She remembered Glenn quoting: "The world is too much with us. . . . Getting and spending, we lay waste our powers." What were our powers? What did God intend men to do with hands and bodies and gifts and souls? She gazed back over the bleak land and then out across the broad sea. Only a millionth part of the surface of the unsubmerged earth knew the populous abodes of man. And the lonely sea, inhospitable to stable homes of men, was thrice the area of the land. Were men intended, then, to congregate in few places, to squabble and to bicker and breed the discontents that led to injustice, hatred, and war? What a mystery it all was! But Nature was neither false nor little, however cruel she might be.

————

Once again Carley fell under the fury of her ordeal. Wavering now, restless and sleepless, given to violent starts and slow spells of apathy, she was wearing to defeat.

That spring day, one year from the day she had left New York for Arizona, she wished to spend alone. But her thoughts grew unbearable. She summed up the endless year. Could she live another like it? Something must break within her.

She went out. The air was warm and balmy, carrying that subtle current which caused the mild madness of spring fever. In the Park the greening of the grass, the opening of buds, the singing of birds, the gladness of children, the light on the water, the warm sun—all seemed to reproach her. Carley fled from the Park to the home of Beatrice Lovell; and there, unhappily, she encountered those of her acquaintance with whom she had least patience. They forced her to think too keenly of herself. They appeared carefree while she was miserable.

Over teacups there were waging gossip and argument and criticism. When Carley entered with Beatrice there was a sudden hush and then a murmur.

"Hello, Carley! Now say it to our faces," called out Geralda Conners, a fair, handsome young woman of thirty, exquisitely gowned in the latest mode, and whose brilliantly tinted complexion was not the natural one of health.

"Say what, Geralda?" asked Carley. "I certainly would not say anything behind your backs that I wouldn't repeat here."

"Eleanor has been telling us how you simply burned us up."

"We did have an argument. And I'm not sure I said all I wanted to."

"Say the rest here," drawled a lazy, mellow voice. "For Heaven's sake, stir us up. If I could get a kick out of *anything* I'd bless it."

"Carley, go on the stage," advised another. "You've got Elsie Ferguson tied to the mast for looks. And lately you're surely tragic enough."

"I wish you'd go somewhere far off!" observed a third. "My husband is dippy about you."

"Girls, do you know that you actually have not one sensible idea in your heads?" retorted Carley.

"Sensible? I should hope not. Who wants to be sensible?"

Geralda battered her teacup on a saucer. "Listen," she called. "I wasn't kidding Carley. I am good and sore. She goes around knocking everybody and saying New York backs Sodom off the boards. I want her to come out with it right here."

"I dare say I've talked too much," returned Carley. "It's been a rather hard winter on me. Perhaps, indeed, I've tried the patience of my friends."

"See here, Carley," said Geralda, deliberately, "just because you've had life turn to bitter ashes in your mouth you've no right to poison it for us. We all find it pretty sweet. You're an *un*satisfied woman and if you don't marry somebody you'll end by being a reformer or fanatic."

"I'd rather end that way than rot in a shell," retorted Carley.

"I declare, you make me see red, Carley," flashed Geralda, angrily. "No wonder Morrison roasts you to everybody. He says Glenn Kilbourne threw you down for some Western girl. If that's true it's pretty small of you to vent your spleen on us."

Carley felt the gathering of a mighty resistless force, But Geralda Conners was nothing to her except the target for a thunderbolt.

"I have no spleen," she replied, with a dignity of passion. "I have only pity. I was as blind as you. If heartbreak tore the scales from my eyes, perhaps that is well for me. For I see something terribly wrong in myself, in you, in all of us, in the life of today."

"You keep your pity to yourself. You need it," answered Geralda, with heat. "There's nothing wrong with me or my friends or life in good old New York."

"Nothing wrong!" cried Carley. "Listen. Nothing wrong in you or life today—nothing for you women to make right? You are blind as bats—as dead to living truth as if you were buried. Nothing wrong when thousands of crippled soldiers have no homes—no money—no friends—no work—in many cases no food or bed?. . . Splendid young men who went away in their prime to fight for *you* and came back ruined, suffering! Nothing wrong when sane women with the vote might rid politics of partisanship, greed, crookedness? Nothing wrong when prohibition is mocked by women—when the greatest boon ever granted this country is derided and beaten down and cheated? Nothing wrong when there are half a million defective children in this city? Nothing wrong when there are not enough schools and teachers to educate our boys and girls, when those teachers are shamefully underpaid? Nothing wrong when the mothers of this great country let their youngsters go to the dark motion picture halls and night after night in thousands of towns over all this broad land see pictures that the juvenile court and the educators and keepers of reform schools say make burglars, crooks, and murderers of our boys and vampires of our girls? Nothing wrong when these young adolescent girls ape *you* and wear stockings rolled under their knees below their skirts and use a lip stick and paint their faces and darken their eyes and pluck their eyebrows and absolutely do not know what shame is? Nothing wrong when you may find in any city women standing at street corners distributing booklets on birth control? Nothing wrong when great magazines print no page or picture without its sex appeal? Nothing wrong when the automobile, so convenient for the innocent little run out of town, presents the greatest evil that ever menaced American girls! Nothing wrong when money is god —when luxury, pleasure, excitement, speed are the striven for? Nothing wrong when some of your husbands spend more of their time with other women than with you? Nothing wrong with jazz—where the lights go out in the dance hall and the dancers jiggle and toddle and wiggle in a frenzy? Nothing wrong in a country where the greatest college cannot report birth of one child to each graduate in ten years? Nothing wrong with race suicide and the incoming horde of foreigners?. . . Nothing wrong with you women who cannot or will not stand childbirth? Nothing wrong with most of you, when if you *did* have a child, you could not nurse it?. . . Oh, my God, there's nothing wrong with America except that she staggers under a Titanic burden that only mothers of sons can remove!. . . You doll women, you parasites, you toys of men, you silken-wrapped geisha girls, you painted, idle, purring cats, you parody of the females of your species—find brains enough if you can to see the doom hanging over you and revolt before it is too late!"

CHAPTER ELEVEN

Carley burst in upon her aunt.

"Look at me, Aunt Mary!" she cried, radiant and exultant. "I'm going back out West to marry Glenn and live his life!"

The keen old eyes of her aunt softened and dimmed. "Dear Carley, I've known that for a long time. You've found yourself at last."

Then Carley breathlessly babbled her hastily formed plans, every word of which seemed to rush her onward.

"You're going to surprise Glenn again?" queried Aunt Mary.

"Oh, I must! I want to see his face when I tell him."

"Well, I hope he won't surprise *you*," declared the old lady. "When did you hear from him last?"

"In January. It seems ages—but—Aunt Mary, you don't imagine Glenn—"

"I imagine nothing," interposed her aunt. "It will turn out happily and I'll have some peace in my old age. But, Carley, what's to become of me?"

"Oh, I never thought!" replied Carley, blankly. "It will be lonely for you. Auntie, I'll come back in the fall for a few weeks. Glenn will let me."

"*Let* you? Ye gods! So you've come to that? Imperious Carley

Burch!. . . Thank Heaven, you'll now be satisfied to be let do things."

"I'd—I'd crawl for him," breathed Carley.

"Well, child, as you can't be practical, I'll have to be," replied Aunt Mary, seriously. "Fortunately for you I am a woman of quick decision. Listen. I'll go West with you. I want to see the Grand Canyon. Then I'll go on to California, where I have old friends I've not seen for years. When you get your new home all fixed up I'll spend awhile with you. And if I want to come back to New York now and then I'll go to a hotel. It is settled. I think the change will benefit me."

"Auntie, you make me very happy. I could ask no more," said Carley.

————

Swiftly as endless tasks could make them the days passed. But those on the train dragged interminably.

Carley sent her aunt through to the Canyon while she stopped off at Flagstaff to store innumerable trunks and bags. The first news she heard of Glenn and the Hutters was that they had gone to the Tonto Basin to buy hogs and would be absent at least a month. This gave birth to a new plan in Carley's mind. She would doubly surprise Glenn. Wherefore she took council with some Flagstaff business men and engaged them to set a force of men at work on the Deep Lake property, making the improvements she desired, and hauling lumber, cement, bricks, machinery, supplies—all the necessaries for building construction. Also she instructed them to throw up a tent house for her to live in during the work, and to engage a reliable Mexican man with his wife for servants. When she left for the Canyon she was happier than ever before in her life.

It was near the coming of sunset when Carley first looked down into the Grand Canyon. She had forgotten Glenn's tribute to this place. In her rapturous excitement of preparation and travel the Canyon had been merely a name. But now she saw it and she was stunned.

What a stupendous chasm, gorgeous in sunset color on the heights, purpling into mystic shadows in the depths! There was a wonderful brightness of all the millions of red and yellow and gray surfaces still exposed to the sun. Carley did not feel a thrill, because feeling seemed inhibited. She looked and looked, yet was reluctant to keep on looking. She possessed no image in mind with which to compare this grand and mystic spectacle. A transformation of color and shade appeared to be going on swiftly, as if gods were changing the scenes of a Titanic stage. As she gazed the dark fringed line of the north rim turned to burnished gold, and she watched that with fascinated eyes. It turned rose, it lost its fire, it faded to quiet cold gray. The sun had set.

Then the wind blew cool through the pinyons on the rim. There was a sweet tang of cedar and sage on the air and that indefinable fragrance peculiar to the canyon country of Arizona. How it brought back to Carley remembrance of Oak Creek! In the west, across the purple notches of the abyss, a dull gold flare showed where the sun had gone down.

In the morning at eight o'clock there were great irregular black shadows under the domes and peaks and escarpments. Bright Angel Canyon was all dark, showing dimly its ragged lines. At noon there were no shadows and all the colossal gorge lay glaring under the sun. In the evening Carley watched the Canyon as again the sun was setting.

Deep dark-blue shadows, like purple sails of immense ships, in wonderful contrast with the bright sunlit slopes, grew and rose toward the east, down the canyons and up the walls that faced the west. For a long while there was no red color, and the first indication of it was a dull bronze. Carley looked down into the void, at the sailing birds, at the precipitous slopes, and the dwarf spruces and the weathered old yellow cliffs. When she looked up again the shadows out there were no longer dark.

They were clear. The slopes and depths and ribs of rock could be seen through them. Then the tips of the highest peaks and domes turned bright red. Far to the east she discerned a strange shadow, slowly turning purple. One instant it grew vivid, then began to fade. Soon after that all the colors darkened and slowly the pale gray stole over all.

At night Carley gazed over and into the black void. But for the awful sense of depth she would not have known the Canyon to be there. A soundless movement of wind passed under her. The chasm seemed a grave of silence. It was as mysterious as the stars and as aloof and as inevitable. It had held her senses of beauty and proportion in abeyance.

At another sunrise the crown of the rim, a broad belt of bare rock, turned pale gold under its fringed dark line of pines. The tips of the peak gleamed opal. There was no sunrise red, no fire. The light in the east was a pale gold under a steely green-blue sky. All the abyss of the Canyon was soft, gray, transparent, and the belt of gold broadened downward, making shadows on the west slopes of the mesas and escarpments. Far down in the shadows she discerned the river, yellow, turgid, palely gleaming. By straining her ears Carley heard a low dull roar as of distant storm. She stood fearfully at the extreme edge of a stupendous cliff, where it sheered dark and forbidding, down and down, into what seemed red and boundless depths of Hades. She saw gold spots of sunlight on the dark shadows, proving that somewhere, impossible to discover, the sun was shining through wind-worn holes in the sharp ridges. Every instant Carley grasped a different effect. Her studied gaze absorbed an endless changing. And at last she realized that sun and light and stars and moon and night and shade, all working incessantly and mutably over shapes and lines and angles and surfaces too numerous and too great for the sight of man to hold, made an ever-changing spectacle of supreme beauty and colorful grandeur.

She talked very little while at the Canyon. It silenced her. She had come to see it at the critical time of her life and in the right mood. The superficialities of the world shrunk to their proper insignificance. Once she asked her aunt: "Why did not Glenn bring me here?" As if this Canyon proved the nature of all things!

But in the end Carley found that the rending strife of the transformation of her attitude toward life had insensibly ceased. It had ceased during the long watching of this cataclysm of nature, this canyon of gold-banded black-fringed ramparts, and red-walled mountains which sloped down to be lost in purple depths. That was final proof of the strength of nature to soothe, to clarify, to stabilize the tried and weary and upward-gazing soul. Stronger than the recorded deeds of saints, stronger than the eloquence of the gifted uplifters of men, stronger than any words ever written, was the grand, brooding, sculptured aspect of nature. And it must have been so because thousands of years before the age of saints or preachers—before the fret and symbol and figure were cut in stone—man must have watched with thought-developing sight the wonders of the earth, the monuments of time, the glooming of the dark-blue sea, the handiwork of God.

————

In May, Carley returned to Flagstaff to take up with earnest inspiration the labors of homebuilding in a primitive land.

It required two trucks to transport her baggage and purchases out to Deep Lake. The road was good for eighteen miles of the distance, until it branched off to reach her land, and from there it was desert rock and sand. But eventually they made it; and Carley found herself and belongings dumped out into the windy and sunny open. The moment was singularly thrilling and full of transport. She was free. She had shaken off the shackles. She faced lonely, wild, barren desert that must be made habitable by the genius of her direction and the labor of her hands. Always a thought of Glenn hovered tenderly, dreamily in the back of her consciousness, but she welcomed the opportunity to have a few weeks of work and activity and solitude before taking up her life with him. She wanted to adapt herself to the metamorphosis that had been wrought in her.

To her amazement and delight, a very considerable progress had been made with her plans. Under a sheltered red cliff among the cedars had been erected the tents where she expected to live until the house was completed. These tents were large, with broad floors high off the ground, and there were four of them. Her living tent had a porch under a wide canvas awning. The bed was a boxlike affair, raised off the floor two feet, and it contained a great, fragrant mass of cedar boughs upon which the blankets were to be spread. At one end was a dresser with large mirror, and a chiffonier. There were table and lamp, a low rocking chair, a shelf for books, a row of hooks upon which to hang things, a washstand with its necessary accessories, a little stove and a neat stack of cedar chips and sticks. Navajo rugs on the floor lent brightness and comfort.

Carley heard the rustling of cedar branches over her head, and saw where they brushed against the tent roof. It appeared warm and fragrant inside, and protected from the wind, and a subdued white light filtered through the canvas. Almost she felt like reproving herself for the comfort surrounding her. For she had come West to welcome the hard knocks of primitive life.

It took less than an hour to have her trunks stored in one of the spare tents, and to unpack clothes and necessaries for immediate use. Carley donned the comfortable and somewhat shabby outdoor garb she had worn at Oak Creek the year before; and it seemed to be the last thing needed to make her fully realize the glorious truth of the present.

"I'm here," she said to her pale, yet happy face in the mirror. "The impossible has happened. I have accepted Glenn's life. I have answered that strange call out of the West."

She wanted to throw herself on the sunlit woolly blankets of her bed and hug them, to think and think of the bewildering present happiness, to dream of the future, but she could not lie or sit still, nor keep her mind from grasping at actualities and possibilities of this place, nor her hands from itching to do things.

It developed, presently, that she could not have idled away the time even if she had wanted to, for the Mexican woman came for her, with smiling gesticulation and jabber that manifestly meant dinner. Carley could not understand many Mexican words, and herein she saw another task. This swarthy woman and her sloe-eyed husband favorably impressed Carley.

Next to claim her was Hoyle, the superintendent. "Miss Burch," he said, "in the early days we could run up a log cabin in a jiffy. Axes, horses, strong arms, and a few pegs—that was all we needed. But this house you've planned is different. It's good you've come to take the responsibility."

Carley had chosen the site for her home on top of the knoll where Glenn had taken her to show her the magnificent view of mountains and desert. Carley climbed it now with beating heart and mingled emotions. A thousand times already that day, it seemed, she had turned to gaze up at the noble white-clad peaks. They were closer now, apparently looming over her, and she felt a great sense of peace and protection in the thought that they would always be there. But she had not yet seen the desert that had haunted her for a year. When she reached the summit of the knoll and gazed out across the open space it seemed that she must stand spellbound. How green the cedared foreground— how gray and barren the downward slope—how wonderful the painted steppes! The vision that had lived in her memory shrank to nothingness. The reality was immense, more than beautiful, appalling in its isolation, beyond comprehension with its lure and strength to uplift.

But the superintendent drew her attention to the business at hand.

Carley had planned an L-shaped house of one story. Some of her ideas appeared to be impractical, and these she abandoned.

The framework was up and half a dozen carpenters were lustily at work with saw and hammer.

"We'd made better progress if this house was in an ordinary place," explained Hoyle. "But you see the wind blows here, so the framework had to be made as solid and strong as possible. In fact, it's bolted to the sills."

Both living room and sleeping room were arranged so that the Painted Desert could be seen from one window, and on the other side the whole of the San Francisco Mountains. Both rooms were to have open fireplaces. Carley's idea was for service and durability. She thought of comfort in the severe winters of that high latitude, but elegance and luxury had no more significance in her life.

Hoyle made his suggestions as to changes and adaptations, and, receiving her approval, he went on to show her what had been already accomplished. Back on higher ground a reservoir of concrete was being constructed near an ever-flowing spring of snow water from the peaks.

This water was being piped by gravity to the house, and was a matter of greatest satisfaction to Hoyle, for he claimed that it would never freeze in winter, and would be cold and abundant during the hottest and driest of summers. This assurance solved the most difficult and serious problem of ranch life in the desert.

Next Hoyle led Carley down off the knoll to the wide cedar valley adjacent to the lake. He was enthusiastic over its possibilities. Two small corrals and a large one had been erected, the latter having a low flat barn connected with it. Ground was already being cleared along the lake where alfalfa and hay were to be raised. Carley saw the blue and yellow smoke from burning brush, and the fragrant odor thrilled her. Mexicans were chopping the cleared cedars into firewood for winter use.

The day was spent before she realized it. At sunset the carpenters and mechanics left in two old Ford cars for town. The Mexicans had a camp in the cedars, and the Hoyles had theirs at the spring under the knoll where Carley had camped with Glenn and the Hutters. Carley watched the golden rosy sunset, and as the day ended she breathed deeply as if in unutterable relief. Supper found her with appetite she had long since lost. Twilight brought cold wind, the staccato bark of coyotes, the flicker of camp fires through the cedars. She tried to embrace all her sensations, but they were so rapid and many that she failed.

The cold, clear, silent night brought back the charm of the desert. How flaming white the stars! The great spire-pointed peaks lifted cold pale-gray outlines up into the deep star-studded sky. Carley walked a little to and fro, loath to go to her tent, though tired. She wanted calm. But instead of achieving calmness she grew more and more towards a strange state of exultation.

Westward, only a matter of twenty or thirty miles, lay the deep rent in the level desert—Oak Creek Canyon. If Glenn had been there this night would have been perfect, yet almost unendurable. She was again grateful for his absence. What a surprise she had in store for him! And she imagined his face in its change of expression when she met him. If only he never learned of her presence in Arizona until she made it known in person! That she most longed for. Chances were against it, but then her luck had changed. She looked to the eastward where a pale luminosity of afterglow shone in the heavens. Far distant seemed the home of her childhood, the friends she had scorned and forsaken, the city of complaining and striving millions. If only some miracle might illumine the minds of her friends, as she felt that hers was to be illumined here in the solitude. But she well realized that not all problems could be solved by a call out of the West. Any open and lonely land that might have saved Glenn Kilbourne would have sufficed for her. It was the spirit of the thing and not the letter. It was work of any kind and not only that of ranch life. Not only the raising of hogs!

Carley directed stumbling steps toward the light of her tent. Her eyes had not been used to such black shadow along the ground. She had, too, squeamish feminine fears of hydrophobia skunks, and nameless animals or reptiles that were imagined denizens of the darkness. She gained her tent and entered. The Mexican, Gino, as he called himself, had lighted her lamp and fire. Carley was chilled through, and the tent felt so warm and cozy that she could scarcely believe it. She fastened the screen door, laced the flaps across it, except at the top, and then gave herself up to the lulling and comforting heat.

There were plans to perfect; innumerable things to remember; a car and accessories, horses, saddles, outfits to buy. Carley knew she should sit down at her table and write and figure, but she could not do it then.

For a long time she sat over the little stove, toasting her knees and hands, adding some chips now and then to the red coals. And her mind seemed a kaleidoscope of changing visions, thoughts, feelings. At last she undressed and blew out the lamp and went to bed.

Instantly a thick blackness seemed to enfold her and silence as of a dead world settled down upon her. Drowsy as she was, she could not close her eyes nor refrain from listening. Darkness and silence were tangible things. She felt them. And they seemed suddenly potent with magic charm to still the tumult of her, to soothe and rest, to create thoughts she had never thought before. Rest was more than selfish indulgence. Loneliness was necessary to gain consciousness of the soul. Already far back in the past seemed Carley's other life.

By and by the dead stillness awoke to faint sounds not before perceptible to her—a low, mournful sough of the wind in the cedars, then the faint far-distant note of a coyote, sad as the night and infinitely wild.

———

Days passed. Carley worked in the mornings with her hands and her brains. In the afternoons she rode and walked and climbed with a double object, to work herself into fit physical condition and to explore every nook and corner of her six hundred and forty acres.

Then what she had expected and deliberately induced by her efforts quickly came to pass. Just as the year before she had suffered excruciating pain from aching muscles, and saddle blisters, and walking blisters, and a very rending of her bones, so now she fell victim to them again. In sunshine and rain she faced the desert. Sunburn and sting of sleet were equally to be endured. And that abomination, the hateful blinding sandstorm, did not daunt her. But the weary hours of abnegation to this physical torture at least held one consoling recompense as compared with her experience of last year, and it was that there was no one interested to watch for her weaknesses and failures and blunders. She could fight it out alone.

Three weeks of this self-imposed strenuous training wore by before Carley was free enough from weariness and pain to experience other sensations. Her general health, evidently, had not been so good as when she had first visited Arizona. She caught cold and suffered other ills attendant upon an abrupt change of climate and condition. But doggedly she kept at her task. She rode when she should have been in bed; she walked when she should have ridden; she climbed when she should have kept to level ground. And finally by degrees so gradual as not to be noticed except in the sum of them she began to mend.

Meanwhile the construction of her house went on with uninterrupted rapidity. When the low, slanting, wide-eaved roof was completed Carley lost further concern about rainstorms. Let them come. When the plumbing was all in and Carley saw verification of Hoyle's assurance that it would mean a gravity supply of water ample and continual, she lost her last concern as to the practicability of the work. That, and the earning of her endurance, seemed to bring closer a wonderful reward, still nameless and spiritual, that had been unattainable, but now breathed to her on the fragrant desert wind and in the brooding silence.

———

The time came when each afternoon's ride or climb called to Carley with increasing delight. But the fact that she must soon reveal to Glenn her presence and transformation did not seem to be all the cause. She could ride without pain, walk without losing her breath, work without blistering her hands; and in this there was compensation. The building of the house that was to become a home, the development of water resources and land that meant the making of a ranch—these did not altogether constitute the anticipation of content. To be active, to accomplish things, to recall to mind her knowledge of manual training, of domestic science, of designing and painting, to learn to cook —these were indeed measures full of reward, but they were not all. In her wondering, pondering meditation she arrived at the point where she tried to assign to her love the growing fullness of her life. This, too, splendid and all-pervading as it was, she had to reject. Some exceedingly illusive and vital significance of life had insidiously come to Carley.

One afternoon, with the sky full of white and black rolling clouds and a cold wind sweeping through the cedars, she halted to rest and escape the chilling gale for a while. In a sunny place, under the lee of a gravel bank, she sought refuge. It was warm here because of the reflected sunlight and the absence of wind. The sand at the bottom of the bank held a heat that felt good to her cold hands. All about her and over her swept the keen wind, rustling the sage, seeping the sand, swishing the cedars, but she was out of it, protected and insulated. The sky above showed blue between the threatening clouds. There were no birds or living creatures in sight. Certainly the place had little of color or beauty or grace, nor could she see beyond a few rods. Lying there, without any particular reason that she was conscious of, she suddenly felt shot through and through with exhilaration.

Another day, the warmest of the spring so far, she rode a Navajo mustang she had recently bought from a passing trader;

and at the farthest end of her section, in rough wooded and ridged ground she had not explored, she found a canyon with red walls and pine trees and gleaming streamlet and glades of grass and jumbles of rock. It was a miniature canyon, to be sure, only a quarter of a mile long, and as deep as the height of a lofty pine, and so narrow that it seemed only the width of a lane, but it had all the features of Oak Creek Canyon, and so sufficed for the exultant joy of possession. She explored it. The willow brakes and oak thickets harbored rabbits and birds. She saw the white flags of deer running away down the open. Up at the head where the canyon boxed she flushed a flock of wild turkeys. They ran like ostriches and flew like great brown chickens. In a cavern Carley found the den of a bear, and in another place the bleached bones of a steer.

She lingered here in the shaded depths with a feeling as if she were indeed lost to the world. These big brown and seamy-barked pines with their spreading gnarled arms and webs of green needles belonged to her, as also the tiny brook, the blue bells smiling out of the ferns, the single stalk of mescal on a rocky ledge.

Never had sun and earth, tree and rock, seemed a part of her being until then. She would become a sun-worshiper and a lover of the earth. That canyon had opened there to sky and light for millions of years; and doubtless it had harbored sheep herders, Indians, cliff dwellers, barbarians. She was a woman with white skin and a cultivated mind, but the affinity for them existed in her. She felt it, and that an understanding of it would be good for body and soul.

Another day she found a little grove of jack pines growing on a flat mesa-like bluff, the highest point on her land. The trees were small and close together, mingling their green needles over-head and their discarded brown ones on the ground. From here Carley could see afar to all points of the compass—the slow green descent to the south and the climb to the black-timbered distance; the ridged and canyoned country to the west, red vents choked with green and rimmed with gray; to the north the grand upflung mountain kingdom crowned with snow; and to the east the vastness of illimitable space, the openness and wildness, the chased and beaten mosaic of colored sands and rocks.

———

Again and again she visited this lookout and came to love its isolation, its command of wondrous prospects, its power of suggestion to her thoughts. She became a creative being, in harmony with the live things around her. The great life-dispensing sun poured its rays down upon her, as if to ripen her; and the earth seemed warm, motherly, immense with its all-embracing arms. She no longer plucked the bluebells to press to her face, but leaned to them. Every blade of gramma grass, with its shining bronze-tufted seed head, had significance for her. The scents of the desert began to have meaning for her. She sensed within her the working of a great leveling process through which supreme happiness would come.

June! The rich, thick, amber light, like a transparent reflection from some intense golden medium, seemed to float in the warm air. The sky became an azure blue. In the still noontides, when the bees hummed drowsily and the flies buzzed, vast creamy-white columnar clouds rolled up from the horizon, like colossal ships with bulging sails. And summer with its rush of growing things was at hand.

Carley rode afar, seeking in strange places the secret that eluded her. Only a few days now until she would ride down to Oak Creek Canyon! There was a low, singing melody of wind in the cedars. The earth became too beautiful in her magnified sight. A great truth was dawning upon her—that the sacrifice of what she had held as necessary to the enjoyment of life—that the strain of conflict, the labor of hands, the forcing of weary body, the enduring of pain, the contact with the earth—had served somehow to rejuvenate her blood, quicken her pulse, intensify her sensorial faculties, thrill her very soul, lead her into the realm of enchantment.

One afternoon a dull, lead-black-colored cinder knoll tempted her to explore its bare heights. She rode up until her mustang sank to his knees and could climb no farther. From there she essayed the ascent on foot. It took labor. But at last she gained the summit, burning, sweating, panting.

The cinder hill was an extinct crater of a volcano. In the center of it lay a deep bowl, wondrously symmetrical, and of a dark lusterless hue. Not a blade of grass was there, nor a plant. Carley conceived a desire to go to the bottom of this pit. She tried the cinders of the edge of the slope. They had the same consistency as those of the ascent she had overcome. But here there was a steeper incline. A tingling rush of daring seemed to drive her over the rounded rim, and, once started down, it was as if she wore seven-league boots. Fear left her. Only an exhila-rating emotion consumed her. If there were danger, it mattered not. She strode down with giant steps, she plunged, she started avalanches to ride them until they stopped, she leaped, and lastly she fell, to roll over the soft cinders to the pit.

There she lay. It seemed a comfortable resting place. The pit was scarcely six feet across. She gazed upward and was astounded. How steep was the rounded slope on all sides! There were no sides; it was a circle. She looked up at a round lake of deep translucent sky. Such depth of blue, such exquisite rare color! Carley imagined she could gaze through it to the infinite beyond.

She closed her eyes and rested. Soon the laboring of heart and breath calmed to normal, so that she could not hear them. Then she lay perfectly motionless. With eyes shut she seemed still to look, and what she saw was the sunlight through the blood and flesh of her eyelids. It was red, as rare a hue as the blue of sky. So piercing did it grow that she had to shade her eyes with her arm.

Again the strange, rapt glow suffused her body. Never in all her life had she been so absolutely alone. She might as well have been in her grave. She might have been dead to all earthy things and reveling in spirit in the glory of the physical that had escaped her in life. And she abandoned herself to this influence.

She loved these dry, dusty cinders; she loved the crater here hidden from all save birds; she loved the desert, the earth—above all, the sun. She was a product of the earth—a creation of the sun. She had been an infinitesimal atom of inert something that had quickened to life under the blazing magic of the sun. Soon her spirit would abandon her body and go on, while her flesh and bone returned to dust. This frame of hers, that carried the divine spark, belonged to the earth. She had only been ignorant, mindless, feelingless, absorbed in the seeking of gain, blind to the truth. She had to give. She had been created a woman; she belonged to nature; she was nothing save a mother of the future. She had loved neither Glenn Kilbourne nor life itself. False education, false standards, false environment had developed her into a woman who imagined she must feed her body on the milk and honey of indulgence.

She was abased now—woman as animal, though saved and uplifted by her power of immortality. Transcendental was her female power to link life with the future. The power of the plant seed, the power of the earth, the heat of the sun, the inscrutable creation-spirit of nature, almost the divinity of God—these were all hers because she was a woman. That was the great secret, aloof so long. That was what had been wrong with life—the woman blind to her meaning, her power, her mastery.

So she abandoned herself to the woman within her. She held out her arms to the blue abyss of heaven as if to embrace the universe. She was Nature. She kissed the dusty cinders and pressed her breast against the warm slope. Her heart swelled to bursting with a glorious and unutterable happiness.

———

That afternoon as the sun was setting under a gold-white scroll of cloud Carley got back to Deep Lake.

A familiar lounging figure crossed her sight. It approached to where she had dismounted. Charley, the sheep herder of Oak Creek!

"Howdy!" he drawled, with his queer smile. "So it was you-all who had this Deep Lake section?"

"Yes. And how are you, Charley?" she replied, shaking hands with him.

"Me? Aw, I'm tip-top. I'm shore glad you got this ranch. Reckon I'll hit you for a job."

"I'd give it to you. But aren't you working for the Hutters?"

"Nope. Not any more. Me an' Stanton had a row with them."

How droll and dry he was! His lean, olive-brown face, with its guileless clear eyes and his lanky figure in blue jeans vividly recalled Oak Creek to Carley.

"Oh, I'm sorry," returned she haltingly, somehow checked in her warm rush of thought. "Stanton?. . . Did he quit too?"

"Yep. He sure did."

"What was the trouble?"

"Reckon because Flo made up to Kilbourne," replied Charley, with a grin.

"Ah! I—I see," murmured Carley. A blankness seemed to wave over her. It extended to the air without, to the sense of the golden sunset. It passed. What should she ask—what out of a thousand sudden flashing queries? "Are—are the Hutters back?"

"Sure. Been back several days. I reckoned Hoyle told you. Mebbe he didn't know, though. For nobody's been to town."

"How is—how are they all?" faltered Carley. There was a strange wall here between her thought and her utterance.

"Everybody satisfied, I reckon," replied Charley.

"Flo—how is she?" burst out Carley.

"Aw, Flo's loony over her husband," drawled Charley, his clear eyes on Carley's.

"Husband!" she gasped.

"Sure. Flo's gone an' went an' done what I swore on."

"*Who?*" whispered Carley, and the query was a terrible blade piercing her heart.

"Now who'd you reckon on?" asked Charley, with his slow grin.

Carley's lips were mute.

"Wal, it was your old beau thet you wouldn't have," returned Charley, as he gathered up his long frame, evidently to leave. "Kilbourne! He an' Flo came back from the Tonto all hitched up."

CHAPTER TWELVE

Vague sense of movement, of darkness, and of cold attended Carley's consciousness for what seemed endless time.

A fall over rocks and a severe thrust from a sharp branch brought an acute appreciation of her position, if not of her mental state. Night had fallen. The stars were out. She had stumbled over a low ledge. Evidently she had wandered around, dazedly and aimlessly, until brought to her senses by pain. But for a gleam of campfires through the cedars she would have been lost. It did not matter. She was lost, anyhow. What was it that had happened?

Charley, the sheep herder! Then the thunderbolt of his words burst upon her, and she collapsed to the cold stones. She lay quivering from head to toe. She dug her fingers into the moss and lichen. "Oh, God, to think—after all—it happened!" she moaned. There had been a rending within her breast, as of physical violence, from which she now suffered anguish. There were a thousand stinging nerves. There was a mortal sickness of horror, of insupportable heartbreaking loss. She could not endure it. She could not live under it.

She lay there until energy supplanted shock. Then she rose to rush into the darkest shadows of the cedars, to grope here and there, hanging her head, wringing her hands, beating her breast. "It can't be true," she cried. "Not after my struggle—my victory —not *now!*" But there had been no victory. And now it was too late. She was betrayed, ruined, lost. That wonderful love had wrought transformation in her—and now havoc. Once she fell against the branches of a thick cedar that upheld her. The fragrance which had been sweet was now bitter. Life that had been bliss was now hateful! She could not keep still for a single moment.

Black night, cedars, brush, rocks, washes, seemed not to obstruct her. In a frenzy she rushed on, tearing her dress, her hands, her hair. Violence of some kind was imperative. All at once a pale gleaming open space, shimmering under the stars, lay before her. It was water. Deep Lake! And instantly a hideous terrible longing to destroy herself obsessed her. She had no fear. She could have welcomed the cold, slimy depths that meant oblivion. But could they really bring oblivion? A year ago she would have believed so, and would no longer have endured such agony. She had changed. A cursed strength had come to her, and it was this strength that now augmented her torture. She flung wide her arms to the pitiless white stars and looked up at them. "My hope, my faith, my love have failed me," she whispered. "They have been a lie. I went through hell for them. And now I've nothing to live for. . . . Oh, let me end it all!"

If she prayed to the stars for mercy, it was denied her. Passionlessly they blazed on. But she could not kill herself. In that hour death would have been the only relief and peace left to her. Stricken by the cruelty of her fate, she fell back against the stones and gave up to grief. Nothing was left but fierce pain. The youth and vitality and intensity of her then locked arms with anguish and torment and a cheated, unsatisfied love. Strength of mind and body involuntarily resisted the ravages of this catastrophe. Will power seemed nothing, but the flesh of her, that medium of exquisite sensation, so full of life, so prone to joy, refused to surrender. The part of her that felt fought terribly for its heritage.

All night long Carley lay there. The crescent moon went down, the stars moved on their course, the coyotes ceased to wail, the wind died away, the lapping of the waves along the lake shore wore to gentle splash, the whispering of the insects stopped as the cold of dawn approached. The darkest hour fell— hour of silence, solitude, and melancholy, when the desert lay tranced, cold, waiting, mournful without light of moon or stars or sun.

In the gray dawn Carley dragged her bruised and aching body back to her tent, and, fastening the door, she threw off wet clothes and boots and fell upon her bed. Slumber of exhaustion came to her.

When she awoke the tent was light and the moving shadows of cedar boughs on the white canvas told that the sun was straight above. Carley ached as never before. A deep pang seemed invested in every bone. Her heart felt swollen out of proportion to its space in her breast. Her breathing came slow and it hurt. Her blood was sluggish. Suddenly she shut her eyes. She loathed the light of day. What was it that had happened?

Then the brutal truth flashed over her again, in aspect new, with all the old bitterness. For an instant she experienced a suffocating sensation as if the canvas had sagged under the burden of heavy air and was crushing her breast and heart. Then wave after wave of emotion swept over her. The storm winds of grief and passion were loosened again. And she writhed in her misery.

Some one knocked on her door. The Mexican woman called anxiously. Carley awoke to the fact that her presence was not solitary on the physical earth, even if her soul seemed stricken to eternal loneliness. Even in the desert there was a world to consider. Vanity that had bled to death, pride that had been crushed, availed her not here. But something else came to her support. The lesson of the West had been to endure, not to shirk

—to face an issue, not to hide. Carley got up, bathed, dressed, brushed and arranged her dishevelled hair. The face she saw in the mirror excited her amaze and pity. Then she went out in answer to the call for dinner. But she could not eat. The ordinary functions of life appeared to be deadened.

The day happened to be Sunday, and therefore the workmen were absent. Carley had the place to herself. How the half-completed house mocked her! She could not bear to look at it. What use could she make of it now? Flo Hutter had become the working comrade of Glenn Kilbourne, the mistress of his cabin. She was his wife and she would be the mother of his children.

That thought gave birth to the darkest hour of Carley Burch's life. She became possessed as by a thousand devils. She became merely a female robbed of her mate. Reason was not in her, nor charity, nor justice. All that was abnormal in human nature seemed coalesced in her, dominant, passionate, savage, terrible. She hated with an incredible and insane ferocity. In the seclusion of her tent, crouched on her bed, silent, locked, motionless, she yet was the embodiment of all terrible strife and storm in nature. Her heart was a maelstrom and would have whirled and sucked down to hell all the beings that were men. Her soul was a bottomless gulf, filled with the gales and the fires of jealousy, superhuman to destroy.

That fury consumed all her remaining strength, and from the relapse she sank to sleep.

Morning brought the inevitable reaction. However long her other struggles, this monumental and final one would be brief. She realized that, yet was unable to understand how it could be possible, unless shock or death or mental aberration ended the fight. An eternity of emotion lay back between this awakening of intelligence and the hour of her fall into the clutches of primitive passion.

That morning she faced herself in the mirror and asked, "Now—what do I owe *you?*" It was not her voice that answered. It was beyond her. But it said: "Go on! You are cut adrift. You

are alone. You owe none but yourself!. . . Go on! Not backward
—not to the depths—but up—upward!"

She shuddered at such a decree. How impossible for her! All
animal, all woman, all emotion, how could she live on the cold,
pure heights? Yet she owed something intangible and inscrutable
to herself. Was it the thing that woman lacked physically, yet
contained hidden in her soul? An element of eternal spirit to
rise! Because of heartbreak and ruin and irreparable loss must
she fall? Was loss of love and husband and children only a test?
The present hour would be swallowed in the sum of life's trials.
She could not go back. She would not go down. There was
wrenched from her tried and sore heart an unalterable and
unquenchable decision—to make her own soul prove the evolution of woman. Vessel of blood and flesh she might be, doomed
by nature to the reproduction of her kind, but she had in her the
supreme spirit and power to carry on the progress of the ages—
the climb of woman out of the darkness.

Carley went out to the workmen. The house should be
completed and she would live in it. Always there was the
stretching and illimitable desert to look at, and the grand heave
upward of the mountains. Hoyle was full of zest for the practical
details of the building. He saw nothing of the havoc wrought in
her. Nor did the other workmen glance more than casually at
her. In this Carley lost something of a shirking fear that her loss
and grief were patent to all eyes.

That afternoon she mounted the most spirited of the
mustangs she had purchased from the Indians. To govern him
and stick on him required all her energy. And she rode him hard
and far, out across the desert, across mile after mile of cedar
forest, clear to the foothills. She rested there, absorbed in gazing
desertward, and upon turning back again, she ran him over the
level stretches. Wind and branch threshed her seemingly to
ribbons. Violence seemed good for her. A fall had no fear for her
now. She reached camp at dusk, hot as fire, breathless and
strengthless. But she had earned something. Such action

required constant use of muscle and mind. If need be she could drive both to the very furthermost limit. She could ride and ride —until the future, like the immensity of the desert there, might swallow her. She changed her clothes and rested a while. The call to supper found her hungry. In this fact she discovered mockery of her grief. Love was not the food of life. Exhausted nature's need of rest and sleep was no respecter of a woman's emotion.

Next day Carley rode northward, wildly and fearlessly, as if this conscious activity was the initiative of an endless number of rides that were to save her. As before the foothills called her, and she went on until she came to a very high one.

Carley dismounted from her panting horse, answering the familiar impulse to attain heights by her own effort.

"Am I only a weakling?" she asked herself. "Only a creature mined by the fever of the soul!. . . Thrown from one emotion to another? Never the same. Yearning, suffering, sacrificing, hoping, and changing—forever the same! What is it that drives *me?* A great city with all its attractions has failed to help me realize my life. So have friends failed. So has the world. What can solitude and grandeur do?. . . All this obsession of mine—all this strange feeling for simple elemental earthly things likewise will fail me. Yet I am driven. They would call me a mad woman."

It took Carley a full hour of slow body-bending labor to climb to the summit of that hill. High, steep, and rugged, it resisted ascension. But at last she surmounted it and sat alone on the heights, with naked eyes, and an unconscious prayer on her lips.

What was it that had happened? Could there be here a different answer from that which always mocked her?

She had been a girl, not accountable for loss of mother, for choice of home and education. She had belonged to a class. She had grown to womanhood in it. She had loved, and in loving had escaped the evil of her day, if not its taint. She had lived only for herself. Conscience had awakened—but, alas! too late. She had overthrown the sordid, self-seeking habit of life; she had awakened to real womanhood; she had fought the insidious spell of modernity and she had defeated it; she had learned the thrill of taking root in new soil, the pain and joy of labor, the bliss of soli-tude, the promise of home and love and motherhood. But she had gathered all these marvelous things to her soul too late for happiness.

"*Now* it is answered," she declared aloud. "That is what has happened?. . . And all that is *past*. . . . Is there anything left? If so *what?*

She flung her query out to the winds of the desert. But the desert seemed too gray, too vast, too remote, too aloof, too measureless. It was not concerned with her little life. Then she turned to the mountain kingdom.

It seemed overpoweringly near at hand. It loomed above her to pierce the fleecy clouds. It was only a stupendous upheaval of earth-crust, grown over at the base by leagues and leagues of pine forest, belted along the middle by vast slanting zigzag slopes of aspen, rent and riven toward the heights into canyon and gorge, bared above to cliffs and corners of craggy rock, whitened at the sky-piercing peaks by snow. Its beauty and sublimity were lost upon Carley now; she was concerned with its travail, its age, its endurance, its strength. And she studied it with magnified sight.

What incomprehensible subterranean force had swelled those immense slopes and lifted the huge bulk aloft to the clouds? Cataclysm of nature—the expanding or shrinking of the earth—vast volcanic action under the surface! Whatever it had been, it had left its expression of the travail of the universe. This mountain mass had been hot gas when flung from the parent sun, and now it was solid granite. What had it endured in the making? What indeed had been its dimensions before the millions of years of its struggle?

Eruption, earthquake, avalanche, the attrition of glacier, the erosion of water, the cracking of frost, the weathering of rain and wind and snow—these it had eternally fought and resisted in vain, yet still it stood magnificent, frowning, battle-scarred and undefeated. Its sky-piercing peaks were as cries for mercy to the Infinite. This old mountain realized its doom. It had to go, perhaps to make room for a newer and better kingdom. But it endured because of the spirit of nature. The great notched circular line of rock below and between the peaks, in the body of the mountains, showed where in ages past the heart of living granite had blown out, to let loose on all the near surrounding desert the streams of black lava and the hills of black cinders. Despite its fringe of green it was hoary with age. Every looming gray-faced wall, massive and sublime, seemed a monument of its mastery over time. Every deep-cut canyon, showing the skeleton ribs, the caverns and caves, its avalanche-carved slides, its long, fan-shaped, spreading taluses, carried conviction to the spectator that it was but a frail bit of rock, that its life was little and brief, that upon it had been laid the merciless curse of nature. Change! Change must unknit the very knots of the center of the earth. So its strength lay in the sublimity of its defiance. It meant to endure to the last rolling grain of sand. It was a dead mountain of rock, without spirit, yet it taught a grand lesson to the seeing eye.

Life was only a part, perhaps an infinitely small part of nature's plan. Death and decay were just as important to her inscrutable design. The universe had not been created for life, ease, pleasure, and happiness of a man creature developed from lower organisms. If nature's secret was the developing of a spirit through all time, Carley divined that she had it within her. So the present meant little.

"I have no right to be unhappy," concluded Carley. "I had no right to Glenn Kilbourne. I failed him. In that I failed myself. Neither life nor nature failed me—nor love. It is no longer a mystery. Unhappiness is only a change. Happiness itself is only change. So what does it matter? The great thing is to see life—to understand—to feel—to work—to fight—to endure. It is not my fault I am here. But it is my fault if I leave this strange old earth

the poorer for my failure. . . . I will no longer be little. I will find
strength. I will endure. . . . I still have eyes, ears, nose, taste. I
can feel the sun, the wind, the nip of frost. Must I slink like a
craven because I've lost the love of *one* man? Must I hate Flo
Hutter because she will make Glenn happy? Never!. . . All of this
seems better so, because through it I am changed. I might have
lived on, a selfish clod!"

Carley turned from the mountain kingdom and faced her
future with the profound and sad and far-seeing look that had
come with her lesson. She knew what to give. Sometime and
somewhere there would be recompense. She would hide her
wound in the faith that time would heal it. And the ordeal she
set herself, to prove her sincerity and strength, was to ride down
to Oak Creek Canyon.

Carley did not wait many days. Strange how the old vanity
held her back until something of the havoc in her face should be
gone!

One morning she set out early, riding her best horse, and she
took a sheep trail across country. The distance by road was much
farther. The June morning was cool, sparkling, fragrant. Mocking
birds sang from the topmost twig of cedars; doves cooed in the
pines; sparrow hawks sailed low over the open grassy patches.
Desert primroses showed their rounded pink clusters in sunny
places, and here and there burned the carmine of Indian paintbrush. Jack rabbits and cotton-tails bounded and scampered
away through the sage. The desert had life and color and movement this June day. And as always there was the dry fragrance on
the air.

Her mustang had been inured to long and consistent travel
over the desert. Her weight was nothing to him and he kept to
the swinging lope for miles. As she approached Oak Creek
Canyon, however, she drew him to a trot, and then a walk. Sight
of the deep red-walled and green-floored canyon was a shock
to her.

The trail came out on the road that led to Ryan's sheep camp, at a point several miles west of the cabin where Carley had encountered Haze Ruff. She remembered the curves and stretches, and especially the steep jump-off where the road led down off the rim into the canyon. Here she dismounted and walked. From the foot of this descent she knew every rod of the way would be familiar to her, and, womanlike, she wanted to turn away and fly from them. But she kept on and mounted again at level ground.

The murmur of the creek suddenly assailed her ears—sweet, sad, memorable, strangely powerful to hurt. Yet the sound seemed of long ago. Down here summer had advanced. Rich thick foliage overspread the winding road of sand. Then out of the shade she passed into the sunnier regions of isolated pines. Along here she had raced Calico with Glenn's bay; and here she had caught him, and there was the place she had fallen. She halted a moment under the pine tree where Glenn had held her in his arms. Tears dimmed her eyes. If only she had known then the truth, the reality! But regrets were useless.

By and by a craggy red wall loomed above the trees, and its pipe-organ conformation was familiar to Carley. She left the road and turned to go down to the creek. Sycamores and maples and great bowlders, and mossy ledges overhanging the water, and a huge sentinel pine marked the spot where she and Glenn had eaten their lunch that last day. Her mustang splashed into the clear water and halted to drink. Beyond, through the trees, Carley saw the sunny red-earthed clearing that was Glenn's farm. She looked, and fought herself, and bit her quivering lip until she tasted blood. Then she rode out into the open.

The whole west side of the canyon had been cleared and cultivated and plowed. But she gazed no farther. She did not want to see the spot where she had given Glenn his ring and had parted from him. She rode on. If she could pass West Fork she believed her courage would rise to the completion of this ordeal. Places were what she feared. Places that she had loved while blindly believing she hated! There the narrow gap of green and blue split the looming red wall. She was looking into West Fork. Up there stood the cabin. How fierce a pang rent her breast! She faltered at the crossing of the branch stream, and almost surrendered. The water murmured, the leaves rustled, the bees hummed, the birds sang—all with some sad sweetness that seemed of the past.

Then the trail leading up West Fork was like a barrier. She saw horse tracks in it. Next she descried boot tracks the shape of which was so well-remembered that it shook her heart. There were fresh tracks in the sand, pointing in the direction of the Lodge. Ah! that was where Glenn lived now. Carley strained at her will to keep it fighting her memory. The glory and the dream were gone!

A touch of spur urged her mustang into a gallop. The splashing ford of the creek—the still, eddying pool beyond—the green orchards—the white lacy waterfall—and Lolomi Lodge!

Nothing had altered. But Carley seemed returning after many years. Slowly she dismounted—slowly she climbed the porch steps. Was there no one at home? Yet the vacant doorway, the silence—something attested to the knowledge of Carley's presence. Then suddenly Mrs. Hutter fluttered out with Flo behind her.

"You dear girl—I'm so glad!" cried Mrs. Hutter, her voice trembling.

"I'm glad to see you, too," said Carley, bending to receive Mrs.Hutter's embrace. Carley saw dim eyes—the stress of agitation, but no surprise.

"*Oh, Carley!*" burst out the Western girl, with voice rich and full, yet tremulous.

"Flo, I've come to wish you happiness," replied Carley, very low.

Was it the same Flo? This seemed more of a woman—strange now—white and strained—beautiful, eager, questioning. A cry of gladness burst from her. Carley felt herself enveloped in strong close clasp—and then a warm, quick kiss of joy. It shocked her, yet somehow thrilled. Sure was the welcome here. Sure was the strained situation, also, but the voice rang too glad a note for Carley. It touched her deeply, yet she could not understand. She had not measured the depth of Western friendship.

"Have you—seen Glenn?" queried Flo, breathlessly.

"Oh no, indeed not," replied Carley, slowly gaining composure. The nervous agitation of these women had stilled her own. "I just rode up the trail. Where is he?"

"He was here—a moment ago," panted Flo. "Oh, Carley, we sure are locoed. . . . Why, we only heard an hour ago—that *you* were at Deep Lake. . . . Charley rode in. He told us. . . . I thought my heart would break. Poor Glenn! When he heard it. . . . But never mind *me*. Jump your horse and run to West Fork!"

The spirit of her was like the strength of her arms as she hurried Carley across the porch and shoved her down the steps.

"Climb on and run, Carley," cried Flo. "If you only knew how glad he'll be that you came!"

Carley leaped into the saddle and wheeled the mustang. But she had no answer for the girl's singular, almost wild exultance. Then like a shot the spirited mustang was off down the lane. Carley wondered with swelling heart. Was her coming such a wondrous surprise—so unexpected and big in generosity—something that would make Kilbourne as glad as it had seemed to make Flo? Carley thrilled to this assurance.

Down the lane she flew. The red walls blurred and the sweet wind whipped her face. At the trail she swerved the mustang, but did not check his gait. Under the great pines he sped and round the bulging wall. At the rocky incline leading to the creek she pulled the fiery animal to a trot. How low and clear the water! As Carley forded it fresh cool drops splashed into her face. Again she spurred her mount and again trees and walls rushed by. Up and down the yellow bits of trail—on over the brown mats of pine needles—until there in the sunlight shone the little gray log cabin with a tall form standing in the door. One instant the canyon tilted on end for Carley and she was riding into the blue sky. Then some magic of soul sustained her, so that she saw clearly. Reaching the cabin she reined in her mustang.

"Hello, Glenn! Look who's here!" she cried, not wholly failing of gayety.

He threw up his sombrero.

"Whoopee!" he yelled, in stentorian voice that rolled across the canyon and bellowed in hollow echo and then clapped from wall to wall. The unexpected Western yell, so strange from Glenn, disconcerted Carley. Had he only answered her spirit of greeting? Had hers rung false?

But he was coming to her. She had seen the bronze of his face turn to white. How gaunt and worn he looked. Older he appeared, with deeper lines and whiter hair. His jaw quivered.

"Carley Burch, so it was *you?*" he queried, hoarsely.

"Glenn, I reckon it was," she replied. "I bought your Deep Lake ranch site. I came back too late. . . . But it is never too late for some things. . . . I've come to wish you and Flo all the happiness in the world—and to say we must be friends."

The way he looked at her made her tremble. He strode up beside the mustang, and he was so tall that his shoulder came abreast of her. He placed a big warm hand on hers, as it rested, ungloved, on the pommel of the saddle.

"Have you seen Flo?" he asked.

"I just left her. It was funny—the way she rushed me off after you. As if there weren't two—"

Was it Glenn's eyes or the movement of his hand that checked her utterance? His gaze pierced her soul. His hand slid along her arm to her waist—around it. Her heart seemed to burst.

"Kick your feet out of the stirrups," he ordered.

Instinctively she obeyed. Then with a strong pull he hauled her half out of the saddle, pellmell into his arms. Carley had no resistance. She sank limp, in an agony of amaze. Was this a dream? Swift and hard his lips met hers—and again—and again.

"Oh, my God!—Glenn, are—you—mad?" she whispered, almost swooning.

"Sure—I reckon I am," he replied, huskily, and pulled her all the way out of the saddle.

Carley would have fallen but for his support. She could not think. She was all instinct. Only the amaze—the sudden horror —drifted—faded as before fires of her heart!

"Kiss me!" he commanded.

She would have kissed him if death were the penalty. How his face blurred in her dimmed sight! Was that a strange smile? Then he held her back from him.

"Carley—you came to wish Flo and me happiness?" he asked.

"Oh, yes—yes. . . . Pity me, Glenn—let me go. I meant well. . . . I should—never have come."

"Do you love me?" he went on, with passionate, shaking clasp.

"God help me—I do—I do!. . . And now it will kill me!"

"What did that damned fool Charley tell you?"

The strange content of his query, the trenchant force of it, brought her upright, with sight suddenly cleared. Was this giant the tragic Glenn who had strode to her from the cabin door?

"Charley told me—you and Flo—were married," she whispered.

"You didn't *believe* him!" returned Glenn.

She could no longer speak. She could only see her lover, as if transfigured, limned dark against the looming red wall.

"That was one of Charley's queer jokes. I told you to beware of him. Flo is married, yes—and very happy. . . . I'm unutterably happy, too—but I'm not married. Lee Stanton was the lucky bridegroom. . . . Carley, the moment I saw you I knew you had come back to me."

THE END

PUBLISHER'S NOTE

This book was produced as part of the Publishing master's degree program at Western Colorado University, Graduate Program in Creative Writing. The students worked cooperatively to produce these fine new editions of worthy public-domain works. The intent is to bring literary classics to a new readership. For the enjoyment of a modern audience, some minor revisions to archaic terms or punctuation may have been made.

Because these works were written in a different time, some attitudes and phrasing may seem outdated to a modern audience. After careful consideration, rather than revising the author's work, we have chosen to preserve the original wording and intent.

ABOUT THE AUTHOR

Pearl Zane Grey, the fourth child of Alice Josephine Zane and Lewis Gray, was born in Zanesville, Ohio. After Zane's birth, the family changed their last name from Gray to Grey. Lewis Grey, a dentist, did not want his son to waste his time writing stories. Lewis ripped up Zane's first story when he was only fifteen. The only thing Zane wanted to do was play baseball and write, but he was forced into dentistry for practical reasons.

Zane attended the University of Pennsylvania on a baseball scholarship. He was a decent athlete and played in the minor leagues. After graduation with a degree in dentistry, Zane moved to New York and opened his dentistry business where he struggled with his need to write. He went camping and fishing with his brother in Pennsylvania where he met Lina Roth, known as Dolly. Zane and Dolly were married in 1905. He warned her he would not stop being a free spirit and had numerous affairs after his marriage.

In 1918, the Zanes moved to California and settled in Altadena in 1920. Dolly, a former schoolteacher, edited all of Zane's manuscripts and managed his career including all his contracts. Zane traveled and explored the west, went fishing, and wrote. He had a cabin in Oregon on the Rogue River, and in the desert by the Mogollon Rim near Payson, Arizona. He wrote articles for magazines, serializations, and novels. His most famous novel was *Riders of the Purple Sage*. In 1939, Zane Grey died at the age of 67. After his death, his wife and son published some of his unfinished novels. At least fifty movies were made based on his novels.

ABOUT THE EDITOR

Eva Eldridge has edited three editions of *Sandscript*, an award-winning art and literary magazine. Recently she curated and edited *Trouble in Tucson*, an anthology of mystery stories located in the Tucson, Arizona, area. She is currently enrolled in the Publishing cohort of Western Colorado University's Graduate Programs.

Traveling to cooler climates is one of the ways Eva manages to avoid the desert heat, but she always returns to Tucson where she enjoys gardening, food, summer storms, and writing about her travels. Eva's travel writing and podcasts can be found at https://blendradioandtv.com/.

She lives with her husband and Sera, a pushy old dog. Her website can be found at http://evaeldridge.com.

WORDFIRE CLASSICS

The Lost World
The Poison Belt
by A. Conan Doyle

The Wolf Leader
by Alexandre Dumas

The Cthulhu Stories of Robert E. Howard
by Robert E. Howard

The Detective Stories of Edgar Allan Poe
by Edgar Allan Poe

The Jewel of Seven Stars (Annotated)
by Bram Stoker

From the Earth to the Moon and Around the Moon
by Jules Verne

The Complete War of the Worlds
The War in the Air
Kipps: The Story of a Simple Man
The Sleeper Awakes and Men Like Gods
by H.G. Wells

Mother of Frankenstein: Maria: or, The Wrongs of Woman & Memoirs of the Author of A Vindication of the Rights of Woman
by Mary Wollstonecraft

We: The 100th Anniversary Edition
by Yevgeny Zamyatin

One Stormy Night : A Story Challenge That Created the Gothic Horror Genre
by Lord Byron, Dr. John William Polidori, and Mary Shelley

HOLIDAY CLASSICS

The Ghost of Christmas Always
by Charles Dickens & Kevin J. Anderson

The Santa Claus Stories
by L. Frank Baum

Our list of other WordFire Press authors and titles is always growing. To find out more and to shop our selection of titles, visit us at:
wordfirepress.com

f facebook.com/WordfireIncWordfirePress
X x.com/WordFirePress
instagram.com/WordFirePress
BB bookbub.com/profile/4109784512

www.ingramcontent.com/pod-product-compliance
Lightning Source LLC
Chambersburg PA
CBHW020138120726
47903CB00007B/2315